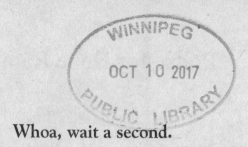
Whoa, wait a second.

When Laurie had met Andrew's gaze, something sparked in her that hadn't been there before. But someone should have briefed her girl parts on the plan. Her libido, which had been slumbering for years, stretched, yawned, and woke up *hungry*. It fixed on Andrew Lyndon and got all hot and bothered. In his faded blue jeans, worn-out loafers, and gray T-shirt, Andrew looked about as yummy as a box of Krispy Kremes.

She slid into the facing chair and studied him for a moment. Andrew was like a deep, still pond that reflected whatever anyone projected onto him. Even now, gazing right into his eyes, Laurie had trouble reading him. But then the corners of Andrew's mouth turned up, and a certain mischievous light danced in his dark eyes. Yearning of a kind she'd never known took flight inside her like a caged bird.

Praise for Hope Ramsay

A Small-Town Bride

"Ramsay charms in her second Chapel of Love contempo-rary...[and] wins readers' hearts with likable characters, an engaging plot (and a hilarious subplot), and a well-deserved happy ending."
—Publishers Weekly

A Christmas Bride

"Happiness is a new Hope Ramsay series."
–FreshFiction.com

"I'm so glad that *A Christmas Bride* is the first of Ramsay's Chapel of Love series because there are more stories to be told—and I'll be reading them."
—HeroesandHeartbreakers.com

Last Chance Hero

"Fans will enjoy another visit to Last Chance, the quintes-sential Southern small town. The characters in this town are priceless...Readers can expect to have a whole lot of fun."
—RT Book Reviews

"I love visiting Last Chance and getting to revisit old friends, funny situations, the magic and the mystery that al-ways seem to find their way into these wonderful stories."
—HarlequinJunkie.com

Last Chance Family

"4 stars! Ramsay uses a light-toned plot and sweet characters to illustrate some important truths in this entry in the series."

—RT Book Reviews

"[This book] has the humor and heartwarming quality that have characterized the series...Mike and Charlene are appealing characters—unconsciously funny, vulnerable, and genuinely likable—and Rainbow will touch readers' hearts."

—TheRomanceDish.com

Inn at Last Chance

"5 stars! I really enjoyed this book. I love a little mystery with my romance, and that is exactly what I got with *Inn at Last Chance*."

—HarlequinJunkie.com

"5 stars! The suspense and mystery behind it all kept me on the edge of my seat. I just could not put this book down."

—LongandShortReviews.com

Last Chance Knit & Stitch

"Hope Ramsay is going on my auto-read list for sure. *Last Chance Knit & Stitch* may be my first Last Chance book, but it won't be my last."

—HeroesandHeartbreakers.com

"Ramsay writes with heart and humor. Truly a book to be treasured and heartwarming foray into a great series."
—NightOwlReviews.com

Last Chance Book Club

"The ladies of the Last Chance Book Club keep the gossip flowing in this story graced with abundant Southern charm and quirky, caring people. Another welcome chapter to Ramsay's engaging, funny, hope-filled series." ***—Library Journal***

"Last Chance is a place we've come to know as well as we know our own hometowns. It's become real, filled with people who could be our aunts, uncles, cousins, friends, or the crazy cat lady down the street. It's familiar, comfortable, welcoming."
—RubySlipperedSisterhood.com

Last Chance Christmas

"Amazing…This story spoke to me on so many levels about faith, strength, courage, and choices. If you're looking for a good Christmas story with a few angels, then *Last Chance Christmas* is a must-read."
—TheSeasonforRomance.com

"Visiting Last Chance is always a joy, but Hope Ramsay has outdone herself this time. She took a difficult hero, a wounded heroine, familiar characters, added a little Christmas magic, and—voilà!—gave us a story sure to touch the Scroogiest of hearts."
—RubySlipperedSisterhood.com

Last Chance Beauty Queen

"4½ stars! Enchantingly funny and heartwarmingly charming."
—RT Book Reviews

"A little Bridget Jones meets *Sweet Home Alabama*."
—GrafWV.com

Home at Last Chance

"An enjoyable ride that will capture interest and hold it to the very end."
—RomRevToday.blogspot.com

"Full of small-town charm and Southern hospitality...You will want to grab a copy."
—TopRomanceNovels.com

Welcome to Last Chance

"Ramsay's delicious contemporary debut introduces the town of Last Chance, SC, and its warmhearted inhabitants... [she] strikes an excellent balance between tension and humor as she spins a fine yarn."
—*Publishers Weekly* (starred review)

"[A] charming series, featuring quirky characters you won't soon forget."
—Barbara Freethy, *New York Times* bestselling author of *At Hidden Falls*

HERE COMES
THE BRIDE

Hope Ramsay

FOREVER

NEW YORK BOSTON

Forever
Hachette Book Group
1290 Avenue of the Americas, New York, NY 10104
forever-romance.com
twitter.com/foreverromance

First Edition: August 2017

Forever is an imprint of Grand Central Publishing. The Forever name and logo are trademarks of Hachette Book Group, Inc.

The publisher is not responsible for websites (or their content) that are not owned by the publisher.

The Hachette Speakers Bureau provides a wide range of authors for speaking events. To find out more, go to www.hachettespeakersbureau.com or call (866) 376-6591.

ISBNs: 978-1-4555-6488-0 (mass market); 978-1-4555-6486-6 (ebook)

Printed in the United States of America

OPM

10 9 8 7 6 5 4 3 2 1

For Tanni. Thanks for everything.

Acknowledgments

Writing is solitary work, but there are always a few people who deserve special thanks when a project is finally finished. First of all, I'd like to thank Tanni Rednor, who sat down with me one day and helped me come up with the idea that we called "fifty dates with a bride."

I'd also like to acknowledge the singer-songwriter James Taylor, and his song, "Her Town Too," a song about how breakups affect friends and family. I listened to this song on an endless loop as I was writing the first draft.

I'd also like to thank the chat room writers who convened every morning during the Ruby Slippered Sisterhood's 2017 Winter Writing Festival. You kept me sane as I was working on the many revisions this book required.

And speaking of revisions, Alex Logan, my longtime editor, deserves special thanks because the first draft of this book needed a lot of work, and her advice was, as always, invaluable in shaping the second, third, and fourth drafts.

Finally, many thanks to my husband, Bryan, for his support and tolerance for the messy house, the take-out dinners, and the stress of living with an author on a tight deadline.

HERE COMES
THE BRIDE

Chapter One ————————————

If Laurie Wilson could have controlled the weather for her wedding, she would have. She had controlled, planned, organized, and directed every other aspect of her special day. So when it rained for a solid seven days before the ceremony, Laurie exhausted herself with worry.

She could have saved herself the angst because August twenty-sixth arrived with an endlessly azure sky more like September than late summer. And in true silver-lining fashion, the rain had broken the deep August drought leaving the asters, woodbine, and rudbeckia that grew in the meadow beside Laurel Chapel in full, glorious bloom.

The day was as perfect as her dream.

So was her wedding dress.

The full-length mirror in the church's waiting room provided a stunning reflection of the woman who was about to become Mrs. Brandon Kopp. Alençon lace dripped from her gown's bodice while the Swarovski crystals along the sweetheart neckline sent colorful sparks of light along the walls and ceilings. Laurie pressed her hands down into the yards of netting in the skirt, feeling giddy.

"You look gorgeous, princess," Dad said from behind her, a tremor in his voice.

For the first time in her life, Dad's pet name actually fit. The A-line ball gown was princess-worthy, and her thick, unruly tresses had been braided into a crown that now bristled with baby's breath like a living tiara.

She turned around to find Dad, his hands jammed in the pockets of his dark gray suit, his dahlia boutonniere slightly askew. She stepped up to him and fixed the flower. "There," she said, with butterflies flitting around in her core.

He captured her hand and gave it a little kiss. "I can't believe my little princess is getting married," he said, a sheen in his eyes. "But I heartily approve of your groom."

"I do too," she said with a grin. "And I'm happy the planning is finally over. I thought Mom and I would come to blows a few times over the last few months."

The door opened, and Laurie's bridesmaids invaded in a swirl of burgundy chiffon and laughter. Madison Atwood, Emma Raynerson, and Jessica Westbrook were dear friends from college, and Brandon's sister, Roxanne, was the maid of honor.

"We've been sent to let you know that Brandon and the groomsmen are about to take their positions. It's only a few more minutes," Roxy said. "And I just wanted to tell you before the wedding toasts start that I'm so happy you're going to be my sister-in-law. Brandon couldn't have chosen any better."

A wave of joy percolated through Laurie. "Thank you so much." She gave Roxy a fierce hug. "Not just for saying that, but for holding my hand the last few months. All of you have been terrific, really. I know I can get a little OCD about things, and you all have been so supportive, especially when Mom started throwing her weight around."

A tearful and slightly giggly group hug followed, but it didn't last long because Courtney Wallace, the events coordinator for Eagle Hill Manor, opened the door and said, "It's show time, ladies…and gent." The strains of the Air from Bach's *Suite No. 3 in D*—arranged for organ and violin—floated in from the sanctuary. A little flutter of excitement gnawed at Laurie's insides as her friends left the room, lined up in the chapel's small vestibule, and one by one, made their way down the aisle.

She took Dad's arm and looked up at him. He smiled and winked. "I love you, princess," he said.

"I love you too," she murmured as the music changed from the Bach to Pachelbel's Canon in D. She'd had a huge argument with Mom about this music choice. Mom wanted the traditional "Bridal Chorus" from Wagner's opera *Lohengrin*. But Laurie was a bit of an opera buff, and in her estimation, the wedding in *Lohengrin* wasn't one she wanted to emulate since the bride ends up dead at the end of the opera. So no "Bridal Chorus" for her. She regarded it as bad luck.

Without the opening fanfare of "Here Comes the Bride" to signal her arrival, the wedding guests didn't rise to their feet very quickly. But they did eventually get the message. She gripped Dad's arm and looked ahead to where Brandon waited, dressed in a dark gray suit with his curly, almost-black hair falling over his forehead. He aimed his big blue eyes at her, and her heart beat a little faster.

They'd known each other for ten years, since freshman year at George Washington University. They had hooked up a time or two in college but not seriously until five years ago. Brandon was the love of a lifetime. The only man she'd ever slept with. Her heart swelled in her chest as she arrived at the altar without tripping on the train of her dress. Thank God. She could check that worry off her list of possible disasters.

She looked up into Brandon's eyes. She'd imagined this moment thousands of times. His eyes would sparkle, maybe with unshed tears of joy. His mouth would curl at the corner and expose his adorable dimple. He'd wink...

Wait. She'd never imagined him frowning at her. What? Did he hate her dress? Was it too princessy? She knew it; she should have gone with the mermaid dress even though Mom hated it. Crap. The moment was spoiled forever.

The minister interrupted her inner rant. "*Dearly beloved. We have come together in the presence of God to witness and bless the joining together of —*"

"Wait," Brandon said.

"What?" The minister laid his finger down to mark his place in the *Book of Common Prayer*. Then he looked up at Brandon over the rims of his half-glasses.

The bodice of Laurie's dress chose that moment to become a tourniquet, shutting off her air supply.

"What on earth are you doing?" In the front pew, Brandon's father stood up with a thunderous look on his face.

Brandon ignored his dad. He kept staring at Laurie with panic in his eyes. "Uh, Laurie, um..."

"How dare you!" This came from Mom in the pew on the opposite side. Like Brandon, Laurie tried to ignore her mother while simultaneously trying to breathe.

"I can't," Brandon said.

"You can't or you don't want to?" Roxy asked. "Because, baby bro, there is a big difference."

"I...Well, both of those, actually."

"What?" Laurie finally managed to push out the word and suck in a gulp of air.

Brandon took her by the hand, and the touch sent ice up her arm. She wanted to pull away from him but she was frozen in place. "Look, Laurie, you're more or less the only girl I ever dated."

"So?" someone asked. Laurie wasn't sure but it sounded like Andrew Lyndon, the best man.

"I just don't think either of us is ready for this. I mean, we don't have enough experience."

"What?" That was definitely Mom's voice. "You're twenty-eight years old, for goodness' sake. You're not a couple of teenagers."

"Is there someone else?" Laurie could only whisper the words as the foundation of her world crumbled beneath her.

Brandon's eyes widened. "No, never. I swear, Laurie, I have never cheated on you. But I think we got on the wedding carousel and..." He stabbed a hand through his hair. "Shit," he said under his breath as he turned away.

"If there's no one else, then—"

"I just want a break, okay? Like six months. You know, like a trial separation."

"For crap's sake, how can you have a separation if you're not even married?" Dad asked in a tense voice.

Laurie glanced at Dad, still standing there waiting to give her away. His face had gone pale and grave. He turned toward Brandon. "What is it you want, son?"

"I just need time. You know, to make sure this isn't a mistake." And then he gave Laurie a sweet, sad smile and said, "And you need time too, Laurie. I think it would be good if we saw other people. Really. And then we can decide."

"Are you crazy? I love you. I don't want to see other people."

He shook his head. "I'm really sorry. I know you spent a lot of time and money planning all this." He turned and strode down the aisle and out of the chapel. His father climbed over a couple of wedding guests and hit the aisle at a dead run. Laurie hoped the old guy didn't give himself a heart attack chasing after his son.

Roxy must have had the same thought because she dropped her bouquet and tore after Mr. Kopp, saying, "Daddy, don't kill yourself."

Dad glanced at Mom and snarled something obscene while the wedding guests went ominously silent, except for Mom, who collapsed in the front pew, openly weeping and maybe even wailing a little.

Someone grabbed Laurie by the hand. "Come on, let's get you out of here."

She looked up. Andrew Lyndon, the best man. Funny how he'd stayed and Roxy had gone. He tugged her forward, and she followed him down the aisle like a confused puppy. Behind her, the bridesmaids and the groomsmen followed in a disorderly retreat, and all Laurie could think about was that the musicians were supposed to play Mendelssohn's "Wedding March" during the recessional.

Andrew marched out of the chapel and down the path to the inn, his little sister, Amy, running ahead of him clearing the way. Behind him, the remaining bridesmaids and groomsmen, including his brother, Edward, and cousins Matt and Jason, followed like a formally clad flash mob.

They hurried across the lawn, into the inn, up the sweeping staircase, and arrived at the Churchill Suite—Eagle Hill Manor's signature guest room on the second floor. Amy, who was also an assistant wedding planner at the inn, opened the door with her passkey.

"C'mon, boys, let's go get wine," Amy said, snagging Andrew's brother and cousins. She looked up at Andrew. "We'll be back. In the meantime, you hold down the fort. I can't think of anyone better. You are the most levelheaded member of the Lyndon family." She winked and gave him a sisterly smile.

Wow, Amy had really grown up in the last year. Instead of a spoiled brat without ambition or focus, she had grown up to become a clever and competent woman. She'd married Dusty McNeil earlier in the summer over everyone's objections, including his own. But as it turned out, everyone was wrong. Amy and Dusty were wildly happy, and Dusty had been exactly the medicine Amy had needed to heal the broken places in her once-aimless life.

Amy took charge of Andrew's younger brother and cousins like a mother hen and ushered them down the hall, leaving Andrew to deal with the distraught bride. He guided Laurie into the room, which was cluttered with suitcases packed and ready for a five-day honeymoon in Bermuda.

He came to a stop on the Persian rug just inside the door. Now what?

In his professional life, he'd mediated plenty of disputes, from simple divorce cases to complicated disagreements between litigants. This situation had Humpty Dumpty written all over it. No one was going to put this back together.

He turned and allowed himself to look Laurie in the face. Her big hazel eyes stared back, oddly vacant. She might have been a wax statue, the way she stood stiff and unmoving without real expression. A beautiful wax statue, with her golden hair braided with flowers.

What kind of idiot walks away from a woman like this?

Before he could act, Madison, Emma, and Jessica closed ranks around Laurie and guided her to one of the wing chairs in the sitting room. She sank down into it, her big skirt billowing up around her, making her look like a frothy white cupcake.

"I think we should find Brandon's Camaro and mess it up," Emma said.

"Screw that, I want to kill him, not his car," said Jessica.

"Can I castrate him first?" Madison asked.

"But I love him," Laurie said in a watery voice as the first tear escaped the corner of her right eye.

"Oh, baby, don't cry for that SOB," Madison said and then hurried into the bathroom, returning a moment later with a big wad of tissues, which she pressed into Laurie's hand. Laurie accepted the tissues but did nothing to stanch the slow drip of tears. That controlled release of emotion wrenched Andrew's heart more than sobs could have. She ought to be disconsolate. She ought to be angry.

Fury boiled down in the pit of his stomach. He hadn't felt rage like this since last spring, when he'd gone after Amy's boyfriend in the mistaken belief that Dusty was taking advantage of his sister. Dusty, who knew how to settle disputes with his fists, had put a serious hurt on him.

So much so that he'd enrolled in a weekly aikido class, where he'd learned something he'd always known. That the only way to defuse a fight was not to fight at all, but to find a way to make peace. And yet, despite all the training in the dojo, Andrew still wanted to strangle Brandon. How could his best friend do something so outrageously hurtful? Andrew knew what being dumped felt like. Val had walked out on him two years ago without any kind of warning. He'd almost moved on, but he would never forget that feeling of lost trust.

The door banged open and in walked Andrew's younger cousins, Matt and Jason, with several bottles of champagne and a big bucket of ice. Amy trailed behind with a tray filled with champagne flutes.

"We nabbed some of the champagne reserved for the wedding toast. We figured since it was already paid for, we—"

"Shut up, Matt," Andrew said, rolling his eyes toward Laurie. "And what happened to Edward?"

"Our dear darling brother decided to find Brandon and talk to him," Amy said, her voice unusually grave.

Damn. That should have been Andrew's job. Not only was he the best man, but he and Brandon were almost like brothers. They'd been in nursery school together, and their parents were old and dear friends. Maybe he could defuse the situation. Although if he were honest with himself, the only things he wanted to say to Brandon at the moment would probably not calm the situation down.

So instead of leaving the bride to talk to the groom, he nabbed a bottle of champagne and started pouring. When everyone had received a glass, Jessica raised hers and said, "Here's to castrating and then murdering Brandon Kopp, but only after we destroy his car."

The bridesmaids chorused, "Hear, hear."

Jason and Matt looked uncomfortable. Laurie just sat there holding her wineglass without drinking.

"Uh, I don't really feel like killing or castrating Brandon, and if you mess up his Camaro, he's going to be really pissed," Matt said, ever the socially insensitive one.

Everyone looked at him as if he'd just farted in church. But Matt held his ground. "Look, you guys, Brandon is a friend. He's more than a friend, really, since we all grew up with him and Roxy. I'm just saying that he should be praised for walking away if he wasn't three hundred percent sure about getting married."

"Get the hell out of here." Jessica got right up into Matt's face and almost pushed him out of the room. Good for her. It saved Andrew from doing the same thing.

"I think I'll go too," Jason said, leaving his untouched champagne glass on a side table.

"Uh-oh," Amy said, once Jason was gone. "This is going to get messy, isn't it? Like a divorce. Edward was pretty blunt with us. He said Laurie had enough support and someone should be thinking about Brandon."

"Yeah," Jessica said, "in order to torture him, slowly."

Amy touched his arm, and Andrew looked down into his sister's dark eyes. "You really need to do something before everyone gets angry with everyone else," she said. "I hate it when the family's in turmoil. And the Kopps are like members of the family." There were tears in Amy's eyes.

Why me? Andrew wondered. But he already knew the answer. He often played referee. But this time, keeping the peace might be impossible. Brandon breaking up with Laurie would shatter the dynamic of their tight-knit circle of friends and family.

Negotiating those fissures and cracks would be doubly difficult because Laurie's father, Noah Wilson, was Andrew's boss at Wilson Kavanaugh, a law firm with a nationally respected mediation practice. For the last five years, Andrew had been busting his butt trying to make partner. This breakup would put him in an awkward position to say the least.

He downed his champagne and stepped across the room, sinking into the ottoman beside Laurie's chair. "Laurie," he said gently.

She looked up at him, her face marred by tear tracks. He wanted to pull her into his arms and tell her to weep and sob and yell, even though he knew from experience that none of those things would change the situation. Still, there was something to be said for the cathartic property of throwing things. He'd broken an entire set of dishes the day Val walked out on him.

No one knew he'd done that, of course. Andrew kept his emotions tightly reined when he was in public. Laurie was like that too. It was something he admired about her.

"What would fix this situation for you?" he asked.

"I love him," she whispered, her voice so tight, it sounded brittle.

"So you'd be okay if he changed his mind and we started over? You still want to marry him?"

She nodded, biting her lower lip. "I certainly don't want to kill or maim him." She glanced at Madison. "Or mess up his car."

"Let me go talk to him, okay?" Andrew said gently.

"You can't be serious." Emma downed the last drop of her champagne and glared at him. "That asshole left her at the altar. That's like the worst humiliation a woman can suffer. It's like he—"

"Shut up," Laurie said, her voice surprisingly strong. "I'd take him back," she said.

"Okay, let me see what I can do." Andrew got up and headed toward the door, but Emma followed him.

"You aren't seriously thinking about talking Brandon into going forward with the ceremony, are you?"

"Why not?"

She rolled her eyes. "Because he's a dickwad, and Laurie deserves better."

"He wasn't a dickwad two hours ago, was he? Maybe he just had a moment of—"

"Doesn't matter who he was two hours ago. He walked away from her on her wedding day. And it's not her place to grovel and ask him to come back."

"I wouldn't ask her to grovel, Emma. But if she's willing to take him back, don't you think it's worth trying to see if that's possible? The object is to find a win-win situation for both of them."

"You're unbelievable. Laurie is not capable of judging what she wants right now." Emma's fists landed on her hips.

"And you are?" he asked, suddenly annoyed at Laurie's best friend.

Emma shook her head. "No. But I think Laurie loves the idea of Brandon. I think she's been overlooking a lot of problems with the real Brandon."

Andrew let out a long breath. "Look, she asked me to talk to him, okay? I'm the best man—reasoning with the groom comes with the territory. And besides, I'm a mediator so talking to people in crisis is sort of my thing."

Emma folded her arms across her chest. "Knock yourself out. But you aren't going to change Brandon's mind. My guess is that he's been cheating on Laurie." She turned and ducked back into the Churchill Suite.

Was there someone else? Andrew didn't think so. But he'd certainly been surprised that day when he'd come home from work and found Val all packed and ready to run off to her lover.

Laurie looked down at the champagne flute, studying the way the late afternoon sun sparkled on the bubbles and her two-carat pavé-set Tiffany engagement ring. She remembered the day Brandon had put that ring on her finger. It was at her birthday party, two years ago. She hadn't thought too much about the fact that members of their close group of friends each brought a balloon to the party with a single letter on it. But it all became clear when Brandon suggested a group picture with the balloons, which, when lined up in the right order, spelled out: LAURIE, WILL YOU MARRY ME?

Brandon had gotten down on his knee and presented the ring in its beautiful robin's-egg-blue Tiffany box. She'd loved the ring from the first moment she'd laid eyes on it. It was classic and maybe a tiny bit old-fashioned.

And now she would have to give it back.

Something broke inside her heart, and the tears she'd been trying not to shed welled up like a fountain. How could such a romantic man walk away from their wedding?

She slipped the ring from her finger. "Someone needs to give this back," she managed to choke out.

"Aw, honey," Jessica said, "you are not giving that back. You're going to sell it on eBay and pocket the ten grand. You'll need the money to fix up that house Brandon talked you into buying. Now drink your champagne. It'll take the edge off."

She did as she was told, and just as soon as she'd drained the flute, Madison refilled it. "I just don't get it," Laurie said through her tears.

"Neither do we," Emma said. "But the important thing is that a man who leaves his bride at the altar is a jerk."

Laurie shook her head. No. Brandon was a great guy. The problem wasn't Brandon. It was her.

She sniffled back her tears and downed another glass of champagne. Yes, definitely. She was the problem. She'd been a fool to think that they had a special relationship that could weather her problems in the bedroom. She needed to accept the fact that she was a dud when it came to sex. She was uptight and OCD and had trouble turning her brain off. Who wanted to be chained to a wife like that?

She downed another glass of champagne.

"So, girls, you know we really can't kill him or castrate

him. But the Camaro…we could really mess it up," Emma said in a solemn tone.

"Maybe we could find a bottle of spray paint and write the words 'Left the Bride at the Altar' across his back window," Madison said.

"You're an amateur," Jessica said. "I vote that we go to Lowes and buy a pickax and turn the Camaro into Swiss cheese."

"That would be too obvious," Emma said. "We should just put sugar in the gas tank."

The girls continued to discuss ways of destroying Brandon's beloved car while they sipped several more glasses of champagne.

Meanwhile Laurie obsessed over all the things she'd done wrong. It was amazing that Brandon hadn't found someone else. Assuming he'd told her the truth. But it didn't matter because he'd lose interest in her as soon as he started playing the field. She bored him in the bedroom, and that's why he wanted her to date other guys. Maybe he thought she needed the experience. Like the opposite of slut-shaming or something. But sleeping around would be like cheating on him.

Except it wouldn't be cheating. Not now.

The truth exploded on her like a stinger missile, and suddenly all the champagne she'd been sipping didn't want to stay down. She didn't make it all the way to the bathroom before she hurled it up.

Well, that was it. Her beautiful $7,000 wedding dress was utterly ruined. Even if Andrew could talk Brandon into marrying her, Laurie now had nothing to wear to the wedding.

Chapter Two ———————

Andrew's uncles Charles and Mark, along with his father, were sitting in the library with Noah Wilson. They hovered around Laurie's father as if they might be undertaking an intervention. Everyone seemed to have a drink, which made perfect sense because, if ever there was a moment for alcohol, this was it.

"Uh, sorry," Andrew said and turned around. He'd been heading toward the French doors in the library when he'd stumbled on the group of elder statesmen.

"Andrew." Noah called him back, and since Noah was his boss, he turned.

"Yes."

"Thanks for getting Laurie out of the church that way. Is she all right?"

"She's upset, but her girlfriends are with her, and I just saw her mother go upstairs. Um, have any of you seen Brandon?"

A muscle in Noah's cheek flexed. His boss was furious, and had every reason to be.

"I think I saw him out at the gazebo," Uncle Charles said. "Thanks."

Andrew crossed the room and headed through the French doors onto the terrace. A few moments later, he found Brandon standing in the gazebo staring out at the panoramic view of the Shenandoah Valley across the west lawn.

"If you're here to talk me out of it, get in line. Dad has expressed his disappointment. Roxy has poured on the sisterly guilt. And Laurie's father has ripped me a new one; I mean, he was red-faced furious with me in a way I've never seen before. For a moment, I thought the guy might try to punch me or something. Your father saved me."

"Yeah, I saw him in the library plying Laurie's father with bourbon. I'm kind of surprised Noah didn't try to initiate mediation."

"I don't think he had mediation on his mind," Brandon said, turning around and leaning into the gazebo's baluster. "I hope you aren't here for that either."

"Laurie still loves you, you know," Andrew said after a moment of silence.

Brandon's lips pressed together. "Yeah, I know. But I'm not changing my mind. One day she'll thank me for this."

"Somehow, Brandon, I don't think so. You hurt her today."

He cocked one eyebrow. "So you're on her side too, huh?"

"I'm not on anyone's side. I'm just speaking the truth."

"Fine."

"Also, you should know that Laurie's friends are so pissed off, they're making plans to do something heinous to your car."

"Thanks."

Wow. Brandon's response was underwhelming given

that he loved his fully restored 1970 Camaro Z28 the way some people loved their pets. The car was practically a member of his immediate family.

"You should know that Jessica is especially vindictive. On the other hand, Laurie continues to express her love and support," Andrew said.

"Is she really upset?"

"Of course she is," Andrew said mildly, swallowing back his own anger. "She expected to marry you today. Right now she's trying to figure out why you did what you did."

"To be honest, Laurie says she loves me, but I'm not sure she knows what love is. I'm not sure I do either. I don't think we belong together," Brandon said.

Andrew was experienced enough in negotiations to know when he was being BS'd. "So if I hear you right, you're saying you don't want to get married to Laurie at all? Earlier you said you wanted a break for a while. Those two positions are in conflict, you know."

Brandon shook his head and looked heavenward in a display of exasperation. "I don't want you to mediate. All I know is that I feel like I'm being rushed into something."

"You've known Laurie for ten years. That's not rushing into anything. So I'm just asking the basic question. Why did you do it? And what do you need to move forward?"

"And I'm saying that I don't want you trying to be my relationship counselor, okay? I'm not looking for a compromise. I just need a friend, is all."

"So you want me to support your decision without question, is that it?"

"No, of course not. I'd like you to understand where I'm coming from. But if you want to rip me a new one like Laurie's father did, go ahead. I don't really give a rat's ass what you do." The anger in Brandon's voice scalded his words.

"I think you do care. And I think you're going to pay a price for this eventually. The people who love you and Laurie are going to be pulled into factions, and once that happens, a resolution that will meet your needs will be hard to find."

"Well, thanks for making me feel better."

"I didn't come here to make you feel better."

"Look, Andrew, if you want to take Laurie's side on this, then fine." Brandon walked past Andrew in a determined stride, the tone of his voice conveying the opposite of his words. Brandon obviously expected his best man to remain loyal no matter what. Unfortunately Andrew saw both sides to this dispute.

Courtney Wallace, the wedding planner at Eagle Hill Manor, hurried up the grand staircase toward the Churchill Suite. This was the second time in her short career as a wedding planner that she'd had to deal with a left-at-the-altar scenario. Last spring, reality TV personality Mia Paquet had dumped Daniel Lyndon at the altar. But in that case, Courtney had practically jumped for joy.

Mia had been the worst bridezilla ever.

Laurie, not so much, although she could be a little OCD about small details. But really, what bride wasn't just a little OCD when it came to her wedding day?

Courtney reached the landing just as her assistant, Amy McNeil, arrived from the opposite direction.

"How is she?" Courtney asked. No need to explain the pronoun. There was only one person on anyone's mind right at the moment.

Amy shook her head. "It's bad. Really bad. I feel so sorry for her. All that work…"

"We should have done something to stop the wedding before today," Courtney said as she pressed a finger to her forehead where a tension headache was starting to blossom.

"What could we have done? I mean, did you know Brandon was planning to pull a stunt like that? I sure didn't see it coming. I've known Brandon all my life, and he's a totally sweet guy."

"Brandon isn't sweet," Courtney said.

"Well, I guess not, I mean after—"

"No, I mean before. He's a classic example of the *Nice Guy, Not.*"

Amy blinked. "Okay, refresh my memory. Which one is that?"

At thirty-five and still single, Courtney had dated extensively and had never once found Mr. Right, although she had lost her heart once, ages ago. In the intervening years, she had developed a list of ten male losers that every woman should avoid at all costs.

"The *Nice Guy, Not* is the one who looks perfect on paper," Courtney said. "Everyone says he's a nice guy. He holds doors. He's not afraid to meet the parents. He even cuddles. But he thinks all that good behavior entitles him to special treatment, as if common decency were something special. That makes him just another entitled male jerk.

"And you know what? Now that I think of it, Brandon also has a few traits in common with the *Belittler.* Don't you remember how he second-guessed every one of Laurie's decisions? And she needed that like a hole in the head, what with her mother constantly expressing her views as well."

Amy nodded. "I guess you do have a point about that. He was annoying as hell about the reception menu. At the time, I thought it was nice that he cared so much about the wedding plans."

Courtney shook her head. "Amy, real men don't care about wedding plans. They just do what they're told."

"So you think he's screwing around on her?"

"I have no clue, but when a man says he wants to take a break, it usually means he has a honey on the side."

"You know, Court, you have a jaded view of love for a woman in your position."

"Yeah, but I'm a hell of a good organizer, and this pays better than nursing. Although on days like this, I sometimes think the burnout potential is just as high."

"Well, there's nothing you can do upstairs. Laurie is in the good hands of her friends. They've got plenty of champagne, and they're already thinking about ways to destroy Brandon's Camaro."

Courtney grinned. "I knew I liked Laurie's friends."

"So, is there anything you need from me?" Amy asked.

Courtney shook her head. "No, most of the guests have left, although your dad and uncles are having some kind of powwow in the library. Pam is in there too. I think they're trying to talk Laurie's father down. He really lost it a while ago. Anyway, I sent in a couple of bottles of Bella Vista wine. I also left directions to keep the bar open until everyone clears out of the Carriage House. We've already made arrangements to send any leftover food to the Jefferson County homeless shelter."

"All right then. I'll go check on Dad and the uncles and make sure everything is okay in the library. Then I plan to head home to Dusty." Amy's eyes lit up the moment she said her husband's name. Amy and Dusty were the epitome of starry-eyed newlyweds. Courtney hoped their happiness lasted.

"You should go home too," Amy said.

"I will, after I make sure everything is buttoned up in the Carriage House."

They turned and walked down the stairway together. At

the bottom, Amy turned right and headed toward the library. Courtney turned left and went through Eagle Hill Manor's front door to the grand portico. She wanted to take the long walk around to the Carriage House in order to clear her mind before handling the last few details of Laurie's wedding-that-never-was.

But one of the Lyndon boys was blocking her way. He sat on the front steps with his elbows on his knees and his head bowed. His tux fit him like it had been hand-tailored just for him, and for an instant, she felt sorry for him. He looked a little sad, sitting there alone.

Which Lyndon was he? They all looked alike from the back. Was it Andrew? Jason? Edward?

Just then, he turned and gave her one of those smiles that a less experienced woman might have fallen for. Oh yeah, she knew this one. Matthew. Amy's first cousin and Daniel Lyndon's brother. And if she remembered correctly, Amy thought he was kind of a jerk.

Although really, the words "man" and "jerk" were interchangeable in Courtney's book. Since she'd already had her fill of jerks today, she started to do a one-eighty when he said, "Don't go." He had a seductively deep, velvet voice.

She froze. Guys with seductive, velvet voices were one of her weaknesses. Every guy she'd ever met with a velvet voice had turned out to be a major player. And Matt Lyndon's reputation preceded him.

"You're the wedding planner, aren't you?" he asked. "A situation like today's must be difficult. For what it's worth, I thought the reception room looked particularly nice. I liked the purple flowers."

"Dahlias," she said without thinking and pressed her lips together. She shouldn't encourage him.

Like every player she'd ever met, the guy knew better

than to use a standard pickup line. Instead he'd opened with a compliment that showed how much he was interested in what she did for a living. Maybe she should tell the guy that his cousin Amy was responsible for the flower arrangements.

Nah, maybe not. Maybe she'd wait to shoot him down. So instead of leaving him there on the portico, she turned and strolled in his direction. Predictably, his eyes sparked, and a smile touched his lips. He was handsome, she'd give him that. But then all of the Lyndon men were handsome.

"This is such a nice spot," he said, his voice as smooth and easy as a shot of Maker's Mark. He was a cool customer, completely at ease. And she gave him points for hitting on her. He was young, maybe twenty-five. And she was much older. It had been a while since anyone—young or old—had so much as catcalled.

Not that she enjoyed catcalls. But still, a woman in her mid-thirties enjoyed being hit on now and again. She purposefully ran her hand through her hair, just to see what he would do. Any player worth his salt would interpret that as a come-on.

He stood up and intercepted Courtney, getting close enough for her to smell his woodsy aftershave. "I imagine the inn is a great place for couples to get away for a weekend," he said. "It's probably a drag for a person like you. I mean, where do you go for a getaway?"

Oh brother, Matt Lyndon was so obvious. He was testing to see if she was available. She gave him a coquettish smile, which he mirrored. "I'm afraid I work too hard to get away on weekends. Besides, I hate leaving my cat alone, you know?"

She didn't have a cat. But letting him think she did was like waving a piece of raw meat in front of a tiger. A woman who would stay home with her cat was automatically unattached. He knew the code as well as she did.

"So, do they make you wear black to work?" he asked. "It's not really your color, although the shape of that dress is nice. You look kind of hot in it."

Uh-huh, there it was, the little passive-aggressive remark designed to send the message that he wasn't desperate, had standards, and maybe if she was nice to him, he would show her a good time. "Thanks," she said, as if she didn't actually know the steps to this dance.

"So you look like a fun person, Courtney. The kind who likes to get out and party, you know? Have a little casual fun."

Casual fun. Like a hookup with no strings attached. At least he was an honest player, she'd give him that. She had no use for players who led a girl on. She said nothing in response to his come-on. She simply turned her back on him and took a couple of steps toward the inn's front door. Then she stopped and looked over her shoulder with what she hoped was a classic come-hither look.

He grinned. "So, do you have anything planned for after work? Since there's no wedding, maybe we could get away somewhere for drinks or something?"

There it was, the classic close.

She wondered if Matt understood the cruelty of his little game. Probably not. He undoubtedly thought that if he used the word "casual," it would absolve him of any damage he might do to any woman who crossed his path.

She turned and faced him head on. "No thanks, Matthew. I know a player when I see one. Oh, and one other thing, you can tell Brandon that I intend to take his ex-fiancée under my wing and teach her exactly how to recognize players like you and heartbreakers like him. And I hope to God she never has to suffer another humiliation at the hands of a man ever again."

Chapter Three ─────────

I t's time to get up."

Laurie cracked her eye and then immediately squeezed it shut. Someone had pulled the curtains back, and the damn sun shone through the big double-hung window like a torture device. Why the hell had it stopped raining anyway? Her head throbbed, but this wasn't one of her killer migraines, thank God. It was merely a basic hangover with a chaser of life-shattering grief.

"Come on, you need to eat." Mom's voice had that steely quality to it, and despite Mom's tears last night, this morning she was dry-eyed.

That was Mom. Her life zigzagged from one emotional disaster to another. She had tons of practice getting over crap with the help of various therapies from classic psychoanalytic to cognitive behavioral. She was self-aware and more than happy to expound on the deeper meaning of life, even though she was totally lost and without any real direction.

Laurie burrowed deeper into the bed and pulled the pillow over her head. She didn't want to get up. She didn't want to eat. She didn't want to face the world. Damn. If she'd been smarter, she would have bypassed the champagne and gotten Jessica to drive her home. She raised her head and checked the digital clock on the bedside table.

Too late to catch the flight to Bermuda.

Laurie pushed her hair out of her eyes and looked up at Mom, a vision in black-and-white polka dots that probably came from Bergdorf Goodman. The dress was so New Yorker-comes-to-Virginia.

That was Mom, all right, a New Yorker born and bred. Dad had temporarily transplanted her to D.C., but when their marriage dissolved, Mom moved back to Manhattan, taking ten-year-old Laurie with her. Despite years of living there, Laurie had never become a New Yorker. She detested the city.

So when she turned eighteen, she came back "home" to attend George Washington University in the nation's capital. She'd been living in D.C. for the last ten years.

"Come on," Mom said in that mommy voice of hers. "I know you would rather hide, but it's better to get up, take a shower, and dress for brunch."

"Brunch? Really?" Laurie's voice sounded vaguely frog-like, a sign that she was dehydrated from the champagne, hurling, and eventual dry heaves.

"It's Sunday, sweetie. And you have to eat. I thought we'd brunch at the Red Fern Inn."

"I don't want brunch. I'll get room service."

"It's too late for that. You've missed the inn's breakfast, and they don't have room service."

As usual, Mom focused on the practicality of things instead of Laurie's desire not to have brunch at all.

"I'm sorry, sweetie. We decided to let you sleep," Mom added in a compassionate tone.

"Who's 'we'?"

"Not your father, that's for sure. You'll be pleased to know that I sent him back to Washington. Honestly, the man is impossible. But you should know that he was so furious yesterday that it took Charles, Jamie, and Mark Lyndon to calm him down. I'm afraid they plied him with a lot of bourbon. He was very grumpy at breakfast this morning." Mom leaned over the bed, and Laurie noticed the glass of water in her hand. "I've got Tylenol for your headache."

Resistance was futile so Laurie pushed herself up from the pillows and discovered that her headache wasn't really all that bad after all. And she was definitely sober, which was a pity. She would have to do something about that.

She took the Tylenol anyway, mostly to give Mom a sense of accomplishment. "Do they have mimosas at the Red Fern?"

Mom glared at her. "The old adage about hair of the dog has been scientifically proven wrong, you know."

Laurie nodded, but an hour later, she and Mom sat in the tap room at the Red Fern Inn sipping a couple of spicy Bloody Marys. The dark room, with its stone walls, heavy beams, and heart-of-pine flooring suited Laurie's mood. Plus it was late for brunch and the crowd was pretty thin, which meant she didn't have to run into anyone she knew.

Not that she knew many people in Shenandoah Falls, since she'd moved here only a month ago. She and Brandon had bought a run-down fixer-upper. Laurie could certainly see the potential of the house, but if she'd had her way, they would have purchased a two-bedroom condo in the new complex down Route 7, closer to Winchester.

Actually, now that she thought about it, if she'd been totally free to make her own decisions, she would have taken the associate professor job at the University of Michigan. In which case she'd be sitting in beautiful Ann Arbor right now. Instead, she'd taken the far less prestigious job at Winchester University just twenty minutes away. She'd made that sacrifice so Brandon could join his father's law firm, Lyndon, Lyndon & Kopp.

Her throat thickened. It took a gargantuan effort to swallow down the tomato juice and vodka. Damn him. Damn him to hell and back again. She took several deep breaths and shoved the overwhelming crap to the back corner of her mind. She could do this. She could make it through this meal without crumbling. She opened the menu and tried to focus. The Red Fern offered no less than seven different varieties of eggs Benedict.

Decisions, decisions. Would she go traditional, or try the Eggs Benedict Huevos Rancheros, or maybe even the Eggs Benedict Cumberbatch? No, nix the Benedict Cumberbatch eggs, they were definitely out of her league. Traditional, then. Not that there was any doubt really. Laurie just liked to pretend to be adventurous.

She was so engrossed in the menu that she practically jumped when Pam Lyndon showed up at the table looking like royalty in a dark gray pencil skirt and a cornflower blue tweed jacket that buttoned up the front with a Mandarin collar.

"Hello," she said. "I know you both probably want to be left alone, but I was just finishing brunch with some of the members of the Harvest Festival steering committee when I saw you come in. I wanted to tell you both how sorry I am about yesterday." Pam cocked her head like a curious dog and inspected Laurie out of a pair of keen blue eyes that matched her jacket. "Laurie, I want you to know that the doors of Charlotte's Grove will always be open for you. After all these years, I feel as if you're part of the family," she said as she pulled up a chair. "I will truly miss you if you don't stay in touch. And, darlin', I know this is a sensitive subject. But I don't want to see you crawl away in some hole."

"You should listen to her," Mom said.

Laurie said nothing because right now all she wanted was to find a nice dark secluded place to lie down and assume the fetal position.

"Darlin'," Pam said. "I know you don't want to hear this, but the best thing you can do for yourself is to pick yourself up and just go on without Brandon as if nothing has happened. I know he's shaken your self-esteem, but you can't let him know that. He says he wants you to go see other people, and in my opinion, you should do it. In fact, if you like, I'd be happy to set you up with one of my nephews. You and Daniel have a lot in common. Both of you have had terrible wedding disasters. And of course, you and Andrew are already friends."

Oh great, just what she needed, a date with some guy who also got left at the altar. And how could she date Brandon's best friend? No thanks. Escape wasn't an option so she looked Pam in the eye. "Thank you, Mrs. Lyndon, really. But I'm not ready to date anyone."

Pam stood up and patted her shoulder. "Of course you aren't. But give it a few days. If you change your mind, give me a call. Now that you've moved to town, we shouldn't be strangers."

"Thanks," Laurie said.

"I heard that you bought a house in town."

"Yes, on Rice Street."

Pam's frown spoke volumes. Laurie already knew that her house wasn't in the fashionable section of town. But Brandon had big plans for fixing it up and selling it for a bundle in a few years when the neighborhood started to improve. That plan was up in smoke too. Damn. She couldn't continue to co-own the house with Brandon. She'd have to sell it.

"Well, I should be going. Darlin', please keep in touch," Pam said, her smile fixed.

"Sure," Laurie said in a pinched voice.

When Pam's back was turned, Laurie picked up her drink and took three or four swallows just to kill the sudden emotional and financial pain.

"Sorry about that. You know this is going to be hard," Mom said, once Pam was out of earshot, "but Pam is right. It's like riding a horse. When you're thrown, you just have to climb back on. You'll survive. I'm here to help you do that. And I think the first thing we should do is make a list."

Laurie was a supremely good list maker. She'd made it through the last year of wedding planning, house shopping, and job hunting with multiple lists. And she'd already started a list of all the things she wanted done to her fixer-upper. Now it looked as if she needed to make a list of the things she had to do to get over her relationship with Brandon.

Couldn't she just wallow in the pain for a while? Maybe spend the next five days—days when she should have been in Bermuda soaking up sun—wearing her pajamas and eating Ben and Jerry's Chubby Hubby ice cream?

No, she couldn't. And the first item on her list would have to be ditching the Chubby Hubby and developing a new relationship with something else, like Empower Mint or Chocolate Therapy. She took another sip of her drink—a smaller one this time. The vodka was starting to take the edge off.

"I think the first thing we should do is take you to New York for some shopping. I don't want you spending the next five days on your couch eating ice cream. Is that clear?"

Mom knew her so well.

Laurie finished her drink and waggled her empty glass

at the passing waitress, who nodded. Then she turned back toward her mother. "I don't need retail therapy," she said. "Besides, I don't like taking Dad's money. You know that. I want to stand on my own two feet. That's why Brandon and I chose a short honeymoon in Bermuda." Her voice wobbled. She should be there right now.

"Your father and I have only your best interests in mind, and we don't mind spending money on you. In my opinion, you need more than just a shopping trip. You need a total makeover."

"Mom, please..."

"Sweetie, you do. It's terrible when a man lets you down. Take it from me. The first thing I did for my self-esteem after your dad and I split was to get a little work done, you know?"

Yes, Laurie knew. Mom had had more than a *little* work done; she'd had the whole middle-age lift package from her boobs to her butt.

"I don't need any work done," Laurie said as the waitress put another Bloody Mary in front of her.

"I know that. You're still so young. But you do need better hair and...uh..."

"What, Mom? Spit it out." The vodka was bringing out her inner brat.

"Laurie, everyone heard what Brandon said yesterday. When a man says he wants to go sample the rest of the world, it means he's gotten bored with the woman in his life."

"Or it could just mean he's a dick." Laurie spat the words, but the moment she spoke them, her heart wanted to take them back.

"You know that's not true," Mom said. "Brandon has always been so sweet to you."

Mom was right. Brandon wasn't a dick, and she already knew that Brandon had gotten bored with her. She just didn't want to admit it.

"So I think we should focus on redoing you, inside and out. A new wardrobe that's a little more office hottie and a little less dowdy college professor. And I think you could really use a session with a therapist. In fact, I've already gotten recommendations for a couple of local CBT therapists that might help you relax, you know, about…things."

Laurie was tempted to ask Mom what things she was talking about, but unfortunately Laurie already knew. She wasn't exactly inventive or creative or even exuberant when it came to sex. She was kind of old-fashioned. And maybe as frumpy as her wardrobe, which consisted of pantsuits in all the basic colors—gray, navy, and black.

Laurie finished her second Bloody Mary just as the waitress came by to take their orders. And just to prove that she could do something unexpected, she ordered the Eggs Benedict Cumberbatch.

"So, what do you say?" Mom asked. "The guest bedroom is ready for you, and we can take the train up this evening and spend five days shopping on Fifth Avenue and in SoHo, and maybe even go to the Met."

Mom had just pulled out the stops, hadn't she? A trip to the Metropolitan Opera was a huge inducement. But the cost was too high.

She shook her head. "Mom, I'm not going to change myself. And I'm certainly not going to do what Brandon suggested. I won't spend the next six months sleeping around so I can be a better wife to the guy I fell in love with the first moment I saw him."

"Sweetie, don't—"

"Don't what? Mom, here's the thing. I thought Brandon

loved me for who I am. And trying to change myself won't work. I mean, how'd that work for you and Dad?"

Mom's mouth dropped open, and Laurie knew she'd pushed it too far. Damn. She was so tired of tiptoeing around her parents' broken relationship. And the very last thing she wanted in life was to become her mother. But Brandon had certainly given her a gigantic push in that direction.

The Washington, D.C., office of Wilson Kavanaugh, LLC, occupied space on the thirteenth floor of a new office building at the corner of Connecticut Avenue and K Street. The reception area was paved in marble and paneled in European beech. The partner offices were light and airy, the corridors wide and spacious, the carpets thick and neutral-toned.

The opulence ended when it came to the associate offices, all of which sat in the interior of the suite, without windows except for glass walls open to the common area where the administrative staff labored.

On Monday morning, Andrew found himself at his desk sipping the day's second cup of coffee when Noah darkened his door. "Andrew, I need your help," Noah said as he stepped into the office and closed the door behind him.

Andrew immediately snapped to attention. "What's up? Is there a problem with the Aviation Engineering negotiations?"

Noah shook his head. "No, I read your memo on that, and I think you nailed the health care strategy. Good work on that, by the way." Noah took a seat in Andrew's single side chair.

Andrew tried to relax, but out beyond his glass wall, his assistant was peeking above her cubicle with a worried frown. Kim had good cause to worry. Partners never visited associates at Wilson Kavanaugh.

Andrew took a deep, calming breath and asked, "What can I do for you?"

"It's a personal matter..." Noah's voice faded out, and he moved restlessly in the plastic and steel chair, which looked great but had not been designed for sitting. This had never been a problem before since almost no one ever visited his office. If Andrew needed to speak with Noah, he made an appointment.

Noah finally found a comfortable position and let go of a long breath before he spoke again. "To be honest, I'm here to talk about Laurie and Brandon."

"What about them?" Andrew asked in a cautious tone.

"I was furious with Brandon on Saturday."

"You had good cause to be."

"Your father and uncles calmed me down."

Andrew already knew this, but something about the way Noah said it, while his eyes moved to the left, put Andrew on guard. "Uncle Mark has a long history of calming people down," he said in a neutral voice.

Noah nodded. "I've had a day or two to think about things, and I've come to the conclusion that, if I do nothing, Laurie's self-esteem will be shattered for a very long time. I love my daughter, Andrew. I don't want her living her life alone in some academic ivory tower. I want her to be—" He bit off the end of his sentence and gazed through the window.

Andrew had never seen Noah so emotional.

After a long moment, Noah hauled in big breath, as if to calm himself, and continued. "Brandon's behavior is inexcusable, even if I believe it's a classic example of cold feet, exacerbated by over-the-top wedding plans. Regardless, I need your help to make sure my daughter does exactly what Brandon asked her to do."

"What's that?"

"Go out on dates and see other people. That will give her confidence, and at the same time it will likely drive Brandon crazy. I bet it helps Brandon to see that he's made a mistake."

What the hell? Noah wanted to get Laurie and Brandon back together. Why?

"I see I've surprised you," Noah said.

"Surprised" wasn't the word Andrew was thinking. He nodded and chose his words carefully. "Brandon doesn't want me to mediate his conflict with Laurie. And besides, I'm hardly impartial since Brandon and Laurie's breakup has divided my circle of friends. This is an awkward situation for me, Noah."

"Of course it is. It's awkward for everyone. Nevertheless I want you to drop everything and focus on this problem. From now on, this is your highest priority," Noah said.

Oh boy, Andrew was in serious trouble. But he couldn't say no because Noah had Andrew's career in his hands. Andrew was up for partner this year. "Okay," he said. "I'll give it some thought after we finish the Aviation Engineering negotiations."

Noah shook his head. "No. I don't want you wasting your time with AVIEN. I want you to speak with my daughter right away and convince her of the necessity of dating. Be sure to tell her that going out with other men has the potential to help Brandon see the enormity of his mistake. And then I want you to facilitate her dates."

"Facilitate her dates? What does that mean?"

"It means introducing her to some of your friends."

Andrew's mouth almost dropped open. "But—"

"Make it happen for her, understand?" Noah stood up, cutting off all objections. "I know this is going to be difficult, but I have faith in you, Andrew."

The managing partner of Wilson Kavanaugh turned and stalked through the door. A moment later, Kim scurried into Andrew's office and hovered over his desk. "Did he fire you?" she asked.

"No. We were discussing private client matters."

"Which matters? I saw his face. He was kind of agitated. Did you mess up on AVIEN? I told you that idea for pushing health care was a loser; they'll never agree to anything except a wage hike."

He ground his teeth. "Kim, if you don't mind, I'd—"

"Good morning." Tobin Grant, who was obviously hooked into the office grapevine, stopped at the door to Andrew's office and lounged there looking every inch the successful D.C. lawyer on the make.

"I heard Noah came to visit," he said, his blue eyes twinkling. "Should I genuflect or offer my condolences? The last time Noah entered an associate's office was three years ago, and it didn't go well for old Steve."

Andrew leaned back in his chair, trying to exude confidence. "Look, guys," Andrew said, "Noah just gave me a new assignment. If you don't mind, I have work to do."

"What assignment?" Kim and Tobin asked in unison.

"Something confidential."

They shared a conspiratorial glance that told Andrew everything he needed to know about Kim's nonexistent loyalties. But then he already knew his odds in the partnership pool were much longer than Tobin's. Tobin Grant was the fair-haired boy who was practically assured of making partner at the end of the year.

Andrew not so much. He'd had to work harder and suck up more than Tobin ever had to. And now, his chances in the partnership sweepstakes were fading, and all because his best friend had left the boss's daughter at the altar.

Chapter Four

Mom had spent most of Sunday trying to get Laurie on a train to New York, but Laurie had dug in her heels. Mom could be a pain in the ass sometimes, but she also had a short attention span. She'd finally given up Sunday evening and had taken the last Acela back to the Big Apple.

Unfortunately, Mom knew how to use a cell phone. She called and texted hourly until Laurie put her phone into airplane mode. Then, on Monday evening, Mom pulled out the big guns and sent in the police. Not the entire SFPD, of course, but a nice, polite, and handsome policeman named Ryan Pierce, who refused to leave her door until he made certain she wasn't suicidal.

Ryan had a soft Virginia accent, a pair of big blue eyes, and a cowlick. He also had a nasty-looking scar on the right side of his neck where it looked as if he'd been burned. But a single girl could overlook that small defect since he didn't have a wedding ring on his left hand. If she were at all interested in climbing back on the horse, as Mom had suggested on Sunday, then Ryan Pierce just might be the guy. At least he wasn't connected with the Lyndon family like Daniel or Andrew.

But Laurie wasn't ready. She filed Ryan Pierce away for a rainy day and assured him that she was not thinking about offing herself. Although she was killing her waistline with her days-long ice cream, popcorn, and pizza binge. But hey, she didn't have to worry about fitting into the beautiful lace wedding dress anymore. And binging on junk food and all twenty-six episodes of the first two seasons of *House of Cards* kept her mind off her troubles.

So on Tuesday morning, she grabbed some cold pizza, made herself a cup of coffee in the Keurig coffeemaker someone had given her as a wedding present, and settled in for season three. But she hadn't watched more than fifteen minutes before someone knocked on her front door.

Damn. Couldn't people just leave her alone? She ignored the doorbell and snuggled down into Brandon's Washington Capitals throw. But concentrating on Francis Underwood and his brand of amoral politics was hard when someone continued to ring the bell and knock on the door. And then whoever it was decided to peep through the gigantic living room window that overlooked her rickety porch.

Laurie's heart soared. The visitor who pressed his face up against the grubby window pane was definitely male. For an instant, she thought it might be Brandon, come to tell her that it was all a horrible mistake.

But the guy on her porch was taller and thinner than Brandon. "C'mon, Laurie, open the door," he said as he raised a green and red donut box. "I brought Krispy Kremes."

Speak of the devil. Andrew Lyndon himself. With donuts. She wondered if his aunt had sent him.

She hauled herself up from the couch and padded to the front door. She cracked it open. "I'll take the donuts, please." She reached her hand through the narrow opening.

He cocked his head like an adorable puppy with big soulful eyes. "You don't get the donuts unless you let me in."

"I'm not dressed for company," she said, glancing down at her pink bunny slippers, gray sweatpants, and George Washington University sweatshirt. She'd been wearing these clothes since Sunday afternoon.

"I'm not company," he said.

"No? Then why are you here bearing bribes? Did your aunt send you?"

He frowned. "My aunt? Why would she have sent me?"

Clearly Andrew didn't know about his aunt's matchmaking plans. "Okay, then why are you here?"

Andrew's mouth twitched. "Actually your dad sent me."

How could you not like Andrew when the guy always told the truth? He was dependable. And honest. An ex-fiancé's perfect best friend. "Why did he send you and not come himself?"

"I don't know. I'm here to talk to you about an idea."

"What kind of idea?"

Andrew looked away and to the left, his body language screaming discomfort.

Laurie was suddenly intrigued. "Is Daddy pissed at Brandon?"

Andrew huffed out a breath. "Yes. And no. Look, can I come in, please?"

She opened the door wide and knew a moment of humiliation as he scanned her from head to toe. She hated the look in his eyes. Was it pity? She didn't want anyone, least of all Brandon's best friend, to pity her. "So what is this idea?"

"Teaching Brandon a lesson."

"How? And why would you be interested in doing that? I mean, you're his friend, right?"

He looked her straight in the eye. "Yes, I am. And I also work for your father."

"Right. So conflicted."

He nodded.

"Well, you can relax because I don't want to teach Brandon a lesson."

"No? Then what do you want, Laurie?"

She blinked. "Oh my God, you sounded just like Daddy right then. What is he up to?"

"Noah wants to help you and Brandon get back together. He's enlisted my help."

She snatched the box of donuts from his hands. "Really?"

"That's what he told me yesterday. He'd like me to see what I can do about it."

She snorted a laugh. "What you really mean is that he's using his leverage over your partnership prospects to force you into doing something you don't want to do. I'm totally aware of Dad's high-handed tactics. I'm really sorry, Andrew. He can be a pain in the butt. But thanks for these." She clutched the box of donuts to her breast and tried to shut the door in Andrew's face.

Unfortunately, Andrew had good reflexes. He wedged his foot in the door and forced it open.

She retreated in the face of his superior strength, but not without a snarky retort. "I'm not sharing the donuts."

"That's fine, I brought them just for you because I know how much you love Krispy Kremes."

She gave him a sideways look. "How do you know that?"

He shrugged. "I don't know how. I just do. You're part of the family or something, you know?"

"No, I don't. I'm not part of your family. Your aunt said the same thing to me on Sunday."

He arched his brow. "Has Aunt Pam been to visit?"

"No. Mom and I ran into her on Sunday at the Red Fern Inn."

"Ah," he said as he strolled into the living room, his wingtips sounding as hollow as the house. He didn't ask if he could stay; he merely dropped into one of the ugly IKEA recliner chairs that belonged to Brandon. He leaned back, cocked one leg over his knee, and assumed a mild and utterly unreadable expression. Laurie had often wondered if that nondescript demeanor was a mask or whether Andrew Lyndon was, truly, incapable of strong emotions.

In all the years Laurie had been with Brandon, she'd seen Andrew lose that cool reserve only once—when he'd gone after Dusty McNeil. Laurie could hardly fault him for that since Andrew had told everyone that he thought Dusty was taking advantage of his sister. If Laurie had an older brother, she would want him to be protective and concerned like that.

But most of the time, Andrew wasn't that passionate about anything. In fact, he was the responsible guy at every party. The one you could count on to be the designated driver or to pull everyone back from the brink of stupidity. He was, always, the voice of reason.

She climbed back under the Capitals throw on the couch, selected a donut from the box, and nodded her head at him. "Okay, you've got exactly five minutes for whatever it is you came to say."

He leaned forward and dropped his leg. "On Saturday, when I asked you what you wanted, you told me that you were willing to forgive Brandon. Do you still feel that way?"

A rush of sugar coursed through her as she sank her teeth into the donut. There was nothing in the world—not even sex—as good as a Krispy Kreme. She thought carefully about Andrew's question as the donut melted in her mouth. "I don't know," she said honestly.

Andrew nodded, as if her answer hadn't surprised him in the least. His nonreaction ticked her off for some unfathomable reason. "He broke my heart," she added, just to be clear. "How can I forgive that?"

"Easy. If you love him and want to be his wife."

"Not so easy. I mean, why did Brandon do that to me? We were together for so long."

"What if that's the problem?" he asked.

"What? That we've been together? Like it's okay for him to get bored?" Although that's exactly what had happened.

Andrew shook his head. "No, it's more like fear of better options."

"What does that mean?"

"Maybe he feels as if he never took the time to...I don't know, play the field, sow some wild oats, whatever."

"Right." She took another bite of the donut. In a minute, she would ask Andrew to leave, and she would forget this unsettling conversation.

Andrew said nothing for the longest time, and it was almost as if he used the silence as a weapon to pry her open. She busied herself devouring the donut and refused to give in.

"So," he said when she was down to licking the sugar off her fingers, "what if we showed Brandon the consequences of looking for better options?"

"Okay. And what, in your judgment, are the consequences?"

"I'm pretty sure Brandon hasn't thought through how he might feel if you decided to go out and play the field."

"You mean he might be a victim of his own double standard?" she asked and then shook her head. "But what if he's already gone out and played the field? What if there's someone else?" Her voice wavered, and she had to admit that the prospect of Brandon cheating on her was soul-sucking.

Andrew shook his head. "Laurie, I truly don't think Brandon has been going out with other women on the side. I think he just got cold feet because he's never played the field, and it suddenly dawned on him that he'd never have the chance again if he got married. That can be a terrifying realization."

"So you're saying that if I do what Brandon asked me to do—go explore other options—it will make him jealous?"

"Well, sort of. See, I'm not suggesting that you actually date other people. I'm suggesting that you give the *appearance* of dating other people. In order to make him realize what an idiot he's being."

"Okay, how do I give the appearance of dating? What do I do, just go directly to Match.com and post a sexy profile?"

"There's an idea."

"But if I did that, I would lose Brandon forever, wouldn't I?"

"Maybe not." He leaned back in the chair, looking so completely comfortable that it irked her. "Instead of Match.com, I was thinking along the lines of setting you up on a series of show dates, with guys Brandon either knows or admires or even hates. In short, guys that will annoy the crap out of him. We'd arrange them so that Brandon either sees you out with someone else, or hears about it. I'm betting that seeing you out with someone else will drive him crazy, and he'll realize there are no better options out there."

Her mouth actually dropped open. "You're not serious."

"Do you have a better idea?"

She shook her head. "No, I don't. But if I did what you suggest and it worked, I'd spend the rest of my life wondering if I'd tricked Brandon into marriage."

"But you do love him, right?"

"I do, but I can't manipulate him that way. It's wrong."

"You won't even try?"

She shook her head. "Look, I'm sorry Dad sent you here. I shouldn't have to trick Brandon into coming back to me. That's just crazy." She stood up, walked to the door, and opened it. "You can tell Dad that I'm fine. And thanks for the donuts. Now if you don't mind, Netflix is calling my name."

Laurie probably should have called Dad and told him not to send Andrew on any more missions designed to make Brandon come back to her. But she didn't call her father because she was a little afraid that Dad would talk her into doing what Andrew had suggested. Dad could be incredibly persuasive, and he was a master manipulator.

So she pushed Andrew's visit—and his ridiculous idea—out of her mind and dived back into *House of Cards* for a few more hours. But by Tuesday evening, she'd grown tired of Frank Underwood and his Machiavellian schemes—not to mention his monologues delivered in a not-quite-authentic Southern accent. So when the doorbell rang at a little before six o'clock, she was ready to admit that her self-imposed exile had reached the point of tedium.

But she wasn't about to let just anyone in. She peeked

through the side window and discovered that her visitor wasn't Mom, Dad, Andrew, or Officer Pierce, but Courtney Wallace carrying a reusable grocery bag from Food Lion. Suddenly real food sounded appealing, so she opened the door.

"Hi," Courtney said with a grin, ignoring Laurie's sweats, bunny slippers, and messy ponytail. "I brought all the fixings for margaritas, including the Don Julio. But to be honest, homemade margaritas are my fallback plan. I'm hoping to get you out of the house and down to the Jay Bird Café. Rory, the bartender there, makes better margaritas than I do. And Wednesday is open mic night. My friend Arwen will be singing. It's my opinion that all single women need to hear Arwen's songs about relationships. The woman has a gift for cutting right to the heart. Oh, and no one cares if you cry during open mic nights. I mean, sometimes the music is really bad."

Courtney didn't wait to be welcomed in; she simply marched through the door like a general and captured the territory. "So," she said, scanning the living room in a way she had not studied Laurie and her dirty clothes and hair, "I see you haven't gotten much done with the place."

"Uh, no, I…"

"Well, don't worry. I have friends. We'll get the place good enough to sell and make a profit if that's what you need. And if I were you, the first thing I'd do is burn Brandon's furniture." She turned and actually made eye contact, her big blue eyes full of concern but not pity. "So, what's it gonna be? Margaritas here or at the Jay Bird?"

"I need a shower," Laurie said, making up her mind right then that Courtney was someone she wanted as a forever friend. Emma, Madison, and Jessica were forever friends too, but Madison lived in California, Jessica lived in New

York, and even though Emma lived in Washington, she was more than sixty miles away. Having a friend who lived around the corner was a godsend.

"Yeah, you do kinda need a shower," Courtney said, "but I can wait. The show doesn't start until eight o'clock. You want a 'rita for the road?" She held up the grocery bag that apparently didn't contain any groceries except maybe limes and salt.

"Uh, no, just give me a few minutes."

It took Laurie almost an hour to clean herself up. During that time, Courtney must have disposed of the pizza boxes, cleared the dirty dishes, and folded the Capitals fleece blanket because when Laurie came down from the bedroom, the living room looked semipresentable. How had Laurie allowed herself to go like that? Being a slob wasn't her thing. "You didn't have to clean—" she began.

"Nope, I didn't. But I did. The thing is, you don't have to face this problem alone. I've had my heart broken so many times, it hardly bleeds anymore. But I still remember the first asshole who took me for granted. His name was Mark, and when he broke up with me, he issued those fatal words I will never forget. 'Court,' he said, 'I'm breaking up with you because I love you too much and I don't want you to be hurt.' Now, you tell me what the hell that means?"

Laurie shook her head. "I don't know. It's kind of oxymoronic."

"Forget the oxy, it was just plain moronic. Being told that your boyfriend loves you too much is like one of those WTF moments, you know? I cried my eyes out, and I mourned that relationship for two whole years of my life. I still can't believe I wasted that much time on him.

"In the end, I realized that Mark was one of those guys

who seemed to care about me, but the moment Sheryl Roth crossed his path with her blond hair and size double-D's, he justified his decision to ditch me by inventing that weaselly excuse. The amazing part is that he actually thought telling me he loved me too much would spare my feelings. He actually thought he was doing *me* a big favor. It's truly unbelievable what some guys think."

"I guess," Laurie said without much conviction. Listening to Courtney's experiences in the world of dating and hookups was depressing.

Courtney put her arm around Laurie's shoulder. "Chin up, babe. There's an antidote to how you're feeling right now. It's called good booze and girlfriends, both of which are waiting for us at the Jay Bird."

The bar was only a short walk from the neighborhood where Laurie and Courtney lived. When they arrived, two of Courtney's friends, Arwen and Melissa, were waiting for them with a big plate of nachos and a pitcher of margaritas. Once Courtney and Laurie had settled in at the table, Courtney raised her glass and said, "Here's hoping Brandon Kopp has a miserable, unhappy life."

Arwen and Melissa said, "Hear, hear." But Laurie refrained. Did she want Brandon to have a miserable life? No. She actually wanted him to be happy. And the wounded part inside her heart wanted him to come back and be happy with her.

"C'mon. Drink up," Courtney said.

Laurie took a sip of her margarita, the salt and lime filling her mouth with its complicated tastes.

Arwen patted Laurie's back. "Just remember that Brandon deserves whatever he gets. I work at Lyndon, Lyndon, & Kopp as a paralegal, and I just heard through the office grapevine that he's decided not to join his father's law firm."

Laurie almost choked on her drink. "He's not moving here?" she asked.

"I don't think so," Arwen said. "I was in the copy room yesterday, and I overheard Charles Lyndon telling his secretary that they were looking for a new associate attorney. They wouldn't be doing that if Brandon was joining the firm and working in the Virginia office. Lyndon, Lyndon & Kopp is growing but not enough to justify two associate attorneys."

"I can't believe it," Laurie said in a choked voice. "Honestly I'm starting to think I never knew Brandon at all."

How could he do this to her? How could he have demanded that she give up her dream job at the University of Michigan for him and then choose not to join his father's firm? The sudden fury was almost cleansing.

"Don't you worry, Laurie," Courtney said. "We'll find some way of making his life miserable. We just need to put our minds to it."

And just like that she knew what she needed to do. "Actually," Laurie said, straightening her shoulders, "I think I have a plan. It's not exactly mine, but it's a good one."

"Whose is it?"

"Andrew Lyndon's. He dropped by to see me this morning."

"Andrew? Brandon's best man? I wouldn't trust that guy any farther than I could throw him," Courtney said.

"He also works for my dad, so you're probably right about the trust thing. But he still had a killer idea for making Brandon see the error of his ways."

"Do tell," Melissa said, leaning in.

Laurie launched into a summary of Andrew's visit and his plan. When she finished, Arwen leaned forward and said, "Wait a sec. That plan is all about you and Brandon getting back together; it's not about making him miserable. You can't—"

"Taking him back would be a mistake," Courtney said.

"Listen to her," Melissa said. "I lost my heart to this guy who was an English professor. So smart and so cute, but all he ever did was make me feel small and stupid. When we broke up, I was devastated. But in retrospect, it was the best thing that ever happened to me."

"That's because Christopher was a Belittler," Courtney said with authority.

"A what?" Laurie asked.

"A Belittler," Courtney said. "There are ten distinct male types: the Belittler, the Ogler, the Space Invader, the Slut Shamer, the Player, the Too Selfless to Be True, the Not Emotionally Available, the Clueless Guy, the Manbaby, and the Nice Guy, Not." Courtney ticked the types off on her fingers.

Laurie's mouth fell open. She didn't know whether to laugh or cry.

"Yeah, but here's the thing you should keep in mind," Courtney continued. "Assuming you did want to take Brandon back, Andrew's plan would only work if Brandon is a Manbaby. A Manbaby is the kind of guy who breaks up with you expecting to remain friends, but the minute you go out with someone else, he'll be all over you about how you hurt his feelings. A Manbaby's feelings are the only ones that matter."

This description rendered Laurie speechless. She took a big gulp of her drink.

"Well," Arwen said, "Manbaby or not, Brandon made you change your career plans in deference to him, and then he dumped you. In my book, that makes him a jerk. And I have to wonder why in the world your father would send

Andrew with this plan of his. If any man did what Brandon did to me, my daddy and all three of my brothers would give the guy something to think about for the rest of his life."

Laurie sat there for a moment processing Arwen's words, and a light suddenly pierced the haze in her head. "Wait, you guys. What if Dad isn't trying to get Brandon and me back together? What if he's using Andrew to jack Brandon around?"

"Would he do something like that?" Courtney asked.

Laurie nodded. "Dad is a master manipulator. He has this uncanny ability to read people and move them around like pieces on a chessboard. Mom told me he was so pissed off on Saturday that some of the wedding guests had to make an intervention. That just doesn't sound like he wants Brandon and me to get back together. But knowing Dad, and Mom for that matter, they're both worrying that I'm going to become a spinster with five cats. Mom wants to make me over. And I think Dad wants me to exact some kind of revenge on Brandon."

"So your father lied to Andrew?" Courtney asked.

"I think so," Laurie said. "I think he's using Andrew."

The four women sat together in silence for a long moment before Courtney finally said, "Oh my God, it's brilliant. Your father gets Andrew Lyndon to think he's trying to solve this problem between you and Brandon, when all the while he gets manipulated into doing stuff that will drive Brandon bat-shit crazy."

Arwen laughed out loud. "I love this idea. I can just imagine it. You go out with one of Andrew's friends—preferably someone Brandon knows and likes or admires—take a selfie with him, post it on Facebook, and then direct tweet it at Brandon with the hash tag #HowDoYouLikeMeNow. And the coolest thing is that you're only doing what Brandon told you to do, going out and exploring other options."

Yeah. It was brilliant, all right. And kind of cruel. But then revenge always was. And it might just make Brandon crazy, which would be okay. There was only one small problem: It would probably destroy Andrew's friendship with Brandon. And for some strange reason, as furious as Laurie felt right now, it didn't seem fair that Andrew should be the collateral damage in her father's cruel game of revenge.

Chapter Five————————

On Wednesday morning, Laurie got up, cleaned the house, and then headed off to Winchester University. She figured she might as well finish organizing her office before the term began the following Tuesday. Besides, if she had to spend one more hour in Brandon's fixer-upper, she might lose her mind.

She parked her ten-year-old Subaru in the faculty lot and walked to her tiny office in the Social Sciences Building. She told herself over and over again that she was one of the lucky ones. She'd landed an associate professorship at a good school. Many of her grad school peers hadn't been so fortunate.

Still, it was hard not to second-guess her decisions. She'd worked her butt off as a graduate student. She'd even landed a research grant that had allowed her to produce a ground-breaking study of independent voter behavior for her thesis. Several polling organizations had already put her concepts into practice and had correctly forecast the Electoral College victory in the last presidential election. Among political science nerds, Laurie was a rising star.

So she'd been courted by a number of universities across the country but had decided to take the position at Winchester, not because of its prestige in her field, but because it was convenient for Brandon and his career aspirations. Now, looking at that decision with the clarity of the post-wedding debacle, she could see how stupid she'd been.

Why had she given up so much for Brandon? The short, disturbing answer was that she'd grown up watching her mother, who'd made a science of deferring to the men in her life.

There wasn't much she could do about it now except look on the positive side and make the best of a bad situation. Winchester University might be small, but it was still part of Virginia's impressive state university system, which included institutions such as William & Mary, the University of Virginia, and Virginia Tech, among others. There were opportunities here. She could put this college on the map as a center for the study of American voter behavior.

She spent several hours organizing books and supplies and was feeling almost hopeful about her life so, when her cell phone lit up, she foolishly decided to accept the call, even though it was from Mom.

"Hi," Laurie said. "And before you ask, I'm fine. I haven't tried to commit suicide, the cop you sent was kind of cute, and I'm at work right now organizing my office. So really, I don't need a makeover or a therapist."

"You will when I tell you what I was calling about."

That was so Mom. It was almost as if she liked raining on people's parades. "Maybe I should hang up," Laurie said.

"Don't be snotty, sweetie. You know the best thing you can do at a time like this is to look reality in the eye."

What was it about parents? They could take hypocrisy to incredible levels. When reality knocked, Mom would go on a bender and then drunk-dial Dad or one of her endless boyfriends. It was ugly when reality arrived in Susan Wilson's life.

But Laurie didn't want to fight about it. So she leaned back in her chair and braced herself. "Okay, lay it on me. But make it fast, you know, like pulling off a Band-Aid."

"I promise I'll make it quick, sweetie. I spoke with Pam Lyndon this morning. And she had some troubling news."

What the heck was Pam Lyndon up to? It was bad enough having Mom and Dad trying to run her life. "Since when are you and Pam Lyndon such good friends?"

"She's been very nice to me, and she's really concerned about you. She wants to introduce you to one of her nephews. Speaking of which, she called this morning because one of them, I can't remember which one, Edward maybe? Anyway, he happened to mention to her that Brandon went to Bermuda on the honeymoon."

"What?" Laurie's heart started to pound as fury spilled through her.

"It gets worse," Mom said, almost as if she were enjoying the process of bursting every single one of Laurie's balloons.

"Okay." This was like slow torture.

"He apparently didn't go alone," Mom said.

A knot swelled in Laurie's throat. Damn. Damn. Damn. How could she have been so stupid? So he'd been cheating on her after all. Laurie took a big breath and tried to calm down. Of course Brandon had been cheating. Why else would he have stopped the wedding?

"Sweetie," Mom said into the silence, "it's not what you think."

"What?"

"He took another man."

"Oh my God, he's gay. How could I have—"

"No. No, no. You misunderstood. He went with his friend. He's not gay."

"Which friend?"

"One of the Lyndon boys."

"Andrew?" The moment she said his name, she knew it wasn't him. Andrew had been here in Northern Virginia yesterday.

"No, one of the other ones. I can't remember their names. Really, sweetie, Pam has a lot of nephews."

"Jason, Matt?"

"Matt, that's the one. Now brace yourself."

Mom clearly didn't know how to deliver bad news quickly. "I'm braced," Laurie said.

"This Matt fellow is something of a ladies' man, according to Pam. And he went with Brandon to teach him how to pick up women."

Laurie thought about this for a moment and actually found a tiny bit of comfort in it. Matt was a player for sure, but the fact that Matt went with Brandon sort of suggested that Brandon was clueless when it came to dating other people.

"I'm so sorry, sweetie. Are you sure you don't want to come up to New York for some shopping?"

"I'm fine, Mom. Really. Stop worrying about this."

"Wow, you're taking this news well."

Yeah, for the moment. But she'd binge on Ben and Jerry's later tonight and probably cry herself to sleep. Right now she was merely furious that Brandon and Matt had gone on the vacation she'd paid for. The nerve of some people.

"Look, Mom, I'm at work. I've got to go," she said.

Of course, Mom kept her on the phone for another four minutes, alternately cajoling her to come to New York for some shopping and a makeover and suggesting that she let Pam Lyndon set her up with one of her nephews. When Laurie finally extricated herself from the call, she felt restless, so she headed off to the faculty lounge in search of coffee and some sanity.

She'd just poured herself a cup when Michael Altimari, the chair of the political science department, entered the room.

"What are you doing here? Aren't you supposed to be on your honeymoon?" he said in that deep mellifluous voice that probably mesmerized freshman coeds. He was divorced, according to the departmental gossip, and had a reputation as a ladies' man. He certainly dressed the part in a tweed jacket and plaid shirt with a knitted tie. His salt-and-pepper hair, heavy-lidded dark eyes, and absurdly square chin gave him the look of the quintessential middle-aged college professor on the make.

"I didn't go," she said.

"What?"

"I didn't go on my honeymoon. In fact, I didn't get married." She scored it as a major victory when her voice remained firm even though her hands shook a little as she raised the Winchester University coffee mug to her lips.

"What happened?" Michael asked.

"I walked down the aisle, and he walked the other way."

Michael's posture changed instantaneously from one of curiosity to one of avid interest. Laurie realized that in Michael's mind she'd moved from the column labeled

"Married" to the column labeled "Available." Michael's gaze intensified as he studied her body from top to bottom. Laurie couldn't help feeling that he was trying to pinpoint the reason Brandon had walked.

He gave her a big, toothy grin and ran his hand through his hair. "Gee, I'm really sorry, Laurie." His voice dripped a fawning kind of concern.

She looked down at her coffee and willed her hands to stop shaking. "Thanks," she said.

"I'm glad you came in today because there's something I need to speak with you about."

"Oh?"

"More bad news, I'm afraid."

She glanced up at him. She didn't need any more bad news. "What?"

"The funding we were expecting from the Walter Jephson Foundation for the Study of Social Science has fallen through. That means we don't have the resources for your study on the factors that weaken party identification. In fact, we need to pare things back for a semester or two while we find alternate research funds. I'm going to need you to teach a couple of extra seminars."

The universe must have put a big fat bull's-eye on her this morning. First Mom and then Michael. A primal scream would have been so cathartic, but she swallowed it back and simply said, "Okay."

But it wasn't okay. It was a freaking disaster, like the cherry on top of a whole sundae of disasters. She let Michael drone on about the difficulties of funding and running a department on the cheap while she let her fury run rampant through her.

The more Michael tried to explain the situation, the edgier Laurie became until it dawned on her that Michael might not be particularly interested in seeing her light shine here at Winchester University.

Michael had tenure so he didn't have to work all that hard to impress anyone. He certainly didn't need a young associate professor who had been actively recruited by the faculty committee because she'd already published important research. Michael, for all his ogling, viewed her as a threat.

This realization astonished her. She'd never seen herself as being a threat to anyone. But maybe the time had come to step out of the comfortable shell she'd been living in. She didn't need to defer to Michael. She could go around him and find her own research money. She'd done it as a grad student. She could do it as an associate professor.

And she didn't need to lie down and take Brandon's humiliation either. There was something she could do about that. Something her mother never would have done. But something her father wanted her to do.

She hurried back to her office, closed the door, and called Andrew Lyndon.

Wednesday afternoon found Andrew sitting at his desk popping his umpteenth antacid of the day. He had yet to tell Noah that Laurie truly wasn't ready to date anyone. Andrew understood exactly how Laurie felt. Val had left him two years ago, and he still wasn't ready to get back into the dating scene.

He'd been killing time playing Candy Crush on his phone most of the morning because Noah had taken him off the AVIEN negotiations. He'd spent something like thirty bucks buying extra lives, and he was bored out of his mind so, when his personal cell phone buzzed with Laurie's name, he wanted to jump for joy. Maybe she'd reconsidered.

He pressed the talk button. "Laurie, I'm so glad you called. How are you?" He tried to keep the desperation out of his voice.

"To be honest, I'm pissed off. Do you know anything about Brandon going to Bermuda with Matt?"

"If you're calling to confirm that rumor, it is apparently true."

"Why didn't you tell me that yesterday?"

"Because I didn't know anything about it until this morning. My aunt called with the news."

"Wow. She's making the rounds, isn't she? She called my mother too, and of course Mom called me. Honestly, Andrew, your aunt is a busybody."

"Yes, she is. And also the chief gossip. I'm really sorry, Laurie."

"So I have another question," she said in a staccato voice that underscored her annoyance.

"Fire away."

"Is it true Brandon has decided not to join the Shenandoah Falls office of Lyndon, Lyndon & Kopp?"

"Uh, well, I don't know the answer to that."

"Would you find out for me?"

"Of course I will," he said.

"Thanks. Now I want to talk some more about this idea of yours."

Andrew could hardly contain his surprise, or the sudden surge of relief that made him acutely aware of just how tight his shoulders had been all morning. "So I guess you changed your mind about manipulating Brandon after you heard that he went to Bermuda," he said.

"No, actually it was when I heard that he changed his mind about joining his father's firm. Also, I've been thinking about what you said. But there is one thing—my father may have told you that his goal is to get me to take Brandon back. But really that's not what he wants."

Andrew got up and started pacing his office. "What makes you say that?"

"He probably thinks you'll be more likely to help him mess up Brandon's life if you believe you're doing it for some high-minded purpose, like salvaging the relationship."

Andrew stopped in mid-pace. "Messing up Brandon's life? Is that what you think he wants?"

"I'm sure Dad thinks you would rebel if he asked you to help him take Brandon down a few pegs," Laurie said.

Andrew resumed his pacing. Well, it appeared that Laurie had reached the anger phase. He didn't blame her for wanting to mess up Brandon's life. He also knew that Noah had a hidden agenda of some kind. Noah always had a hidden agenda when it came to complicated negotiations.

Noah was capable of seeing both sides of every argument. He wasn't the type of man who sought revenge—quite the opposite, in fact. Noah spent a lot of time subtly moving people around, pushing them from conflict to compromise. Everything Noah had done and said in the last few days suggested that he wanted Laurie and Brandon to get back together. And knowing Noah, he would use every asset at his disposal, including Andrew, to help the litigants see a path toward reconciliation.

But, of course, Laurie wasn't ready to hear this yet. She had to work through her anger first.

"I'm sure your father only has your best interests in mind," Andrew said in a neutral tone.

"Oh, come on. Dad wants to teach Brandon a lesson. And to be honest, I'm starting to get totally down with that idea."

"And you want me to help you?"

She huffed out a breath. "Yeah, I do. And while I'm at it, I'm thinking that maybe I can help you avoid my father's machinations."

Andrew doubted it, but he wasn't about to discourage Laurie if she wanted to help him extricate himself from this problem. "Okay, I'm listening."

"It's pretty easy. I want you to set me up on a date with someone and let Brandon know all about it. In fact, your aunt suggested someone."

"Aunt Pam is the worst matchmaker in the universe. Take it from me, you do not want her messing with your life."

"I'm not looking for a match, Andrew."

"Oh yeah, right. So who did Pam suggest?"

"Your cousin Daniel."

Well, that was a surprise. "Really?"

"Yes," she said. "She seems to think we have a lot in common since we were both left at the altar."

"Is that sarcasm in your voice?" he asked.

"Maybe," she said. "So what do you think about Pam's idea?"

"Well, it will annoy Brandon, that's for sure. It will probably also break Roxy's heart. She and Danny were an item all this summer. Are you ready for that?"

"Hmmm. I hadn't thought of that. But, you know, I'm not serious about Daniel. And Roxy and Daniel broke up. So…"

"Good point," he said.

"So, do you think Daniel would be willing to go out with me?" she asked.

"He might. Let me see what I can arrange."

Chapter Six ─────────────

The Union Jack Pub in old-town Winchester occupied a Victorian cast-iron building that had once housed a bank. The place was an Anglophile's dream, featuring dark oak paneling, a zillion different stouts, ales, porters, lagers, and a spot in the back for darts.

Laurie hated the place because its menu was heavy on the meat and potatoes. Over the years, she and Brandon had argued more than once about dining at the Union Jack. Brandon loved the burgers. Laurie hated the salads.

This made it the perfect locale for her first show-date.

Laurie was running late because Michael the departmental ogler had cornered her in her office for fifteen minutes to talk about absolutely nothing. In her first week on the job at Winchester University, Laurie had come to despise her boss, and even though she knew this date with Daniel was mostly about making Brandon crazy, she was still sort of looking forward to it. She planned to have a glass of wine and unwind.

She scanned the dining room and found Daniel sitting at a booth by the tall front windows. She took off in his direction, tottering on the Nine West heels she'd pulled from the back of her closet this morning before work. The last time she'd worn these pumps, they'd blistered her feet, which was why she hadn't been foolish enough to teach her five seminars in them. She had slipped them on just as Michael had darkened her office door. They had definitely done the trick because Michael had studied her legs as if he were doing research in the college library. She didn't wear skirts very often, and now, knowing Michael, she promised never to put on this black pencil skirt again.

She slid into the booth facing Daniel, who looked up from his cell phone and gave her a wary smile. He'd been there for a while, judging by the half-full drink sitting in front of him. It looked like he was drinking scotch or bourbon on the rocks.

"Sorry I'm late," she said, checking her watch, only to discover that she'd kept him waiting almost twenty minutes. "I had to stop and chitchat with my department head."

Daniel Lyndon cocked his head and gave her an assessing stare. She forced herself to stare right back. He was handsome, of course. The Lyndon genes didn't permit anything else. But unlike his cousins and brothers, Daniel avoided the usual Brooks Brothers suit. Instead he had a refined casual look going for him in a pair of faded jeans, a gray V-neck sweater, and a battered leather aviator jacket. His face sported a dark shadow of beard, as if he'd forgotten to shave this morning. He also desperately needed a haircut.

In short, Daniel Lyndon was not remotely her type.

"It's okay, Laurie. I don't turn into a pumpkin at nine thirty, and I've got a babysitter all lined up. I've got nothing but time on my hands."

"Still, I shouldn't have kept you waiting. I'm sorry."

"It's okay. It gave me time to get the lay of the land, so to speak. Andrew and Brandon are behind you on the other side of the bar. Brandon knows I'm here. He came over to say hi."

"Uh, wait. You said that like you know this isn't a real date."

His ironic half-smile morphed into something practically brilliant. "Andrew briefed me on the plan. To be honest, and don't take this the wrong way, I wouldn't have agreed to it otherwise."

His words shook her confidence. Not that she wanted Daniel Lyndon to think she was all that. But still. Being left at the altar really had screwed up her self-esteem. She gave him a forced smile and remembered that Daniel Lyndon was just another jerk who fit nicely into Courtney's master list of jerks and losers.

She could use this date as practice for the real thing.

A waitress came by, and Laurie ordered a glass of Bella Vista Vineyards Pinot Noir. Daniel ordered another scotch on the rocks.

"You didn't have to order the Lyndon family wine to impress me, you know," he said. "Like I said, I'm doing this as a favor to Andrew."

"I wasn't trying to impress you. I ordered it because it's good wine. Also it's one of the less expensive items on the wine list. I'm an untenured college professor. I have to watch my pennies."

He leaned forward, an intense look in his eyes. "You know, I'm not a total jerk. This might be a fake date for Brandon's benefit, but you don't have to worry about the bill. It's on me. It's the least I can do."

"How do you figure that?"

"Because you're saving me from Aunt Pam and her matchmaking activities. She's determined to match me up with anything in a skirt. In fact, I told her that I was having dinner with you, and she's overjoyed. She thinks we have a lot in common."

"Because of our bad wedding experiences?" she asked.

He laughed. "Very funny and yes. The truth is, I'm happy to help you do whatever it is you're trying to do to Brandon." He paused for a moment. "What is it you're trying to do? I mean, you don't really want him back, do you?"

"No," she said, shaking her head. But down in the depths of her heart, she wasn't so sure. As the days passed, her anger waxed and waned like the moon. Sometimes late at night when she couldn't sleep, she'd lie awake wondering if there was some kind of bargain she could make with God in order to get Brandon back.

She missed him. In fact, it was unsettling to know that he was somewhere in the dining room. She had to forcibly stop herself from turning around and looking over her shoulder to see if she could spot him in the crowd. Brandon was like an itch she needed to scratch.

"I'm glad you don't want him back," Daniel said. "I don't think he's the right guy for you."

She didn't respond. Instead she picked up the menu and stared at it without really seeing it at all. Everyone on the face of the planet seemed to have an opinion about her relationship with Brandon, and they all felt free to express it. It was kind of rude, and it certainly underscored the fact that no one had any faith in Laurie's ability to make the right choices.

The waitress came back with her wine and Daniel's scotch. He ordered the crab cakes, and she bypassed the fish and chips and the bangers and mash, and ordered a burger.

And then she spent a few minutes aligning the salt and pepper shakers and her silverware.

"Are you always this nervous on dates?"

She looked up at him. He had that rebel-without-a-cause thing going for him, and his eyebrow arched just enough to make her feel utterly incompetent.

"Yeah, I guess I am nervous. I haven't dated all that much."

"Right, because you and Brandon were together for ten years, but not exactly married." His voice had an ironic edge to it that was as sharp as honed steel.

"So you think I should have forced him to marry me sooner?"

He snorted a laugh. "I think you should have realized he wasn't interested in commitment when it took ten years to get him to the altar."

She took a long gulp of her wine. "I know you think I probably want to spend this evening running Brandon down. I mean, I suppose he deserves it. But it doesn't really help me, you know, to be sitting here talking about him."

Something changed in Daniel's eyes. "Really? Then why are you here?"

She didn't really have a good answer. So she decided to turn the tables on him.

"So, tell me, how did you feel when your fiancée left you standing at the altar?"

He laughed. "My situation isn't at all like yours. I was relieved when Mia ditched me."

"Because you're afraid of commitment? That makes you just like Brandon."

He stilled. "No, that's not the reason. Mia was a bitch."

"Why do guys always do that?"

"Do what?"

"Start calling women names when things go wrong. Come on, Daniel, you were relieved because you are scared of commitment."

"Why do women always do that?" he asked.

"What?"

"Use the failure-to-commit card every time a relationship fails. The truth is that I tried to get Mia to marry me for two solid years. I was perfectly happy to commit, Laurie. It was Mia who wasn't. I'm not a jerk like Brandon."

"Oh," she said in a small voice. "Then why did you dump Roxy?"

"What?"

"You heard me. You and Roxy were kind of a thing this summer, and then boom, suddenly you weren't."

"We weren't ever a thing. Honestly, we used to fight like cats and dogs when we were kids."

"Yes, you were a thing. You went out a few times. And Roxy helped you with your custody battle. And Roxy talked about you all the time. You guys were definitely a thing."

He shrugged, the gesture so out of sync with the look in his eyes. "Come on, Laurie, what woman wants to take on a two-year-old?"

"Lots of women want children. Are you telling me that Roxy walked away because you have a child? I don't believe that for a minute. She loves children. She raises money for childhood cancer research. I'm thinking it was more a case of you using your daughter as an excuse not to get in too deep."

He stilled. "What is this? Did you organize this meeting to dump all over me?"

"I'm just asking a question, Daniel. Did you ever ask Roxy how she felt about your daughter?"

He blinked a few times. "No. But I didn't need to," he snarled. "Can we change the subject?"

"Sure," she said with a nod.

But instead of talking about the weather, or books, or movies, or any of a dozen other safe date topics, Daniel ordered another drink and then spent most of the time talking about Roxy and the fun they'd had over the summer when they weren't dating and they weren't a thing.

Daniel, it turned out, was not really a jerk. He was just another confused person trying to figure out relationships in the twenty-first century.

"What the hell is she doing here? She hates this place," Brandon said as he slammed his beer glass down on the table, his expression delightfully annoyed.

Andrew pretended innocence, since his back was to the door. "Who?"

"Laurie. Don't turn around," Brandon said, picking up his glass of Sam Adams Oktoberfest once again. "I can't believe it. She's sitting down at Danny's table."

"Really?" Andrew invested just the right amount of incredulity into his voice.

A muscle worked in Brandon's jaw. "The asshole. You'd think he would have told me he was meeting Laurie here. I mean, I went over there to say hi, and he acted like there was nothing going on."

"Um, Brandon, Danny doesn't need to ask your permission to have dinner with Laurie."

Brandon shifted his gaze and blinked a couple of times. "Yeah, I guess you're right."

"Of course I am." Andrew played it cool.

Brandon turned his attention back toward the menu

while Andrew observed him. He didn't glance in Danny's direction. Not once. It was a little disappointing.

The waitress came over, and they ordered a couple of burgers. It was only after she'd left that Brandon looked over Andrew's shoulder a second time. "What the hell?"

"What?" Andrew started to turn.

"No, don't stare."

"What is it?"

"She ordered a burger. Can you believe that?"

"Yeah. The burgers here are pretty good."

"No, it's not that. She never eats red meat. I mean, it's like a religion with her or something. That's why she hates this place. We used to argue about it all the time. You know I love the burgers here."

Oh yeah, Andrew knew, which was why he'd suggested that Laurie's date with Daniel be staged here. He gave Brandon a what-are-you-worried-about shrug. "Maybe she ordered the burger because their salads suck."

"Why would she come here for dinner in the first place?"

"Maybe Danny picked the place."

"Yeah, maybe he did." Brandon frowned down at his beer before he continued. "No, that's not right. This isn't Danny's kind of place either. California kind of rubbed off on him, you know. He eats a lot of salads too."

"Maybe Laurie suggested it, thinking that it was."

Brandon drummed his fingers on the table and looked up again. "Maybe she did."

"Hey, relax, maybe they're just sharing their common experiences."

Brandon scowled. "Is that a reference to the wedding?"

"Yeah, Brandon, it is. I mean, it was probably inevitable that Laurie and Danny went out together, given that both of them were dumped at the altar. And by now I'm sure Laurie has heard that you went on the honeymoon with Matt. So I'm thinking she has a lot to unload on someone who's willing to listen."

Brandon nodded as if he was taking it all in stride. "Maybe I should go over there and tell her that I didn't have much fun. Matt is a total jerk."

"You just discovered this?"

Brandon let go of a long sigh. "I didn't really enjoy the pick-up scene as much as I thought I would."

"Ah."

"But," he said as his gaze shifted away from Laurie and Danny, "at least I can say I've experienced it. That's something." His gaze shifted again. "What the hell is Danny trying to prove anyway?"

"What do you mean?"

"He's gone ghost on my sister, and now here he is hitting on my ex-fiancée. What a creep...Oh my God, that's disgusting."

Andrew once again attempted to look over his shoulder but Brandon grabbed his arm. "Don't."

"What's disgusting?"

"Danny is like all over her."

"What?" This time Andrew turned. To his surprised relief, Danny wasn't all over Laurie, but Daniel was leaning toward her, talking, and she was smiling at him as if she was enjoying herself. Damn. They looked as if they were having a pretty good time together.

She might be all hell-bent to make Brandon pay for what he'd done, but Andrew was doing this because Noah wanted to make sure that Laurie didn't retreat from the world. Maybe Noah was on to something.

But watching Laurie smile at Danny made Andrew's gut churn for some reason. What if something real blossomed between Danny and Laurie? What would Noah think about having a son-in-law like Danny? Andrew had a feeling Noah wouldn't much like Danny with his long hair and leather jacket. Plus Danny didn't fish or play golf or share Noah's conservative politics. Damn.

Andrew turned around and attempted a smile. "Well," he said, "you did tell her to go out and experience the world while you did the same. You took Matt to Bermuda. She's here with Danny. It's a difference without any distinction."

Brandon almost spewed the sip of beer he'd just taken. After a few coughs, he leaned forward with an angry light in his eyes. "You think letting Danny seduce her is a positive experience?"

"For God's sake, she's only having dinner with him. I don't see any kind of seduction happening." Andrew fixed his mediator face in place, even though a small part of him was a little worried. What if Danny did seduce Laurie? What would Noah think about that?

Shit. This whole shame dating thing was fraught with pitfalls and booby traps, wasn't it?

"Look," Brandon said, slamming his beer down on the table for the second time, "I know Danny is your cousin and all, but he's as big a jerk as Matt."

"Brandon, why is this bothering you so much?" Andrew asked in his best nonconfrontational voice.

"Come on, don't pull that crap on me. You know Danny can be a jerk."

"In what way?"

"Well, how about how he's treated Roxy all these years? Don't tell me you don't remember how he used to make her cry. And he's still doing it. I don't know what my sister sees in him. I'd hate to see Laurie get caught up with a guy who doesn't know what he wants in life."

Andrew let himself smile. "Brandon, what happened between Roxy and Danny when they were younger is just kid stuff. He may be reevaluating his future right at the moment, but Laurie could do a whole lot worse than him. I mean, he's unmarried, has money, and has already proven himself to be good father material." Andrew laid it on thick, even though, down deep, he didn't see a good fit between Laurie and Danny either.

"I'm not blaming her." The words exploded out of Brandon's mouth. "I mean, I'm proud of her for actually getting off her butt and setting up a date with someone. Really proud. But why'd she have to pick Danny?"

"Because she's dating. You know, it's like trying on clothes before you buy them."

Brandon gave a short nod. "Okay, that's fair, I guess. And just because she's having a burger with Danny doesn't mean she's going to let him into her life, right?"

"Uh, well, we don't know, do we?" An unsettling thought.

Brandon pushed up from the table. "I think I'll go over and say hi."

Andrew grabbed his friend by the arm and yanked him back into his seat. "No. Bad move. Laurie doesn't want her ex showing up when she's out with someone else. If you want to say something to Laurie, you should call her. Or text her. Or, hey, you could visit her and have a conversation about the house you bought together. No more public scenes, Brandon, especially since she's only doing what you asked her to do."

Brandon sank into his chair. "Yeah, she is, isn't she? I never really thought she'd have the balls."

"No?"

He drained his glass and waved it at the waitress before

turning back with a shake of his head. "No. I mean, she's a little bookish and shy and...I don't know. She's not the hottest tamale out there, you know? But look at her tonight. She's wearing high heels and a tight skirt. Since when does she dress like that?"

"Since you told her to go out and have fun. Pat yourself on the back. She's coming out of her shell. You did a good job." And Andrew found himself regretting the fact that his back had been turned when Laurie had arrived. He would have liked to have seen her wearing a tight skirt and high heels. She'd probably turned a few heads.

"Yeah, I guess. But Danny?" Brandon sounded morose. Damn, maybe Noah knew what he was doing. Maybe he really could get Brandon and Laurie back together.

Andrew could happily and truthfully report to Noah that Brandon was absolutely miserable at the idea of Laurie dating Danny. "Why not Danny?" Andrew asked.

"It's absurd. Honestly, if she wants to get back at me by dating one of the Lyndon boys, she should have picked you, not him. She'd be safe with you."

Andrew almost opened his mouth to ask why but then decided against it because the answer was self-evident. She would be safe with him because she was the boss's daughter and his best friend's ex-fiancée. And also because he was still halfway in love with Val, and everyone knew it.

Chapter Seven————————

The tiny dining room at Bean There Done That always got crowded around 11:00 a.m. on Saturdays. A lot of old-timers still went down the street to Gracie's diner to get their fried eggs, but the new urbanites who'd flocked to Jefferson County from Washington, D.C., preferred the gluten-free, exorbitantly priced breakfast scene.

Laurie stood in the doorway for a long moment, scanning the room with its dark wood floors and walls covered with local artists' work. Andrew had wisely taken a table in the extreme back corner, away from the coffee bar and the windows.

He glanced up out of his dark, masked eyes, and for an instant the whole setup felt like some kind of clandestine meeting with her secret lover. Which was absurd.

She met Andrew's gaze, and to her astonishment, something sparked in her that hadn't been there before. Whoa, wait a second. She was here for a "debrief" of last night's date with Daniel and nothing more than that.

But someone should have briefed her girl parts on the

plan. Her libido, which had been slumbering for years, stretched, yawned, and woke up *hungry*. It fixed on Andrew Lyndon and got all hot and bothered. In his faded blue jeans, worn-out loafers, and gray T-shirt, Andrew looked about as yummy as a box of Krispy Kremes.

She slid into the facing chair and studied him for a moment. Like all the male members of his family, he had espresso eyes, chiseled cheekbones, a sensuous mouth, and dark hair that curled over his forehead. Every single one of the Lyndon boys was handsome and accomplished. But most of them came with serious personality flaws. Matt was a womanizing jerk, the epitome of Courtney's Player. Jason was so interested in public policy that he fit the profile of the Clueless Guy. And Edward, who loved to play sports and who had equipment ranging from a full set of goalie pads to no less than three pairs of skis, definitely fit the profile of the Space Invader.

Andrew, on the other hand, was like a deep, still pond that reflected whatever anyone projected onto him. Pigeonholing him was hard. Even now, gazing right into his eyes, Laurie had trouble reading him. A part of her wanted to take a sledgehammer and demolish that mask the way Brandon had demolished that wall separating the dining room from the kitchen in their fixer-upper. But then Brandon had left his drywall mess for her to clean up. So maybe smashing walls was not a good idea.

The corners of Andrew's mouth turned up, and a certain mischievous light danced in his dark eyes. Yearning of a kind she'd never known took flight inside her like a caged bird.

"I took the liberty of getting you a cup of coffee," he said. "The line in here is ridiculous. To be honest, I would have preferred Gracie's Place, but on Saturday mornings it's like gossip central over there."

"Are you afraid to be seen with me?" she asked. The idea of asking him out was right on the tip of her tongue.

"Of course not. But I don't want Brandon to find out you and I were seen together. He might realize what we're up to."

Right. Andrew was so focused on the whole make-Brandon-jealous plan that he was missing the forest *and* the trees. She thought about challenging him the way she'd challenged Daniel, but decided it wasn't worth it. He was just doing what Dad had asked him to do.

So she picked up her paper cup and took a sip of her lukewarm coffee, which had too much sugar and not enough milk, proving that Andrew didn't know her at all. "So," she said, once she'd swallowed the less-than-satisfactory brew, "I'm dying to know how Brandon reacted to what went down last night."

Andrew's gaze shifted down and to the left, and he paused for a moment as if deep in thought. Or maybe he was just trying to find a way to deliver bad news.

"He wasn't jealous, was he?" she said, a little piece of her heart breaking off. Damn, she needed to remember that she wasn't trying to make Brandon jealous, per se. She was trying to drive him crazy.

Andrew looked up. "Um, well, yes and no."

"What does that mean?"

"He *was* jealous. But I got the feeling he was more worked up over the fact that he didn't think Danny was the right man for you. Honestly, he spent a lot of time talking about how Danny had hurt Roxy. I got the feeling he wanted to protect you and his sister from my big, bad, confused cousin."

"Oh," she said.

"Yeah. Afraid so. He, um, told me that he's still proud of you for going out with someone."

"Well, that's just great," she said in an exasperated tone.

"Brandon is pissed at Daniel for dumping Roxy, while Daniel spent most of the night telling me how much he's in love with her."

"Really? But they broke up."

"They did, but he's still carrying a torch. And you know what? I'm pretty sure Roxy is carrying a torch for Daniel."

"Really?" Andrew had a very adorable frown. She'd never noticed that before.

"I'm serious. I feel like we should do something about that, you know?"

"We? No, thanks."

"Okay, but maybe I should call Roxy or something and tell her how Daniel feels about her."

"Oh no. You should not do that. Let's just move on, okay, and say that this idea of you dating other people to make Brandon jealous was flawed from the start." He drained his coffee. "And I think we should just forget all about me helping you to find dates. I'll figure out some way to make your father see reason."

"Andrew, stop." She leaned forward and touched his hand. She'd only meant the touch to convey her seriousness, but the warmth of his skin sent an intoxicating brew of chemicals flooding her bloodstream. He pulled his hand back as if her touch had scalded him, and for a moment, their gazes locked.

When he finally looked away, she said, "I'm going to call Dad and tell him to quit putting you in the middle, okay?"

He looked up, panic on his face. "No, don't do that. He'll crucify me."

She shook her head. "It'll be fine. Trust me."

She pulled her phone from her purse and dialed Dad's number while Andrew looked on. He really must have been worried about this to let his emotions show.

"Princess," Dad said in that sentimental-daddy way of his, "finally you've returned my calls. I've been worried about you. I know your mother has been filling your head with a lot of nonsense about makeovers. You don't need a makeover. What happened is not your fault. And I'm going to move heaven and earth to fix it for you. Just wait and see, I have a master plan at work."

"I know you do. Honestly, didn't you think I could see through your BS? I'm not stupid. I figured it out. And you're being totally unfair to Andrew."

"Andrew?" He seemed surprised.

"Yes, of course, Andrew. Your associate. The best man. The one who rescued me when Brandon did his thing the other day? Him. You've put him in the middle with this silly plan, and he's way too nice and way too honest to be used that way. Dad, you should know that I like Andrew a lot. Okay?"

"Oh, I didn't realize that you and Andrew were that close."

"We've gotten to know each other better the last few days. You're being unfair to him. And I don't like it."

Dad was silent for a very long moment, as if he was thinking long and hard about what she'd just said or choosing his words carefully. When he finally spoke, it was in his daddy-wise voice. "I'm glad you like Andrew because I trust him. And I want you to listen to him and go with the flow. Let's see what happens, okay?" Dad ended the call before she could even say good-bye. What the hell? Daddy's behavior was kind of odd.

"He didn't listen, did he?" Andrew asked.

Laurie shook her head just as Andrew's cell phone buzzed. He picked it up, glancing at the caller ID and then at Laurie.

"It's him, isn't it?" Laurie asked.

Andrew nodded and took the call, which lasted only half

a minute. Andrew said nothing. He just blinked and said *uh-huh* a couple of times. When he disconnected, he gave Laurie a worried look.

"What did he say?" she asked.

"He told me that he was glad that I had gained your trust, and that he wanted me to continue the good work."

Damn. This was so unfair. She couldn't let Andrew pay for the mess she and Brandon had made of their relationship. Especially since it wasn't all Brandon's fault.

"Well, one thing is totally clear: If I don't let you set me up on dates, my father is going to make your life miserable. And I hate that. So let's just continue on for a little while, okay? Until he loses interest. Also, I'm thinking that the next date should be a real one."

"A real one?"

"Yeah, you know, a real date with a real guy who doesn't know anything about the plan to make Brandon jealous. And you know what? I don't want Brandon in the room this next time. To be honest, it was distracting to know he was there last night."

Andrew studied his empty coffee cup and said nothing.

"Come on, Andrew. I'm trying to help you out."

"Are you?"

"Yes. So who did you have in mind for my next date?"

He looked up, his dark eyes filled with kindness. "Your father suggested that I set you up with some of my friends. I made a list. But it's lame. And I—"

"Let's see it."

He heaved a gigantic sigh as he pulled a folded-up piece of yellow paper from his jeans. "I can't believe I've been sucked into this," he said.

"I can't either. But since we're in this together, we might as well make the best of it. So who's on your list?"

"A couple of college roommates."

"Oh? Tell me about them."

She settled back and listened as Andrew talked about his roommates from the University of Virginia Law School. Each of them was wildly successful. One had been a Supreme Court clerk and was now a hot-shot litigator, and the other, a guy named Connor Strickland, had started a digital legal search firm that was faster and cheaper than LexisNexis. His company had just gone public and was listed on the New York Stock Exchange. The IPO had made him a millionaire, and he'd recently been profiled in *Washingtonian* magazine.

"I'd love to go out with a millionaire. I mean, who wouldn't? And just to help you in your planning, I actually need a plus-one for Emma's wedding coming up in a couple of weeks."

"Okay. I'll see what I can do," he said.

"But I'm totally down with doing something else. Something new and different and maybe a little dangerous."

"Like what? I don't think your father would approve of anything dangerous."

"How about a date at a dance club?" she asked.

"That's not dangerous."

"No?"

He shook his head and took out a pen and made a note on his lined paper.

"What about bungee-jumping?"

He looked up. "No. I am not sending you on any bungee-jumping dates. Your father would have my head on a plate if I did that."

A little more than forty-eight hours later, Andrew sat in his office with a pile of briefs in front of him and a container of not-very-good Chinese at his elbow. He was thinking about that moment at the coffeehouse when Laurie had touched the back of his hand. Every cell in his body had reacted. It was as if he'd suddenly awakened from a long nap, looked around, and remembered that he was still a man capable of being turned on.

Damn. He was compromised. He no longer wanted to see Laurie and Brandon get back together. Somehow he needed to talk Noah out of this mediation. It was wrong. Neither of them was impartial.

Andrew pushed the pile of papers aside and pulled out a legal pad and wrote the words *Why Does Noah Want Laurie and Brandon to Reconcile?* at the top of the page. He focused for a long moment and started making a list:

1. He wants Laurie to be happy.

2. He's suffering early-onset dementia.

Andrew stalled at number three.

Damn. Did Noah really believe that Brandon would make Laurie happy? It was almost inconceivable. Brandon had damaged her career, humiliated her in public, and broken her heart. Surely Noah knew this. Didn't he?

Maybe not. Maybe he *was* demented.

Or maybe there was something Andrew was missing. With Noah, you never knew. He was a master at spinning out plans that he shared with absolutely no one until he sprang them on unsuspecting clients. Oddly, Noah's surprises worked most of the time. He had an amazing track record of bringing people together.

Andrew sat pondering his problem for a long moment. If Noah had a secret plan, what would it be? What benefit did Noah get if Laurie married Brandon?

And there it was. Finally another potential motive for Noah's odd behavior, his single-minded fixation on Laurie and Brandon, and his insistence that Andrew break most of the rules of objective mediation.

Brandon's father, August Kopp, was one of the preeminent Supreme Court litigators in the nation. August had argued many of the seminal cases of the last decade, and he'd won most of them. Andrew didn't know all the details of Lyndon, Lyndon & Kopp's financial situation, but August's practice was clearly lucrative.

Wilson Kavanaugh, which had grown to gargantuan proportions in the last few years by gobbling up law firms right and left, didn't have a Supreme Court litigation team, and the buzz around the office was that they wanted one. Could it be that Laurie and Brandon's marriage was the first step in an effort to convince August Kopp to leave his firm and bring his practice to Wilson Kavanaugh?

Damn. Would August really walk away from Lyndon, Lyndon & Kopp? He and Andrew's uncle Charles were the closest of friends—almost like family. But if Noah's daughter and August's son married, then a merger would truly be all in the family, so to speak. It made a certain amount of sense.

Andrew tore his notes off the pad and ripped them into pieces before throwing them in the trash. He took a deep breath. Was he being paranoid? Maybe.

Dammit. Andrew needed more information. He needed to talk to Uncle Charles, and maybe even August Kopp to lay his worst fears to rest.

Hopefully he was wrong about this, and Noah was merely laboring under the delusion that Laurie wanted Brandon back and that helping them to reconcile would be good for his daughter.

In the meantime, Andrew needed to keep Laurie safe as she ventured out into the world of dating. So when Connor Strickland returned his earlier call and said he'd be happy to take Laurie dancing on Saturday, Andrew cleared his calendar too. Laurie would get her date with a millionaire at a dance club, but she'd also have a secret wingman whether she wanted one or not.

It was customary for Courtney to schedule a meeting with each bride a week or so before her wedding to go over last-minute details. On Wednesday, Emma Raynerson, one of Laurie's bridesmaids, visited Eagle Hill Manor for this pre-event consultation.

In Courtney's experience, it was usually a disaster if a bride and one of her bridesmaids chose the same wedding venue. Drama usually ensued that could literally bust up friendships. But with Laurie and Emma, that didn't seem to be a problem.

For one thing, their weddings couldn't be more different. Laurie and her mother had wanted the whole royal wedding theme: the chapel, the Carriage House, the three-course dinner, and the open bar.

On the other hand, Emma and her fiancé, Nabil Alfarsi, wanted a small wedding officiated by a judge, with a reception for forty staged on the inn's portico. In addition to the reception, Eagle Hill Manor would be hosting a traditional Turkish henna party on the Friday before the wedding. The Raynerson-Alfarsi wedding was one of three events scheduled for Saturday, September twenty-third, which also happened to be the opening day of the Shenandoah Valley Harvest Festival. It was a busy time for the inn.

Emma and Courtney spent an hour in the inn's solarium, where the henna party would take place, sipping tea and going through a punch list of final details. When they reached the end of the list, Emma settled back in her chair and said, "Okay, now that we've gotten through all that, let's discuss the important business. How is Laurie? Really. I call her every day, and she puts on a good face, but I'm really worried about her. Yesterday she didn't even respond to a text I sent her, letting her know that I'd found Brandon's Camaro."

"Oh, was it missing?"

"Well, sort of. You see Andrew tipped him off that we were planning to do something to it. So he moved it from its usual parking place. It took a lot of skullduggery to figure out where he stashed it."

"Awesome." Courtney drew the word out. "Where is it?"

Emma leaned forward and dropped her voice to a near-whisper. "It's here, in Shenandoah Falls. He's hidden it in the garage out behind his father's river house."

"Oh, too bad."

"Too bad? Why?"

"Because if you really want to use a man's car against him, you need to get into his head and ruin all the joy he feels about driving the car. You want to change that joy into fear and dread. And to do that, you kind of have to sabotage it on a continual basis."

"You mean like a siege?"

"Yeah, over a long period. It's like death from a thousand small cuts. But if he's stashed it in a garage and isn't driving it, then there's no real fun in it, you know?"

"No, I don't know. I've never sabotaged a guy's car before. I'm not even sure what we should do."

"Oh, honey, there are a million things an angry woman can do to a man's car. She can cover it in birdseed and let our feathered friends do a number on the paint. Or she can cover it in honey and park it near an ants' nest. She could pour milk onto the carpet and let it ferment, or tape bacon under the driver's seat and let it rot. If she puts a few ball bearings in the door panels—just enough to create a rattle—it will drive him insane. There's also dog poop under the door handles, black shoe polish on the windows, replacing the gas cap with a lockable one. One of my favorites is to loosen the screws holding his plates so that he loses them and has to stand in line at the DMV to get new ones. And then, when he does get new plates, you go back and do it to him a second time. And then there's my personal fave—putting a sign on the bumper that says, *I'm a jerk, honk and give me the finger*."

"Oh my God, Courtney, how much time did you spend researching these ideas? They are phenomenal."

"Are you kidding? I didn't do any research. I've got a world of experience when it comes to unfaithful men and their automobiles."

"So we should start right away."

Courtney shook her head. "Like I said, it won't work. If the car is parked here and Brandon is living in D.C., we can't really get into his head."

Emma leaned back with a sigh. "Okay, I can see that, but if you think for one minute I'm not going to exact revenge on his car, you can—"

"Wait, I've got an idea," Courtney said. "Jessica and Madison are coming to your henna party in two weeks, right?"

Emma smiled. "Yes, they are."

"What if we have a little revenge after-party? We can't stage a series of attacks because he's not using the car regularly, but we could certainly make a point."

"Oh my God, that's a wicked but wonderful idea for a pre-wedding party. Let's do it."

Courtney smiled. "Yes, let's. I'll take care of pulling together everything we need for a midnight raid on August Kopp's garage. In the meantime, though, don't tell Laurie. Let's surprise her, okay?"

"My lips are sealed," Emma said.

Chapter Eight ————————

Laurie officially hit the panic button on Friday afternoon when she Googled the name of the D.C. dance club where she was scheduled to meet Connor Strickland on Saturday. The Park at Fourteenth was apparently the "in" place for D.C.'s young professionals. Local celebs from sports figures to politicos hung out there on a regular basis, and even more appalling, the club's event photos showed only drop-dead gorgeous people with killer bodies draped in designer labels.

She definitely needed a new dress, even though she had no money to buy one since Brandon had left her holding the mortgage to run off to Bermuda on a vacation she'd paid for.

But this was an emergency. And really, Brandon had the money. But Laurie no longer trusted him to pay his share of the bills. Maybe tomorrow, if she could pull up her big girl panties and be sure that she wouldn't cry, she'd call him and make a few demands. She hated to think what might happen if he blew her off. The last thing she wanted to do was to call Dad and ask him to bail her out. Calling Dad was something Mom would do.

She pushed her financial worries out of her mind on Friday night and made the long drive down Route 7 to Tyson's Corner Center, the biggest mall in the D.C. area. She didn't mess around but went straight to the dress department at Bloomingdale's and tried on no less than fifteen different dresses in a rainbow of colors.

In the end, she bought a black sheath dress from a no-name company that was form-fitting and had a daring slit up the side and a sweetheart neck line that showed a modest amount of cleavage. She put the dress on her almost-maxed-out credit card and then went downstairs and let the beauty consultant at the Chanel counter give her a beauty makeover that cost more than her dress.

She could do this thing. She could be beautiful and sexy. She could meet the dress code advice that the club published on its webpage.

Still, she was more than a little anxious when she pulled her ancient Subaru to the curb in front of the club on Saturday evening. She expected the valet to reject her car. People who went to nightclubs like this drove Audis and BMWs. To her relief, the valet didn't seem to care about the dent in the Subaru's right fender or the number on the odometer, which read 150,378 miles.

She also made it past the tight security at the door, where one of the doormen/bouncers actually smiled at her. But that may have been because she dropped Connor Strickland's name. She stepped through the doors and was greeted by the sound of Top 40 music, played just a little too loud for her taste. The music drifted down from the second-floor overlook.

The restaurant on the ground level was classy and elegant with sleek, mid-tone wood paneling and a hand-blown glass chandelier that looked like a fire ball. A stainless steel kitchen opened to the dining room so guests could watch a bevy of white-coated chefs prepare their meals.

The hostess led her to a table near the front windows, where she came face-to-face with Connor Strickland. She recognized him, of course, because she'd checked out his Facebook, LinkedIn, and Twitter profiles. But the guy at the table gave off a different vibe from the carefully posed person in the corporate head shot on his various online profiles. His public persona was definitely button-down, but the real Connor Strickland looked like a player in a pair of tight faded jeans, a body-hugging black T-shirt, and a pair of Toms canvas shoes with holes in the toes.

He stood up and gave her a wink.

WTF?

Then he smiled and said her name in a deep voice that was the definition of hot and manly. A moment later, he moved forward, grabbed her by the arm, and kissed her. Not on the cheek but right on the mouth. No tongue, thank God, but she felt as if her space had been violated.

He gave her a boyish grin and smoothed his dirty-blond hair with one hand. Laurie had to admit he was kind of attractive... from a certain angle.

She squared her shoulders and took a seat at the table, but before she could say a word, Connor ordered her a Park Margarita. She didn't want the drink. She'd planned to stay sober tonight because of the sixty-mile drive back to Shenandoah Falls. Also sobriety seemed wise when one was going out on a blind date.

Obviously she was being way too cautious. But what was wrong with that?

Everything. Cautious people didn't ever live danger-
ously. They never had adventures. They always followed
the straight and narrow.

So when her drink arrived, she threw caution to the wind
and took a sip. It was an excellent margarita, perfectly
sweet and salty at the same time. And Connor seemed nice.
He asked her a few questions about her job and even listened when she launched into a discussion of her research
on the behavior of non-party-affiliated voters. But about
five minutes into her discussion, he had the temerity to argue with her about her research.

Rather than argue back, because the man knew nothing
about voter behavior studies, she turned the conversation
back on him and let him order her a second margarita.

By the time she was halfway finished with the second
drink, she decided that Connor was a natural-born racon-
teur. He kept the conversation going all through the appe-
tizers and her main course of Chilean sea bass. He had the
rib eye steak. But when the coffee arrived, he looked deeply
into Laurie's eyes and asked, "Do you believe in destiny?"

Oh boy. A girl didn't have to have a lot of experience
to know a lame pickup line when she heard one. She was
tempted to launch into a geek girl discussion of free will
but decided against it. He didn't want a conversation with a
smart woman. He wanted someone to wink at and impress.
Besides, he'd already dismissed her research.

She decided she wasn't all that down with dancing with
the guy. She really wanted to leave.

Unfortunately, she was almost finished with margarita
number three, and she didn't have a backup transportation
plan. It wasn't as if she could afford a taxi to drive the sixty
miles back to Shenandoah Falls. Or to book a hotel room in
D.C., which would probably cost more than the taxi. Also,

calling Daddy and crashing at his apartment was not at the top of her list of options.

Connor forced the issue when he reached across the table, grabbed her hand, and forcibly interlaced his fingers with hers. "Laurie, you're an incredibly beautiful and hot woman. And I want to tell you that August Kopp's son, whatever his name is, is a jerk."

She ground her teeth. "Did Andrew tell you about Brandon because—"

"No, no, of course not. Andrew didn't say a word. I did some research on my own. I just want you to know that I understand how life can be really hard sometimes. And also, whatever that guy did, it wasn't your fault. I want to be your friend, and I think we've really hit it off, don't you? Why don't we go somewhere quiet where we can really talk? My apartment is in the Watergate." He squeezed her hand.

Damn. Here it was. The invitation she'd been looking for. And really, who wasn't curious about the Watergate? But curiosity killed the cat, and suddenly she didn't want any part of Connor Strickland.

She pulled her hand away. "Uh, Connor, I, uh, I need to—" She didn't finish the sentence as she stood. She was in full-flight mode, which was complicated by the fact that she was too buzzed to drive. Real escape wasn't even possible, but the ladies' room seemed like a reasonable short-term alternative. She turned and headed across the room, which had become wall-to-wall crowded in the hour and a half that she and Connor had been eating.

She didn't get far before Connor grabbed her from behind. "Hey, what's the deal? I thought we had an understanding, you know?"

She turned, took one look at his face, and realized she was in way over her head.

* * *

For the last two hours, Andrew had occupied a spot at The Park's ground-floor bar, nursing a single beer and a couple of Diet Cokes. He'd kept an eye on the flat-screen television above the bar, where Michigan was clobbering Penn State on the gridiron. Every so often he'd look over toward the couple at the table nearest the window. And every time his gaze landed on Laurie, his worry mounted.

Laurie had certainly come loaded for bear tonight. Her dress clung to her curves, exposed her legs up to mid-thigh, and revealed mouthwatering cleavage. She'd let her hair down too. It fell below her shoulders in a golden waterfall that dared any man to touch it or bury his nose in it.

Connor had taken the dare, grabbing Laurie for a kiss, his hand lingering for a moment on the back of her head. Andrew looked away, his gut tightening. He should stop this. But he didn't. Instead, he watched like a voyeur as Connor ordered Laurie one sweet drink after another.

No question about it, Connor was looking for action tonight, and Laurie was like a hot babe in the woods. But when Laurie abruptly stood up with a wide-eyed panicked look, Andrew sprang into action.

He arrived in the nick of time, grabbing Connor's shoulder and spinning him around. "Leave her alone," he said in a voice that carried above the music floating down from the dance floor upstairs.

"Hey, man, what the hell are you doing here?" Connor asked.

Andrew got right up into Connor's face. "Look, dude, we both know that you can have any woman you want. So don't pick on the ones who are so brokenhearted they don't know what they want."

Connor held his ground, and Andrew feared he might

take a swing so he took a deep breath and centered himself. If Connor followed through, Andrew would be ready to evade him. But as Andrew stared down his old friend, he realized that he'd broken one of the main tenets of aikido. He, not Connor, had picked this fight.

Well, so be it. He needed to keep Laurie safe, and he was ready to do what was necessary. They stood toe to toe for a long moment until Connor gave Andrew a small, non-threatening man-punch to the shoulder. "I'm glad to see you rejoining the human race," he said.

"What?" Andrew was momentarily confused.

Connor leaned in. "She's much better looking than Val," he said with a smile. Then he turned away and was soon lost in the crowd.

Laurie finally found her voice. "What are you doing here?" she asked.

"I'm your wingman," Andrew said as he looked down at her.

The crowd pressed them close as Laurie blinked up at him with a hot, sexy, vulnerable, and buzzed look in her hazel eyes. "I don't understand," she said.

"You insisted on a real date with a real guy. So I made it happen. But I wasn't about to let you do that alone."

She bit her lower lip, and a rush of lust almost leveled Andrew where he stood. No, wait, that was just *wrong*. Wasn't it?

"Thank you," she said. "And I guess I'm also glad you didn't tell me that you had my back. I probably would have stupidly told you to mind your own business." She stumbled a little, and Andrew reached out to steady her. But when he grabbed her shoulders, she leaned into his chest, and his arms just naturally wrapped around her while she tucked her head under his chin.

His worry, which had coiled inside like a spring over the

last two hours, morphed into tension of a different kind. He wanted to pull her more tightly against him, but he didn't make a move. He stood there, holding her up and wondering what he should do next. Take her home to his place? Her place?

And then what? No, he couldn't do that for so many reasons.

"Do you want to dance?" he asked instead. Dancing her into sobriety seemed like a good, safe middle ground.

She pushed back a little and looked up at him with a classic wide-eyed drunken stare. "I hate dancing."

Great. He was out of ideas.

"I have two left feet," she continued. "And I really prefer classical music. Although I can't waltz either."

"No one will notice."

"Doesn't matter." She shook her head with exaggerated care. "I'll know. And self-knowledge is a terrible burden to bear, don't you think?"

He couldn't help but smile. Even drunk, Laurie was smart and witty. "I suppose it is, but didn't you come here to break the chains of your dull life? I distinctly remember that you wanted to have a date at a dance club."

She swayed for a moment. "You know," she said, pointing her finger at his chest, "you are wiser than you look."

"Thanks, I think. Come on, let's dance. It's a great way to sober up." He took her by the hand, uncomfortably conscious of the heat that seemed to flow up his arm and into his core.

They took the elevator to the third floor, bypassing the loud scene on the second floor where the R&B, Top 40, and hip-hop were just beginning to rock the place. The club's third floor was a whole different story. Andrew and Val had come here often in the past. It was more intimate, and on

Saturdays it featured a DJ that played multicultural music, including a lot of Latin music perfect for salsa dancing.

Laurie stalled the moment they exited the elevator. The room wasn't nearly as crowded, but there was a small knot of beautiful people on the dance floor gyrating their hips and doing some pretty fancy footwork. "You're out of your mind," she said.

He leaned down and spoke above the music right into her ear. "Salsa dancing looks way harder than it is. You just walk back and forth. I'll show you." Her slightly floral scent filled his senses and fogged his brain.

It was getting harder by the minute to ignore his attraction. She was so beautiful. And vulnerable. And the touch of her hand in his made him feel alive in ways he hadn't felt in so very long.

But he restrained himself and ignored the obvious as he guided her to a table. He ordered a couple of Cokes, dragged her off to the dance floor, took her in his arms, and proceeded to teach her a few salsa moves.

She was buzzed and inexperienced, and his feet paid a price. But it was a small price for the feel of her in his arms. Within a few minutes, either the beat of the music or the booze in the margaritas kicked in. Laurie Wilson, brilliant but slightly uptight PhD, let go of a whoop and threw herself body and soul into the dancing.

Holy crap! Who knew Laurie Wilson could be so much fun?

When had boring Andrew become so utterly fascinating? Laurie settled into his touch, which was both commanding and gentle, as he led her around the dance floor, coaching her through the steps until they seemed easy and simple.

As the night wore on and her margarita fog lifted, something else happened between them. Their dance posture, which started out distant and formal, began to contract. They inched closer, hips gyrating to the beat of the music. His right hand slipped from its position high on her back downward along her spine until it rested right above her butt, leaving her anticipating and almost aching for the moment when it would dip even lower.

No question about it, the margaritas had loosened her up, but the yearning for Andrew grew as she burned off the alcohol. How was that possible? This kind of carnal longing was new to her.

Unfortunately, as she sobered, she also started to think again, and thinking was a huge buzz kill. She should go. She was definitely sober enough to drive herself home and arrive in one piece. Andrew had rescued her quite thoroughly. Dad's man on the scene had come through again.

Right then, he twirled her around in one of those moves that had her walking backward while he walked forward. Her heart took flight in her chest. This was the stuff of little-girl fantasies. Her inner princess reveled in the idea of dancing with a guy who had rescued her.

But she wanted so much more than just princely behavior and a rescue. Down deep in the place where life frightened her, she wanted something real. Something not so safe.

She looked up at him and momentarily lost her bearings. His dark hair had fallen over his forehead, and his espresso eyes seemed anything but safe. His mask had shattered, and Laurie saw the desire flickering in his eyes, hot, mysterious, and intriguing.

Her breath hitched and her insides clutched. It had never been clearer that she had a choice to make. She could stand there debating all the pros and cons or she could throw caution to the wind and kiss him. Maybe the time for contemplation was over. Maybe it was time to act.

She drew in a breath, closed her eyes, and leaned into him. She had no sense of rhythm so her move was not only a surprise but out of time. Andrew stumbled back a step before his body firmed, allowing her to come up against his chest hard as she cupped the back of his head and pulled him down.

He resisted for an instant, and she almost let go. But something told her that this moment would never come again. It was now, or never.

Their lips met. His firm, warm, slightly open, perhaps in astonishment. Hers surprisingly hungry as she breached the open seam of his mouth with her tongue.

He tasted sweet and bitter and complicated. Like a piece of dark, dark chocolate. His tongue danced away, and she chased it. His body stiffened.

No. No.

She twisted her fingers in his hair and pressed her body into his, breast to chest, thigh to thigh. A giddy and powerful warmth filled her with a sense of being alive and in the moment. And then his tongue changed direction, meeting hers in a dance as skillful as the one they'd been doing all night.

She wrapped her arms around his neck. His hands slipped down to her butt and he clutched her skirt right where the slit exposed her thigh, his fingers brushing against her leg as a torrent of lust took her breath away. It was as if her body suddenly woke up and realized this sort of thing could be fun.

One of the dancing couples bumped into them. "Hey, dudes, get a room," the guy shouted.

Just like that, Andrew's reserve snapped back into place.

He retreated, and Laurie tried to follow, but he held her at arm's length. "I think it's time for us to get some coffee before I take you home."

"Home to your place?" she asked hopefully.

His eyebrow arched. She'd seen that expression on the face of almost every single male member of the Lyndon family. When a Lyndon arched an eyebrow like that, it was never a hopeful sign.

Chapter Nine ——————————————

What had just happened? One minute he'd been in complete control and the next...He stared down at Laurie, surprised and somewhat alarmed. For the first time in *years*, someone other than Val had made him burn.

"No. We're going to get some coffee and then I'm going to drive you back to Shenandoah Falls."

She shook her head and bit her lip, the picture of a not-quite-sober woman. "I'm completely sober."

"No, you're not. And besides, I'm already in enough hot water with your father."

The light in her beautiful eyes dimmed a little. Had he hurt her feelings? Well, too bad. He was not bringing the boss's daughter home for more kisses or whatever. Not even sober.

He escorted her out of the club and up the block to the nearest Starbucks, where he bought her coffee and learned that she liked it heavy on the milk and light on the sugar.

"So what now?" she asked. "Do I have to endure a lecture from you because I kissed you? It's okay. I can take it. God only knows my life is screwed up right at the moment. My job sucks. My mother thinks I'm suicidal. And I spent too much on this dress considering the fact that I don't have the money for the next mortgage payment. I should never have let Brandon talk me into that money pit." Her eyes filled, and her voice definitely wobbled.

"Laurie, it's going to be okay," he said.

She nodded and grabbed a napkin to blot her tears. "I'm sorry. I guess I'm not sober," she said, looking down.

Andrew hated seeing her so upset, especially since he'd caused her tears. Cutting off that incredible kiss had probably shattered her self-esteem. But what was he supposed to do?

Tell her she'd turned him on? Take her home and make love to her?

He couldn't do that. There were rules that governed socially acceptable behavior, and Andrew wasn't about to shatter them. Laurie was beyond his reach. He couldn't kiss her again, but he could help her solve some of her problems. "What's this about the house payment?" he asked.

"Brandon and I had an agreement that I would use my graduation money for the down payment on the house, and he'd make the payments," she said in a surprisingly firm voice. Her tears had dried up, leaving only a little smudge of mascara beneath her eyes.

"Is his name on the note?"

She nodded. "Yes." She took a deep breath, clearly trying to hold back more tears. "Please don't tell Dad about this. He'll swoop in and pay for everything. I don't want Dad's money. I'm not like my mother. I just want Brandon to live up to his obligations and promises. This is so screwed up. I never thought I'd need a divorce before I even got married."

"Have you got a dollar?"

"What?"

"If you have a dollar, get it out of your purse and hand it over."

"Why?"

"Don't ask, just do it."

She dug in her purse and handed him a dollar.

"As of this moment, I'm on retainer as your attorney, and everything you say to me is privileged. That means I can't say a word to your father about anything we discuss. First thing tomorrow I'm going to call Brandon and shake him down for at least half of the house payment. I'm sure it's just an oversight. I don't think Brandon would purposefully leave you high and dry."

"Jeeze, Andrew, I'm kinda glad you think that way. I used to think I knew Brandon, you know, but now..." She couldn't finish the sentence, and tears still pooled in her eyes but stubbornly refused to run down her face.

They sat in silence for a moment before she said, "I guess I've thoroughly humiliated myself tonight, huh?"

"No. Not at all."

She barked a laugh. "You're such a gentleman, Andrew. Really. The sad fact is that I've just become my mother."

"How so?"

She tried to look at anything but Andrew. "Falling for the first strong guy who shows up after a breakup. And Mom used to break up with guys on a regular basis. When things fell apart, she always got drunk and then cried on someone's shoulder. The truth is, I should be strong enough to call Brandon myself."

"First of all, you are entitled to a few tears. Second of

all, you shouldn't have to call Brandon. He's the one who walked away. He should have called you and made arrangements. Tomorrow I want you to e-mail me with a list of the bills associated with the house and anything else that Brandon owes you. For instance, the part of the Bermuda trip that you paid for."

"I paid for all of it. I put it on my credit card, and that payment is overdue too."

Andrew exhaled sharply. "Okay, include that, and anything else you think is important."

"Thanks." She looked down at her coffee, the picture of misery. He empathized with her, but he didn't dare offer her more than his professional help with the bills.

"I'm sorry you've gotten dragged right into the middle of my dispute with Brandon. And I'm sorry I—"

"Laurie, you're not the one who put me in the middle."

"Yeah, I guess Dad did that, huh?"

"No, actually, Brandon set this in motion the day he walked away from you."

Laurie drove herself home, although she and Andrew almost came to blows before he let her go by herself. If she cried over Andrew on the way home, that was no one's business but her own. If she woke up on Sunday with a headache and bloodshot eyes, well, ditto.

She was so ashamed of herself. What had gotten into her? She should have known that Andrew wasn't interested in her kisses.

Still, her self-esteem had taken a hell of a blow last night. It was downright humiliating. All the more so when she checked her e-mail and found one from Andrew, sent at 7:30 a.m., reminding her to send him the details of her financial situation. Did the guy ever sleep?

Yeah, well, that could wait until she had her first cup of coffee. Alas, the milk in her fridge was sour. So she headed off to Bean There Done That for a latte. Once she was sufficiently caffeinated, she planned to hit the Food Lion and The Home Depot. Maybe after that she'd feel like pulling together the financial bad news and sending it off to Andrew.

Or not.

The line at Bean There Done That was ridiculously long, but she endured. She'd been standing there like a hungover zombie for an eternity when someone tapped her on the shoulder.

She turned to find Roxy Kopp and Pam Lyndon standing behind her.

Mrs. Lyndon wore a blue plaid hacking jacket in muted heathers that complemented her gray riding slacks and black boots. Roxy was outfitted all in black, but both of them looked like fashion plates from *Town and Country* magazine.

"Laurie, darlin', how are you?" Pam stepped forward and gave her a little kiss on the cheek, as if they were long-lost friends. It was a tiny bit creepy. Even though she'd had dinner at Charlotte's Grove many times, she didn't know Pam Lyndon well.

Roxy, whom she knew much better, hung back and tried not to make eye contact.

"I'm fine," Laurie said in her best formal-tea-party voice.

"I heard you had dinner at the Union Jack with my nephew a week ago. And surprise, surprise, I heard you were out and about in town with Andrew last night," Pam said in a big voice. "I'm so glad you decided to take my advice."

Uh-oh. How the hell did Pam know about last night?

Had Andrew lied to her about her date with Connor? Had it all been a fake date after all? And worse yet, Pam Lyndon seemed to think Laurie was taking her advice.

Which, actually, was sort of true, since she'd kissed Andrew last night. "Uh, well, I've been staying busy," she said, hoping her red face went unnoticed.

"Good for you. You know your mother and father were both so worried that you would retreat from the world after what happened. Darlin', we're all so proud of you for getting out there and meeting people. Tell me, what do you think of Andrew?"

Damn, damn, damn. Her face was burning up. "He's a good dancer. And he's kind. And—"

Laurie reached the head of the line, which saved her from saying another word. She ordered her latte and wondered if it might be possible to escape. But before she'd even paid her bill, Pam said, "Join us for a moment, darlin'. Let's catch up."

One didn't say no to Pam Lyndon so, a few moments later, she found herself jammed around a tiny table with Roxy on her right and Pam on her left.

"I admit that I'm a little surprised you went out with Andrew," Pam said. "Were you just trying to annoy Brandon? That's what Matt seemed to think."

"Matt? What does he have to do with it?"

"Oh, he's the one who saw you and Andrew. He said you looked like you were enjoying yourself. I know Andrew is reserved, but he can also be fun."

Laurie's face felt like a three-alarm fire. "Uh, well, I think you have the wrong idea. I wasn't out with Andrew last night. I had a blind date with someone else. It didn't go well, I'm afraid. But I ran into Andrew, and we hung out for a little while."

"Ah, so Andrew came to your rescue. How romantic." Pam smiled, and her blue eyes lit up. This was bad. Very, very bad.

Thank God for Roxy, who changed the subject by asking, "Who was your blind date?"

"His name was Connor Strickland."

"Oh my God, the guy who was profiled in *Washingtonian* magazine a couple of months back?" Roxy asked.

"The very same. I thought it might be fun to go out with a millionaire, but he turned out to be a jerk."

"How did you get a date with him?" Roxy asked.

Damn. She'd been cornered. At moments like this, the truth was always best. Besides, she was a terrible liar. "Well, as a matter of fact, he's an old friend of Andrew's."

Pam and Roxy exchanged glances. "So," Roxy said, "Andrew is setting up dates for you and going along as your wingman?"

"I guess so," she reluctantly admitted, looking down at her coffee. This is what happened when one goes out drinking, wakes up with a hangover, and tries to have a conversation before a caffeine infusion.

"So tell me, Laurie, what do you *really* think of Andrew?" Pam asked.

Damn. Mrs. Lyndon had a truly avid look in her eye. Laurie had been warned that Pam fancied herself a matchmaker. Of course, in a way, Laurie wouldn't mind being matched up with Andrew.

But it was impossible. Everyone, with the exception of Pam Lyndon, would be horrified if she went out with Andrew. So she drew herself up straight and said, "He's a good friend."

Pam nodded and smiled. "Ah, just so," she said with an eager smile. "I'm so glad you appreciate Andrew. So many people don't understand him. But, darlin', I'm a bit surprised that you and Daniel didn't hit it off. You two have so much in common."

Roxy's face paled as Pam spoke, and her eyes flicked around the coffee shop as if she were searching for an avenue of escape. Good thing Laurie could put Brandon's sister at ease. "You can relax, Rox. I don't plan on going out with Daniel ever again."

"No?" Roxy sounded so hopeful.

"Why not?" Pam asked.

Laurie glanced at Pam and then back at Roxy. "Daniel isn't interested in me. And I'm not interested in him. The truth is, he's already in love with someone else."

Pam straightened her shoulders. "What? Who? Don't tell me he's heartbroken about that woman who left him at the altar. We were all glad to see her go."

"No, not Mia," Laurie said, and then turned back toward Roxy. "I'm sorry I haven't called you, especially after my date with Daniel. Andrew told me I should stay out of it, but you know, the truth is, Daniel spent the entire dinner date talking about you."

"Me?"

"Roxy?" Pam asked, as if this was something she hadn't thought about. "Roxy and Daniel are like oil and water, Laurie. They have never gotten along."

Roxy looked down at the table, hiding the smallest of smiles.

Laurie ignored Pam and spoke only to Brandon's sister. "Daniel said that he was grateful about the way you helped him with his custody battle. He was blown away by the way you stood with him. But he seems to think that a woman like you isn't ready to be saddled with a two-year-old, probably because Mia wasn't ready and he's projecting his fears.

Bottom line, Rox, you were the main subject of our conversation."

"Really?" Roxy looked up, a sheen in her dark eyes.

"Yeah. And honestly, you'd be a fool if you let your pride get in the way. I know he went ghost on you last summer, but I think it's because he's afraid of being hurt again. So you probably need to make the first move. And I can attest to the fact that being left at the altar plays with a person's self-esteem."

"The hurt can go both ways," Roxy said.

"Yeah, it can. But don't you think Daniel is worth a try? I mean, if he says no to you, or runs away, you haven't really lost anything, right?"

"Except my heart. And maybe my pride for the second or third time."

Pam reached across the table and touched Roxy's hand. "Darlin', why didn't you tell me?"

Roxy's face reddened. "I have. A dozen times. And you keep telling me that Danny hates me."

" 'Hate' is a strong word. But you and Danny have never gotten along."

Roxy nodded. "Pam is kind of right about that. I mean, as kids we fought all the time. And last summer we had our moments. So…"

"Well, at least you know the truth about my plans. Daniel and I went out once but nothing clicked." She picked up her latte and stood. "It's been nice catching up with you, but I have a dozen errands to run."

"Laurie." Roxy stood up too.

"What?"

"I just wanted to say I'm sorry. You know, about Brandon. And about not calling you these last few weeks. I didn't want to…" Her voice faded off.

"It's okay, Roxy. I understand. The truth is, I've gotten plenty of pity calls, and after a while they just get old. I don't want anyone's pity."

Roxy leaned in and spoke in a low tone that Pam couldn't hear. "Good for you. But listen. As you can see, Pam wants to match you up with one of her nephews, but be careful. Not everyone likes that idea. The Lyndon boys are closing ranks around Brandon, and you being seen with Danny and Andrew has ticked everyone off. They think you're stirring the pot. Are you?"

Roxy had just called her out. She *had* gone out with Danny and Connor to annoy Brandon. But something else had happened last night with Andrew. Something she hadn't been looking for. The irony was that she'd known from the start that Andrew was in a precarious situation. Kissing him in public wouldn't make his life any easier. No doubt that's why he'd put a stop to it.

"No, I'm not stirring the pot. I'm just going out on dates. And for the record, Andrew is a friend. Just a friend, that's all."

Chapter Ten

On Monday just before noon, Brandon Kopp dropped by the Wilson Kavanaugh offices unannounced, stalked into Andrew's office, and slammed the door behind him. "What the hell's going on?" he said in a flat, angry tone as he crossed the carpet and leaned over Andrew's desk.

"So I see you got my e-mail about Laurie's finances."

"What?"

"You didn't see my e-mail?"

"I've been busy this morning. What about her finances?"

"She asked me to talk to you about the mortgage. I gather she doesn't have the money to make the payment. And she'd like to be reimbursed for the Bermuda trip. I sent you the details."

"She asked you to talk to me about our finances?"

"Look, she's upset and—"

"Don't BS me, Andrew. Matt was at The Park on Saturday. He saw you dancing with Laurie."

Andrew stood up to meet Brandon's angry stare and tried to decide if this was a good or a bad development. The ambiguity of his feelings was enough to trigger a boatload of guilt. He'd kissed Laurie on Saturday, and even though he'd told her no and sent her home, he couldn't get her out of his mind.

"It's not what you think," he said.

"No? Then you haven't decided to gang up on me?"

"Gang up on—no. I told Laurie I'd try to mediate your financial issues. She deserves to be paid back, Brandon. As for the nightclub, I ran into her on Saturday, and we hung out for a little while."

"Oh my God, you are so naive. Don't you see what she's doing? I mean, first she goes on a date with Danny, and then she's seen dancing with you, and apparently she also throws herself on your good nature and tells you all kinds of lies about our financial situation. Honestly, how did you fall into her trap? She's purposefully creating a shit storm for me. For our friends. For our *families*. And you're helping her."

"Brandon, please, lower your voice." Beyond his glass wall, everyone in the bullpen was watching him. They'd been watching him for a while, ever since Noah had taken him off the AVIEN negotiations and given him no other visible assignment.

"No, I won't be quiet," Brandon said in a belligerent tone. "Don't you see? Laurie's being totally vindictive and manipulative."

"Come on. Laurie's not like that."

"No? Then what's she up to? Look, I don't want you hanging out with her or being her friend or advocate. So if you run into her again, you need to steer clear, understand? When you hang out with her, you're just helping her create chaos. Honestly, I'm furious that you believed her when she told you I hadn't paid the mortgage. I made the September payment before the wedding since I knew we'd be on our honeymoon. I hope you know me better than that. Dammit. She's manipulating the crap out of everyone."

Wow. Brandon was behaving exactly like an angry litigant in a messy divorce. Andrew cast about for something calming to say but he didn't get the chance because Noah strode through the door without knocking and said, "Hello, Brandon."

Brandon turned and physically wilted under Noah's blue-eyed stare. Andrew knew the feeling. Noah could be incredibly intimidating when he wanted to be. "Hello, Noah," Brandon said in a milder tone.

The two men faced off awkwardly for a moment before Noah asked, "What's the problem?"

Andrew jumped on the question before Brandon said something that created more drama than was necessary. Besides, Andrew had nothing to hide. He'd done the right thing by protecting Laurie on Saturday, helping her sober up, and sending her home…alone. "Brandon is upset because my cousin Matt saw Laurie and me on Saturday night at The Park nightclub."

"You went out with Laurie?" A dangerous spark ignited in Noah's bright blue eyes.

"No," Andrew said calmly, "it wasn't a date. She was at the club, and I ran into her. We hung out for a while."

"Come on, Andrew, why on earth would Laurie ever go to a place like The Park? She hates hip-hop music," Brandon said, folding his arms. His best friend was well and truly ticked off. That was kind of surprising.

Noah said nothing, but his brow lowered.

"I don't know," Andrew said in his coolest voice. "Maybe she had a date."

"No way she had a date," Brandon said.

"Why not?" Andrew countered. "She went out with Daniel."

Brandon scowled and shifted his gaze toward Noah and back again. "Andrew, don't be stupid. Her date with Daniel was just a ploy to annoy me. And running into you wasn't an accident. Val used to talk about salsa dancing at The Park all the time. I'm sure Laurie went there hoping to find you. She's using you to get at me."

"Well," Noah said, folding his arms across his chest, mirroring Brandon's stance, "I don't think you have any right to be upset about Laurie going out to a nightclub for any reason. I distinctly heard you tell my daughter that she needed to get out of the house and have some fun."

Brandon ignored Noah and continued to scowl at Andrew. "Look, don't you see what she's doing? We've argued about nightclubs so she decides to go there. We've argued about the Union Jack restaurant so she goes there. She gets on my case about how much time I spend with the guys, and she goes out on dates with my friends. She's being a b—" He bit off the word.

Noah cleared his throat and, in his usual cool voice, said, "I'm going to pretend I didn't hear you almost call my daughter something nasty and uncharitable, considering the fact that you left her at the altar. If she's angry with you, she has good cause.

"Also I will point out that Andrew isn't required to avoid Laurie if he runs into her, whether it's a club or some other place. What's the matter? Are you jealous? Do you regret what you said on your wedding day?"

Brandon's posture changed. He glowered at Noah, his hands forming fists at his side. Noah stood his ground, and in his best, calm mediator voice, he said, "Perhaps the time has come for you and Laurie to sit down and try to work things out between you. I'm happy to give Laurie a call right now and—"

"No." Brandon took several steps toward the door. "I don't have any problem with Laurie dating people. I really mean that. But right now she's playing a game. She should be going out with someone new. Someone I don't know. Until that happens, all this is just her trying to make me feel bad about what happened."

Brandon marched through the door and slammed it behind him. Not too surprisingly, everyone in the bullpen looked up over their cubby dividers as he stalked from the office.

Noah's mouth actually lifted at the corners. "Excellent job, Andrew. And here I thought you were hiding out in here brushing up your résumé. I have to say I'm surprised that you allowed yourself to be seen with Laurie. But then I suppose there's nothing that gets to a man more than the idea of his best friend dating his ex-girlfriend."

Andrew said nothing while his guilty conscience tweaked.

"Did she have a good time?" Noah asked, utterly flooring Andrew.

"Uh, well, um. We danced." His face grew warm, and he was sure that Noah noticed. His boss had taught Andrew everything he knew about reading body language, and Noah had just caught Andrew in a lie. He sat down behind his desk and waited for Noah to pounce.

But he didn't. Instead Noah said, "Salsa dancing sounds like fun. But Laurie isn't much of a dancer. So I'll ask my question again, did she have a good time?" He sat down in the side chair and stared at Andrew as if he could see right through him.

"I taught her salsa dancing." His voice cracked. Damn.

Noah's eyebrows reached for his hairline, and he gave the appearance of being utterly surprised. "Really? You and Latin dancing are two things that don't exactly go together in my mind."

Andrew shrugged. "I used to date a Latina."

"And where is this Latina now?"

"We broke up some time ago."

"Ah." Noah leaned back in the chair and stroked his chin as if deeply in thought.

Andrew kept his mouth shut. If Noah figured out how his feelings for Laurie had changed, Andrew would be in a mess of trouble.

"You know," Noah finally said, "Brandon has a point. We don't want him thinking that Laurie is using you to exact revenge. I think it's time to stop listening to your aunt Pam's advice."

"What?" Andrew was gobsmacked. Had Noah been talking to Pam? Oh no, this was bad.

Noah chuckled. "Yes, I have talked to your aunt. And I know she's the one who suggested that Laurie go out with Daniel. She also told me that she thought Laurie ought to go out with you. I told her I thought that was a bad idea."

"Good thinking," Andrew muttered.

Noah nodded and continued to stroke his chin. "I think we need to change directions, set Laurie up on a date with someone your aunt doesn't know. Someone handsome and well read," he said. "Someone Brandon might regard as a threat or rival." He paused for a moment and then snapped his fingers. "I've got it. Let's send her on a date with Tobin."

Before Andrew could say a word, his boss got up and left, striding in the direction of Tobin's office, three doors down. "Tobin," he said in a voice loud enough to be heard by everyone in the bullpen, "I want you to go on a date with my daughter."

On Monday afternoon, Michael Altimari stopped by Laurie's minuscule office to let her know that Winchester University had decided not to apply for this year's Walter Jephson Foundation grant. The Departmental Executive Committee, composed entirely of tenured professors, had decided at its meeting last Friday that her research proposal needed more work before it was ready to be submitted. Michael recommended waiting a year, working on the premise with him directly, and resubmitting.

When she asked Michael to be specific about the proposal's deficiencies, he gave her a lot of gobbledygook that added up to only one thing: Michael wanted credit for her research, and if she didn't allow him in as a co-author, he would sabotage her career. Of course, he hadn't said as much, but his offer to "work with her to strengthen the premise" was a flashing red light.

She'd have to think about allowing him to co-opt her work. Going against him would make her life miserable, but giving him credit was a nonstarter. It completely chapped her backside when Michael finished delivering his news with a smile and then praised her for being an outstanding teacher. Michael Altimari was an ogler with passive-aggressive tendencies.

So, she was in a black mood when her cell phone buzzed and the caller ID said it was Andrew on the line. Should she answer it?

She considered for a moment, weighing the pros and cons. She definitely wanted to talk with him. Hell, she wanted to corner him in a dark, deserted room and kiss him until they were both senseless. But of course, he'd made it clear that he didn't want to be cornered. And Roxy Kopp had warned her that pursuing Andrew would cause no end of trouble.

Maybe it would be best to let the call go to voice mail. She let it ring three times and then couldn't stop herself from pressing the connect button.

"Hi," she said, trying to sound cool and uninterested while her heart jumped around her chest. She felt like a teenager talking to a boy for the first time.

"Hi," he said, and then paused for a long time, as if he was trying to think of what to say. Maybe he *was* interested.

And maybe she was an idiot.

"What is it, Andrew? Spit it out," she said.

"Well, I've got some good news and bad news."

"Great. Why don't you start with the good news? I've already had enough bad news to last a lifetime."

"Okay. You should expect a call from Tobin Grant."

"Tobin Grant? Isn't he one of the associates at Wilson Kavanaugh?"

"Yeah. He's the associate voted most likely to make partner this year."

"And why is he going to call me?"

"To ask you out on a date."

"That's the good news? I'm underwhelmed."

"Well, there's also the news that Brandon has already paid the September mortgage payment. I haven't yet been able to have a rational discussion with him about the rest."

"What does that mean?"

"That's the bad news."

"Oh?"

"Matt was at The Park on Saturday. He saw us dancing, and he told Brandon all about it. Brandon is furious with you. Sadly, he's not in the slightest bit jealous. He's more or less fig-

ured out what we've been up to and he told me to stay away
from you."

She let go of a long sigh. "I already know that we were
seen at The Park. I ran into Pam and Roxy at the coffee
shop yesterday. Apparently Matt told Brandon and he told
Roxy. For what it's worth, Roxy said that being seen with
you and Daniel has caused a major crap-storm. She warned
me to stay away from you too. On the other hand, your aunt
seemed to be happy that you and I are such good friends."

Andrew let go of a long, audible sigh. "Stay away from
my aunt," he said.

She found herself carefully parsing his admonition and
wondering if he had enjoyed her kiss more than he'd let on.
No, probably not. "Look, I'm sorry. About Saturday. I definitely had too much to drink." And had behaved just like
Mom.

A long, static-filled silence stretched out. "You know,
Laurie," he finally said, "you should go out with Tobin. I
mean, he's great. He's smart, and he dresses well, and your
father loves him. Plus he's not nearly as big of a jerk as
Connor."

She drummed her fingers on the surface of her desk and
thought about quoting Longfellow at him, as in "Speak for
yourself, Andrew." But she had a feeling Andrew had never
read *The Courtship of Miles Standish*. Plus they'd both been
warned to stay away from each other.

"So, are you going to be my wingman again?" she asked,
hoping against hope.

"No. I think you're safe with Tobin. Besides, everyone
thinks you're ready to go on real dates, and it's probably
best if I stay away this time."

"Who's everyone?"

"Your father..."

"And?"

He hauled in another audible breath. "Brandon was here at the office. He was pissed. Accused you of stirring the pot and manipulating things."

"And he suggested that I go on a real date? Doesn't he know I went out with Connor?"

"Uh, no. Not really. All he knows is what Matt told him about seeing us together."

"Oh? Why?"

"Because your dad came into my office while Brandon was ripping me a new one. And I didn't want your father to know about what happened on your date with Connor."

"About how I got drunk, in other words."

"Among other things. So you're good with Tobin? I mean, you can tell him no if you want." Andrew almost sounded like he wanted her to tell this Tobin guy no. But that was probably wishful thinking.

"Yeah. I'm fine. You know what? If he calls, I'll invite him to Emma's wedding next Saturday. I was thinking about asking you, but that's obviously a bad idea."

"Yeah. It is," he said in a flat tone of voice that shattered Laurie's already-broken heart.

Chapter Eleven————————

Laurie's emotions seemed to be on a perpetual roller coaster ride. Some days, she felt strong and ready to take on the world, and at other times, she hit terrible emotional lows. On Friday evening, as she walked up onto the grand portico at Eagle Hill Manor, she hit rock bottom.

It had been exactly four weeks since her wedding disaster, and she hadn't set foot anywhere near the inn in that time. She couldn't help but remember that Friday, when she and her girlfriends checked into the inn. She'd been so happy and excited the night before her wedding.

Twenty-four hours later, her balloon had popped.

She forced a smile as she strolled into the inn's lobby and followed the sign toward the solarium, where Emma's henna party—a combination wedding shower, bachelorette party, and traditional Turkish ceremony—was already in full swing.

Laurie was running late because Michael Altimari had

called her into a meaningless staff meeting in which he'd announced to the entire department that her research proposal had "a few holes in it" and was therefore not quite ready to be submitted as a grant proposal. He'd even had the temerity to suggest that perhaps the problem with her proposal stemmed from the fact that she spent too much time teaching. As if she had any other choice.

It wasn't as if she could complain about her teaching load either. She was the new kid in the department, battling the usual academic inertia. Whining or complaining wouldn't win her any allies or research money.

So she was in a funk when she entered the solarium, where unfamiliar music blared from the speakers, adding to her headache.

"Laurie, we thought you were lost." The fabric of Emma's bright red dress flowed as she crossed the room, and Laurie's breath caught in her throat. The color brought out the olive tones in Emma's skin. She definitely had the bridal radiance thing going in spades.

"I'm sorry," Laurie said, giving her friend a hug. "I got held up at work. And wow, you look fabulous tonight. Red is definitely your color."

Emma grinned. "Thanks. Red is traditional for a henna party. But never mind me, girl. I was worried that maybe coming here would be hard for—"

"I'm fine. Really. It was just a work thing."

"Well, I'm glad. But I'm also angry with you. You haven't been returning my phone calls."

"I'm okay. I'm just busy at work, you know."

Emma gave Laurie another hug, and then pulled her into the room, where Jessica and Madison were already enjoying their drinks—a nonalcoholic blend of orange, apple, and pineapple juices. Laurie had just enough time to grab one for herself before one of the groom's sisters pressed a small red dish containing a mound of mud into her hands.

"It's henna," Nabil's sister said.

Good to know. She had seen henna tattoos before, but the actual henna was a mystery to her. Sticking out of her mud pie was a small blue candle, which the groom's sister set ablaze with a lighter.

When all twenty guests had their dishes of flaming henna in hand, someone killed the music and dimmed the lights. Everyone circled the bride while the groom's mother draped Emma in a red veil, seated her in a straight-backed chair, and then left the room.

Nabil's three sisters and some of their Turkish friends began singing a song in a language Laurie didn't understand. As they sang, they led everyone in a rocking shuffle step that moved clockwise around the bride. The dance was easy enough that even left-footed Laurie mastered it in short order.

Although Laurie didn't understand the words, the dance and the music carried an unmistakable emotion that almost brought tears to her eyes. This circle of light was part of a solemn ritual passed down for generations from mothers to daughters. And it made Laurie wish she had a better relationship with her own mom.

The groom's mother returned to the room bearing a silver tray covered with red lace and a larger mound of henna festooned with more burning candles. The singing and dancing continued for a few more minutes until Emma's soon-to-be mother-in-law entered the circle and took Emma's hand. She pressed a gold coin into Emma's palm, and then Emma's mother covered the coin with henna from the large tray and wrapped Emma's fist—coin and henna included—in a fancy red lace mitten.

"Now, we dance, eat, sing, and get our henna on," Nabil's mother said with a huge smile. The circle broke, the Turkish music swelled from the speakers once again, and the Eagle Hill Manor staff brought in a buffet consisting of steamed salmon, sautéed chicken, and vegetarian penne pasta.

While people ate and chatted, the guests lined up to take their turns with the henna artist who was there to elaborately decorate their hands. Laurie bypassed the henna artist and hit the buffet instead, grabbing a plate of chicken and a glass of water because no alcohol was being served at this event. She found a seat at a small table in the corner and dug in. She was ravenously hungry since her teaching schedule hardly gave her time for lunch.

Jessica eventually found her. "Don't you want to get a henna tattoo?" she asked.

"Nah. I don't think my boss would approve."

"Really? Not even something small, like this?" Jessica displayed the inside of her wrist where a small rose bloomed. The design was intricate and beautiful. "It only lasts a couple of weeks, you know. It's not like a life-changing decision or anything."

"Well…"

"Come on." Jessica gently took her by the arm. "I'm not letting you sit in the corner all night."

"It would help if I had a glass of wine."

"No worries. After this, we're escaping."

"Escaping where?"

"It's a surprise, but trust me, margaritas are involved."

"Is Emma coming with us? I mean, isn't it sacrilegious for her to have margaritas the night before her nonalcoholic wedding?"

"Shhhhh." Jessica put her finger to her lips.

Against her better judgment, Laurie allowed Jessica to drag her over to the henna artist, where she allowed her wrist to be decorated, and not just on the inside either. When the artist finished, the entire circumference of Laurie's right wrist was decorated with a tattoo that looked like a lace cuff. It was gorgeous. And to Laurie's surprise, she found herself admiring it for the rest of the evening.

The party was winding down when Emma finally joined Laurie, Jessica, and Madison at one of the small tables.

"Oh my God, the artist did a fantastic job," she said with a happy gleam in her eye. She had tattoos on the backs of both hands and both feet, in addition to the brown mark on her hand where the coin and henna had been placed. "I love your lace cuff," Emma said, staring down at Laurie's hand.

"I do too, but Michael will say something nasty about it, for sure."

Three pairs of eyes turned in her direction. "Who's Michael?" they asked in near unison.

Laurie snorted a laugh. "Don't get excited. It's not like I've got some new boyfriend or something. Michael is my boss, and he's a total a-hole. Courtney would call him an unholy cross between an Ogler and a Belittler."

"Speaking of Courtney," Emma said, "we have a surprise planned for tonight. I just need to say good night to Nabil's mother and sisters, who I'm sure are not entirely happy about me going off to a bar for a little after-party. But Nabil said he was okay with it, so just hang here for a moment, okay?"

She left them for about ten minutes and returned with Courtney Wallace in tow. "Okay, are you guys ready?"

"I'm more than ready," Madison said. "Let's go get 'em."

Laurie was about to ask what that meant, but Courtney took her by the arm. "I thought we could all drive together," she said. "That way you can leave your car here. I'll be the designated driver, and tomorrow I'll swing by to pick you up for the wedding."

"Um, I don't need you to pick me up," Laurie said.

Once again, her friends stared at her as if she'd lost her mind. "Honey, I know it's hard," Emma said. "But I would be so disappointed if you missed my wedding."

"I'm not going to miss your wedding, Emma. I'm not a basket case. I just don't need a ride." She paused a moment. "I've got a date."

Everyone stopped walking. They were in the parking lot not far from Courtney's SUV. "You have a date for my wedding? Oh my God, I'm not sure we set a place for him. I mean, I..." Emma's voice trailed off.

"But I RSVP'd for me plus one guest."

"I know you did, but that was before...uh..."

"Wait a sec, you have a date?" Jessica asked.

"Yeah, with a guy named Tobin Grant. He works for my father. To tell you the truth, it's kind of a blind date. But still."

"Well, good for you. I hope he's as gorgeous as Brad Pitt," Madison said.

"Me too," echoed Jessica.

"Come on, you guys, time's a-wasting," Courtney said.

They piled into Courtney's car and headed toward town, but when Courtney didn't make the left onto Morgan Avenue, Laurie knew something was up. "Where are we going?" she asked.

"I told you we had a surprise planned," Emma said. "Just sit back and relax. You're going to love this."

Courtney pulled the SUV off the road onto a narrow shoulder beside a wooded area. Just ahead and to the right stood the long, sloping driveway down to August Kopp's country retreat, a 4,000-square-foot luxury log cabin with spectacular views of the Shenandoah Valley to the west. Courtney had cased the property a few nights ago. The car was in a shed out behind the main house. Since the house was a vacation home, it was unoccupied most of the time.

"What the hell, Courtney?" Laurie said.

Emma giggled. Jessica snorted. And Madison leaned forward from the backseat and patted Laurie's shoulder. "We're here to murder Brandon's Camaro," Jessica said.

"Oh my God, I should have known," Laurie said. "And since when does Brandon park his car out here at his dad's place?"

"Since Andrew Lyndon told him we were planning to trash it," Emma said.

"I'm sure Andrew did no such thing," Laurie said in a tone that sounded slightly wounded or affronted. Whoa, what was up with that?

Courtney knew Andrew had set Laurie up with a couple of dates, but there was something in the way she came to Andrew's defense just now that raised a red flag. Laurie had been spending a lot of time with Andrew recently. Was she falling for him? That would be bad.

"It could have just as easily been Jason or Matt who warned Brandon. They were there that day when you guys were talking about the car," Laurie said. "In fact, I remember they were so upset, they left the room in a hurry."

"Okay, whatever. Does it matter? I mean, we found it, right?" Emma said.

"How did you find out where the car was parked?" Laurie asked.

"It was kind of serendipitous," Emma said. "One of Nabil's sisters has a friend who works for Heather Lyndon. Brandon just joined her staff and apparently he hates riding the Metro. He's been complaining to all his coworkers about his precious Camaro being parked out here in the boonies. I told Courtney about the car's location last week, and she was nice enough to scout the terrain for us and assemble the equipment we need to do the car in. Courtney, it turns out, is a whiz at killing cars."

"What?" Laurie gave Courtney a long, sober stare. "You've been planning this for a week and you didn't say one word?"

"I wanted to surprise you."

Laurie gave Courtney a what-the-hell kind of look. "You know, Court, surprises like this are why I really hate to be surprised. Brandon loves his car. It would be wrong for us to do any damage to it."

Clearly it was time to take Laurie in hand. "Yes, Brandon loves his car. He loves it more than he's ever loved you. Which is screwed up if you ask me. So I want you to think about how that man made you feel on your wedding day. About how he went to Bermuda without you. About how he made you take a job you hate and buy a house that you didn't want. Laurie, that man needs to pay for what he's done to you."

Laurie surprised the crap out of Courtney by folding her arms in a defensive posture. "Destroying his car won't solve anything. Honestly, you guys, I don't want anything to do with that. Besides, it's illegal."

Laurie was way too nice for her own good. No wonder she'd stayed with a jerk like Brandon for all those years.

"Come on, Laurie. Courtney is right. We can't let Brandon get away scot-free. What he did was heinous," Jessica said.

"I'm not going to be involved in any scheme to damage his property."

"We aren't going to destroy the car. We're just going to make it no fun for him to drive for a while. And hopefully that will help Brandon think twice before he jacks someone else around," Courtney said.

Laurie shook her head.

"Well," Jessica said, "I'm not letting him get away with it."

"Me neither," chorused Madison and Emma.

Laurie's girlfriends piled out of the car, but Laurie remained unpersuaded.

"Come on, your friends have your back," Courtney said.

Laurie shook her head. "I'm not trashing Brandon's car."

"Because you still love him?"

Laurie shrugged.

"Okay, I'll try to talk them out of it. But I personally think you're giving him a free ride."

Courtney got out of the car and huddled with Laurie's erstwhile bridesmaids. "Laurie has serious cold feet about this. I guess I miscalculated."

"Oh no," Emma said, "it's not you. It's her. She's just scared, I think. Maybe if she saw us going off to kill the Camaro, she'd find her courage and join us."

"I'm not leaving without striking a blow," Jessica said, crossing her arms.

"Well, I guess that's that. Are we all in?"

Everyone nodded.

Courtney opened the SUV's hatch. In the cargo area, she'd organized their supplies in several reusable Food Lion bags. "Each of you grab a sack," she directed. "I'm going to tell Laurie that we're doing this with or without her."

Courtney left the bridesmaids to it, turned away, and

opened the front passenger's door. She leaned down to speak with Laurie. "I don't think I can talk them out of it."

Laurie sat stiff as a board. "I'm not surprised."

"Come with us. It'll be cathartic."

"I told you, it's illegal." She looked up at Courtney.

"Is that the only reason you're chickening out?"

She shook her head. "I don't hate Brandon. I'm not like you. I mean, I want to see the best in people, not the worst."

Whoa, that was kind of harsh. "Is that what you think of me?" Courtney asked, the annoyance coursing through her. "You think I see the worst in people?"

"In men. Yeah, I do. I'm sorry if that upsets you. But your whole man classification system doesn't include a single category for Mr. Right."

"That's because Mr. Right is a myth. And facing that undeniable truth protects me from guys like Brandon. I'm nobody's victim."

"And I am?"

Courtney didn't say a word.

After a moment, Laurie nodded her head. "Do whatever you want, but please don't permanently damage his car, okay?"

"I wasn't planning to."

"No?"

Courtney shook her head. "No. I just want him to learn a lesson is all." Courtney let go of a long sigh. "Look, the car's in the big barn. You know the way, I assume." She reached into her Food Lion bag. "Here's a flashlight in case you change your mind."

Courtney walked away from the car, trying to tamp down her anger. Laurie had a hell of a nerve suggesting that she was a negative person. She was nothing of the kind. Being realistic about the way the world worked was a better way to live. You didn't get dragged down all the time if you knew not to expect much.

She led the girls down a long gravel drive and around the house. The old shed was behind the house, which was completely dark—a good sign that the Kopps were staying in town this weekend.

She'd been prepared to jimmy the lock on the shed, but the door was unlocked, proving that Brandon had crap for brains. Who leaves a vintage Camaro in an unlocked garage?

Courtney ushered the girls inside. "We can't use the lights," she said, "because of the windows. So we'll have to be quiet and rely on the flashlights. Try not to wave them around. It might draw attention."

She stepped over to the car and tried the door. Bless the Lord, it wasn't locked either. "We're in luck," she said and then turned to face her troops.

"In your bags, you'll find some milk to pour on the carpet and some bacon to tape under the driver's seat. You guys take care of that while I put the ball bearings in the door panels. I've also got a lockable gas cap, and we should definitely loosen the screws on his license plates. Let's get to work."

They hopped to their individual jobs with gusto and dedication. So much so that no one heard the footsteps outside the garage until it was too late. The side door burst open, and the overhead lights flashed on.

"Don't move or I'll shoot."

Courtney looked up from the door panel she'd just taken off to find Matthew Lyndon standing there with what looked like a Winchester Model 70 hunting rifle aimed at her head. She froze, and her pulse accelerated like a Camaro on a straightaway.

Chapter Twelve

Andrew saw the arc of flashlights through the shed's windows the moment he pulled up the drive to August Kopp's house. From the backseat, Brandon made an ominous choking noise while Matt jumped from the passenger's seat before Andrew brought his Audi to a complete stop.

"There's a rifle in the house," Brandon said as he and Matt took off toward the main building.

Andrew set the parking brake and followed behind them. "Guys, wait. Let's not do something stupid. Maybe we should call the cops."

But the guys either didn't hear him or weren't listening. Andrew swallowed back a shout that might have alerted whoever was in the shed. He followed them as far as the log home's wide veranda, where he stopped and called 9-1-1. He had just connected with the dispatcher when Brandon and Matt came tearing out of the house.

Matt was in the lead, rifle in hand. Brandon followed behind carrying a handgun.

Shit. If the idiots inside the shed were as hotheaded as Matt and Brandon, someone was going to get hurt.

Andrew didn't try to stop the guys; that could be just as dangerous. Instead he stayed behind long enough to give the 9-1-1 dispatcher the address—maybe thirty seconds— during which time no shots were fired, thank God. He moved up behind Brandon in the barn's doorway, expecting to see some unsavory character with grand theft auto on his mind.

Instead, Courtney, Jessica, Emma, and Madison—each of them dressed as if they'd come from a fancy party in dresses and high heels—stood around the Camaro with their hands above their heads. He scanned the women twice just to make sure, but Laurie was conspicuously absent.

Matt was standing inside the building with his gun trained on Courtney Wallace. There was a stillness about Matt that worried Andrew. The last thing he wanted was for hotheaded Matt to become a lady killer in the literal sense.

Brandon stood behind him, clearly upset and waving the handgun around in a way that was more than merely dangerous. "What the hell do you think you're doing?" Brandon demanded.

Brandon's actions were clearly more than Emma could stand. She burst into tears and sank to the ground, bawling something about how Brandon may have ruined Laurie's day but he damn well wasn't going to ruin hers.

Emma's distress galvanized Jessica and Madison, who rushed to their friend's aid, while Courtney continued to calmly stare down the barrel of the gun Matt had trained on her. Courtney clearly had ice water in her veins.

"C'mon, guys, let's put the guns away, okay?" Andrew said in his calmest voice.

But before either Brandon or Matt could comply, a cop car came rolling up the driveway with its emergency lights ablaze. The strobes sent flashes of red, white, and blue circling the shed's interior.

"Oh my God, you called the cops?" Courtney said, her voice finally showing some emotion.

Matt lowered the rifle. "Not me, babe," he said with a wicked grin. Holy crap, was Matt trying to hit on Courtney? No way.

Andrew stepped into the room and took the handgun away from Brandon. "*I* called the cops. That was before I realized this was a case of revenge and not grand theft."

In the next moment, Officer Ryan Pierce, one of Shenandoah's finest, came through the door with his hand on his holster. "Everybody freeze," he said, and by the look on his face, he meant it.

But neither Jessica nor Madison followed orders. They were too busy calming the agitated Emma, who continued to wail about how her wedding day was ruined. Courtney also failed to follow orders. Instead she put her hands on her hips, looked the cop in the eye, and said, "Honestly, Ryan, do we look like hardened criminals?"

The cop's eyes widened as he took in the scene, especially the pristine, candy-apple red Camaro with the wicked black racing stripe on its hood.

"They were trashing my car," Brandon said.

Officer Pierce aimed a pair of high-beam blue eyes at Courtney and said, "This is getting old, you know. What did you do this time? Bacon under the seats? Milk on the carpet? Ball bearings in the door panels?"

"What?" Brandon wailed. "Did you spill milk on the carpets?" Brandon's tone was both outraged and wounded.

"It's just a car," Andrew said.

"He deserved it," Courtney said. "He loves his car more than he loved Laurie."

"Laurie Wilson? Is this the guy who left her at the altar?" the cop asked.

Courtney nodded.

The cop turned and glared at Brandon. "You know, for once I think Court has a point. You're an asshole for walking out on that woman. Do you know that her mother was so worried about her that the department put her on a suicide watch?"

"Suicide?" Brandon paled.

"Suicide? Really?" The echo came from the door, where Laurie stood, wearing the clingy black dress she'd worn the other night. She looked hot and angry and annoyed. Every synapse in Andrew's body fired at the same time giving him a jolt of pure sexual awareness. Man, he was in some deep trouble here.

The cop looked in Laurie's direction, and a definite blush ran up his face. "Oh, hi, Laurie. You look nice tonight."

Andrew had the overwhelming desire to take a swing at the guy, which would be dumb because Ryan Pierce looked like a guy who knew how to fight. All aikido had ever taught Andrew was how to defend himself. Still, he hated the way Officer Pierce was smiling at Laurie.

"Thanks, Ryan," Laurie said in a sweet tone, and then her gaze shifted toward Brandon. "Hi, Brandon."

Brandon looked down, his shoulders suddenly rounded.

"Ryan is wrong about the suicide stuff," she said. "That was just Mom being dramatic. You know how she can be. She always falls apart whenever she breaks up with someone. But I'm fine. Really. In fact, I'm great. I've been on a couple of dates, which I've enjoyed. And tomorrow I'm going to Emma's wedding with Tobin Grant. Do you know Tobin? He's a pretty gifted litigator."

Brandon looked up, his jaw muscles pulsing. "You can stop now. I'm sorry about the wedding. But all these obviously fake dates you've been going on have done nothing but piss me off. And really, did you think breaking and entering would—"

"We didn't break in," Courtney interrupted. "The garage was unlocked."

"Oh? You know, that makes everything different," Ryan said, giving Laurie a big smile before he turned toward Brandon. "The way I see it, any man who dumps a woman at the altar and then puts his vintage Camaro in an unlocked garage is either asking for it or is a damn fool. Now, since the car seems intact and I gather that one of these ladies is getting married tomorrow, why don't we just call it a day, okay?"

"You mean you aren't going to arrest them?" Brandon asked.

"No. But I might meet them for drinks at the Jay Bird Café in an hour when my shift is done. All in all, I think having a few drinks at the café might be a better way to spend the evening before someone's wedding. And I'm happy to serve as the designated driver for y'all. I have a pretty big van."

With that, Officer Ryan Pierce tipped his police cap at the would-be criminals, gave Laurie the tiniest of winks, and retreated to let them solve things on their own.

An hour later, Ryan Pierce made good on his promise by showing up at the Jay Bird Café and Music Hall right after the live music had ended for the night. He wore civvies and looked freshly showered, his hair damp. Laurie had to admit that he was a nice-looking man, but he didn't thrill her the way Andrew did.

"He's here," Jessica said in a singsong voice as Ryan crossed the room heading their way.

Laurie looked down, studying the margarita she'd been nursing for the last forty-five minutes.

"May I join you?" His voice was deep and manly, and unleashed Laurie's inner nerd girl. Why did guys like him make her nervous? Any other woman would drool over the attention of an American hero. She should be excited that he was interested in her, but instead she just wanted him to go away and keep his distance.

But she was too polite to brush him off. So instead she said, "You didn't really think I was about to commit suicide that day, did you?"

That earned her a slight twitch at the corner of his mouth but no other response. He pulled up a chair and made himself comfortable.

"Did you?" she demanded.

"I didn't know what to think, to tell you the truth. Your mother thought you were in trouble, and it was my job to make sure you weren't." He paused and gave the women at the table a winning smile. "Y'all should know I bent a few rules tonight." His gaze zeroed in on Courtney.

Emma raised her drink. "Well, I for one thank you, and I'm sure my fiancé does too. I don't think Nabil's very traditional Turkish mother would have understood if I'd been dragged off to jail the night before my wedding."

"I'm sure not," Nabil said, standing beside the table. No one had noticed his arrival because everyone had been paying attention to Ryan.

"Oh my God, you're not supposed to gate crash the bachelorette party." Emma put her hands over her face.

Nabil smiled his enigmatic and inscrutable smile, the perfect smile for a man who worked at the State Department. "It's okay," he said, pulling a chair up between Jessica and Emma. "I don't think it's bad luck, and I needed to get away from Mom. She's obsessing." He looked down at Emma's hand. "Very pretty henna." He picked up her hand and pressed a kiss to the back of it.

It was insanely romantic, and the look in Emma's eyes said it all. She and Nabil were hopelessly in love, and when he kissed her hand, everyone at the table said, "Aaaawwww."

Except Courtney, who looked the other way and said, "Uh-oh," just as Brandon strolled into the bar followed by Andrew and Matthew Lyndon.

Just like that, the air in the room became hot and unbreathable while the skin along Laurie's arms puckered up in gooseflesh. Everything flashed hot and then cold, as if her body's internal thermostat had malfunctioned.

Andrew scanned the room with his impossibly dark and sexy gaze, and Laurie found herself simultaneously hoping and dreading that he'd see her. It might be fun to have him at the table, but not with Brandon. Brandon's presence sucked all the fun out of everything.

If Ryan had made her feel like an awkward geek, Brandon made her feel like the worst kind of loser. And Andrew...he made her burn in a totally forbidden way.

She looked down at her drink and thought about paying her bill and walking home. But how could she bolt on Emma's bachelorette party?

"It's okay if you need to leave," Emma said. "I understand."

Laurie looked up into her friend's eyes just as something dark and angry spilled through her. Why should she call it a night? Why did she have to behave? "No," Laurie said, raising her head, "I think we should invite them to join us."

Her friends looked at her as if she'd lost her mind.

"I know," she said, leaning in toward them and lowering her voice. "But I'm tired of running away. I mean, Andrew is a friend, and I've known Brandon for a decade. And Matt is a jerk, as we all know, but he's harmless. Besides, I need to move on, not run away."

"Good point," Madison said, nodding her head as if she'd had one too many drinks. Madison couldn't hold her liquor and proved it when she stood up and waved at Andrew, Matt, and Brandon. "Come on, you guys, we've declared a truce. Laurie says she needs to move on, not run away."

The guys stood stock still with deer-in-the-headlight expressions, and then Andrew took charge, the way he always did. Subtly and without a lot of male bravado or fanfare. He strolled over to the table. "Are you guys sure?" he asked, in that deep, calm, sexy voice of his.

"Absolutely," Jessica said with a goofy smile. "Laurie just said that your presence will help her get over her heartbreak. I have no idea how that works, but she seems to believe it."

Heat crawled up Laurie's face. There was nothing more annoying than a friend who couldn't hold her booze. But maybe Jessica had done her a favor.

"Look," she said, "you might as well sit with us. I mean, if you sat somewhere else, we'd just scowl at you and say nasty stuff about you. This way we can try to be civil. I'm sure Andrew can mediate if it gets too nasty."

She flicked her gaze toward Andrew, and the kindness in

his eyes undid her. She caught fire and melted in the same instant.

Reading body language was essential in Andrew's line of work, and he'd practiced the skill every day since he'd joined the mediation team at Wilson Kavanaugh. Even so, reading the tension between Brandon and Officer Pierce didn't take much expertise.

They both leaned in. They both sat shoulders squared, chest out, head high. Although Ryan's posture was a bit more military. As the evening wore on, the tension between them climbed, especially since Ryan glued himself to Laurie's side as if he'd appointed himself as her personal protector.

Brandon started drinking, and as he moved from buzzed to inebriated, he began to bait Ryan, as if he were ready to have a fight over Laurie. He started making cutting remarks, and then the idiot challenged Ryan to an arm-wrestling match, which Ryan won easily.

Unfortunately, that didn't stop Brandon from behaving like a jerk. He changed tactics, as if he'd decided that if he couldn't best Ryan, he would try to teach Laurie a lesson or something. He turned his big blue eyes on Courtney and tried flirting with her.

His tactics were so awkward and ham-handed that Matt, who had been chatting up Jessica and Madison, stopped what he was doing, squirmed in his chair, and leaned toward Andrew. "We need to rescue him, dude. He's tangling with a woman who eats guys like him for breakfast."

Andrew didn't feel like rescuing Brandon, although he was entertaining a few fantasies about carrying Laurie off to the safety of . . . where? Her place? He flashed on the kiss they'd shared at The Park last Saturday. Oh yeah, he would definitely like to rescue her from this scene for a make-out session on her couch. She deserved better than Brandon. And he truly didn't want her to go home with Ryan Pierce, who, near as Andrew could tell, was the only other adult at this table.

He gave his cousin a quick glance and said, "Brandon's made his bed. He's the guy who has to sleep in it. Alone."

Matt didn't respond. Instead, he got up and took his beer to the other side of the table, where he pulled up a chair between Brandon and Courtney. This left Jessica and Madison high, dry, and slightly ticked off. They immediately turned toward the adjacent table, where a couple of guys with military haircuts were sitting.

Matt didn't seem to care. He'd completely focused his attention on Courtney, and she seemed to be succumbing to his many charms. In the meantime, Brandon had been cut off from every woman sitting at the table. A muscle twitched in his jaw as resentment marched across his face. It certainly looked as if the whole "make Brandon jealous" gambit was working.

Not that Laurie would ever take him back. Would she?

Andrew turned his gaze in her direction just as she glanced up at him. Her eyes were soft and warm and almost swallowed him whole. The noise and activity around him faded out as she cocked her head ever so slightly and bit her lip.

Damn. He wanted to escape. And he wanted to take her with him.

He nodded slightly as the room came back into focus. And then he pulled out his wallet and dropped a few bills on the table. "It's getting late, kids. I'm heading toward my dad's place. Anyone need a ride home?"

Laurie stood up. "I, uh, well, I left my car up at Eagle

Hill Manor. Would you mind dropping me off there? I had a long day at work, and I'm ready to go home."

"No problem, the inn's on my way."

Brandon turned in his chair and gave Andrew a short but meaningful nod, as if to say, *Thanks for pulling her away from Ryan Pierce.* That nod disgusted Andrew. If Brandon wanted Laurie protected and cared for, he ought to have stayed sober.

"Thanks, man," Brandon said, glancing at Matt, who was staring down Courtney's blouse. "I'll see that Matt gets home."

Damn. Maybe he shouldn't leave. Neither Brandon nor Matt was sober enough to drive Brandon's precious Camaro, which was parked outside in two parking spots. Maybe he should run Laurie up to her car and then come back.

He was about to suggest that when Ryan said, "Hey, man, don't worry. I'll make sure everyone has a safe ride home."

Whoa, that was a surprise. Ryan seemed to have no problem letting Laurie leave with someone else.

So Andrew gave Ryan a nod. "Thanks."

He walked Laurie out into the parking lot, with sexual longing corkscrewing through him. He felt just like a teenager on his first date. He wanted to kiss her, but he was afraid to open that Pandora's Box. Instead, he guided her to his Audi and opened the passenger's side for her.

But she didn't get in. She turned toward him and murmured, "Come home with me."

He stilled, his muscles freezing in place. He couldn't. He shouldn't. "Laurie—"

She pressed her fingers against his lips. "Listen to me. I want you to take me home. I want to..." Her voice faded out as she once again cupped the back of his head and pulled him down for a kiss.

Her soft, pliant, sweet lips intoxicated him as nothing else could. He groaned, unable to resist as she opened for him.

What had started soft and warm grew hard and hot and impatient. He stepped deeper into the V of the door, pressing himself against her, the jersey of her dress sliding through his fingers as he ran his hand down to her ass. He pulled her hard against him.

She moaned a little and then whispered, "Oh God, that feels incredible," right into his mouth.

They might have stood there in the open car door making out for hours were it not for the sound of laughter coming from a group leaving the bar. He put his hands on her tiny shoulders and set her back a little. "We should go. I don't want—"

"Yes, we should," she whispered back. "To my place."

He stared down at her for a long time, trying to find the will to say no. He lost that battle. "Yeah, to your place."

Chapter Thirteen ———————

Laurie could hardly believe she had initiated a sexual encounter. She sat silent in the passenger's seat of Andrew's Audi with the erratic cadence of her heart making it hard to think.

Not that she wanted to think. She was too good at thinking at moments like this, and not so good at feeling. At least that's what Brandon always said.

Right now, though, her thoughts had stalled on the way Andrew tasted. On the way his body fit against hers as if they'd been made for each other. On the way he smelled, like clean soap with a hint of citrus. Her brain short-circuited and replayed the kiss over and over again as he fired up the Audi and pulled out of the Jay Bird's parking lot.

When they arrived at the house on Rice Street, he killed the engine, got out of the car, and came around to her side to open the door, as if he were a gentleman from some bygone era. This prompted her to wonder, for just a tiny moment, what Courtney might have to say about a guy who opened doors like that.

She pushed the thought away. She wasn't going to be like Courtney, finding fault with every guy in the universe. Besides, this was Andrew standing in front of her.

"Laurie, are you sure?"

She caressed his cheek and felt another incredible rush of desire. "I'm sure," she whispered.

His eyes grew a shade darker with the spark of the streetlamp in their depths. He kissed her fingers and then gently pulled her hand away. "There are lots of reasons we should—"

"I want to do this," she said in a rush.

"But—"

"Please don't say no. I need the experience, and you are..."

"What?"

"Safe."

His eyes widened. Maybe telling him the truth was a bad idea. "Safe?" he asked.

She nodded, and then tried again. "What I'm trying to say, pretty awkwardly, is that I trust you. You're the perfect guy to... well... you know."

"No, I don't know." He frowned.

"To initiate me."

"What?" The word exploded from him as if he were surprised or something.

"Damn," she said out loud, her throat closing up. "I'm just not good at this."

"Good at what?"

"You know..."

"Sex?"

She nodded, and her face burned. "It's the reason Brandon walked out on me. It's why he wants me to see other people. To get some more experience."

Andrew's expression went through several changes as if he was trying to process the secret she'd just told him. She'd probably given him too much information. As usual, her brain had run away with the rest of her. If she didn't do something quick, Andrew would drop into his impeccable Lyndon manners, walk her to the door, and say good night.

She threw herself against him and pulled him down into another kiss. The moment his lips met hers, a storm of reaction flooded through her. His lips, his tongue, his hand gliding down her back made her feel alive in every cell of her body.

She broke the kiss and looked deep into his eyes. "Please don't say no. I need to learn about pleasure. This is what Brandon wanted me to do when he said we needed time apart."

"I don't think Brandon believes that for an instant," Andrew whispered. "Tonight he was jealous of Ryan."

"Tonight he was coming on to Courtney," she countered. "And you know what? I don't even care. He wasn't the one I was watching all night. And besides, I don't need Brandon's approval anymore." She squared her shoulders. "I want to have sex with you, Andrew Lyndon. And I know you feel the same way. We're both adults. We're both consenting. So what's the big deal?"

For a moment, she thought he might bring up his friendship with Brandon or the fact that he worked for her father, both of which were probably good reasons to back away. But instead, he gave her the tiniest of smiles and said, "Good point," as if he appreciated her logic.

And then he moved in for another kiss that finally put her

brain totally to sleep, while it awakened every other part of her body.

Andrew followed Laurie up the stairway to her bedroom, which looked more like a construction zone than a boudoir. Paint cans stood in lopsided stacks in the corner, the cracked plaster sported patches that were in various stages of sanding, and the curtains consisted of a bed sheet thumbtacked to the window.

But in her defense, the room was otherwise neat and tidy. The bed, which had no headboard, looked as if a drill sergeant had made it to military specifications. Each of the pillows had been squared and smoothed, and the hospital corners looked tight. He could probably bounce a penny off the bedspread.

Not one article of clothing lay on the bed or the chair or the floor, not even a pair of shoes. In fact, the hardwood floors didn't even have any dust bunnies in the corners, which was amazing since the house was in a state of reconstruction.

"Uh, well, I know it's not the Ritz, but..." Laurie stood at the foot of the bed, her body language screaming her unease.

He should go. It would be the adult thing to do. But for just one moment he didn't want to be the adult, responsible one. He just wanted to make love with Laurie. She'd wormed her way into his head and kicked Val right out of it. Besides, if what she'd said downstairs was true, then leaving now might crush her ego. He'd had no idea that she was so uptight about sex.

She turned toward him, her hazel eyes darkening. "I just want to make it clear that I'm not asking for the moon, you know. I mean, I'm doing this for the experience, not..."

Her voice trailed off as she nervously twisted her fingers together.

Andrew wasn't so sure he felt the same way. He'd never been a player. He tended to lead with his heart, and he didn't mind having strings attached. But considering the situation, maybe no-strings was the way to go.

"Okay," he said as he pulled her toward him, settling her against his thighs and chest. That was much better. Her curves were soft, and she fit against him perfectly. "This is all about you having fun," he said. "And that means you have to tell me what you like and what you don't like, okay?"

"Okay."

They were nose to nose now, closer than they'd been the other night at the club. "There are no steps to this dance," he said. "And you don't have to let me lead."

She glanced up at him. "I wouldn't know what to do."

"I doubt that. I mean, you certainly know how to kiss." And he dropped his head and pressed his lips to hers. Wow. For a woman who said she lacked experience, her kisses were erotic as hell. She didn't seem to have a lot of boundaries. Once she got going on his lips, she practically invaded him, her tongue stroking his in a wild and crazy dance that made him groan out loud.

Her fingers dug into his shoulders and then up into his hair. He pressed into that touch as hot, molten desire coursed through him. He truly wanted this woman.

He undid the clip at the back of her head and tossed it aside. The satin texture of her hair spilled through his fingers, sexy as hell. He broke the kiss and trailed little nips along her jawline to her ear. When his tongue touched the spot right below her earlobe, Laurie arched against him with a satisfying whimper and then a breathy "Oh, that feels so good."

Yes. The satisfaction of knowing that she was turned on filled him with lust. He found the zipper for her dress and pulled it down. A moment later it lay pooled around her feet on the floor.

And then something changed, abruptly and without warning. She went still and rigid.

A moment ago, when Andrew had stroked his warm hands down the bare skin of her back, her core had gone into complete meltdown. But when he undid her bra, the giddy feeling retreated like a wave on the shore.

She must have stiffened or something because Andrew backed up a little and made eye contact. Wow, he looked half-drugged, his lips kiss-swollen, his eyes so very dark.

"What is it? Talk to me," he murmured, as if he already knew how she felt about guys groping her boobs.

This was hard. "I..."

He held her gaze, so kind, so safe. She could tell him anything.

"I don't like it when... when... you know, when I'm fondled."

His eyebrow arched in that classic Lyndon look of surprise. "No?"

She shook her head and bit her lip. She was such a loser.

"Thanks for the warning." And then he dipped his head and kissed her again as if she hadn't said anything surprising or embarrassing. Her mind started churning a mile a minute, the way it always did when her clothes came off. She was about to suggest that maybe this wasn't such a great idea when Andrew found that spot below her ear again.

Oh sweet Jesus, when his mouth touched that spot, her whole body exploded with desire. She forgot to be tense. In fact, she got so busy enjoying the sensations that she didn't immediately notice his hands, ghosting up and down her rib cage, approaching the underside of her breasts and then moving away.

Tension coiled inside her with each advance and retreat until she could hardly bear the anticipation. She wanted his hands on her breasts. In fact, they practically ached for his touch.

"Uh, Andrew," she said in a surprisingly husky voice.

"Mmmm," he said into the skin of her shoulder, where he was doing something impossibly hot with his mouth.

"That thing I said about...um...you know...my boobs."

"Mmmm."

"I didn't really mean it. I..." Her voice morphed into a moan as Andrew traced his fingertips around her nipple in a tease that made her go frantic. She arched against him until he had her breast fully in the palm of his warm and wonderful hand.

"Oh, that's so much better," she said. Her head fell back, and Andrew had his way with her breasts. But unlike Brandon, who had always gone after her boobs like a kid with an all-day sucker, Andrew was way softer, and sneakier. He didn't tweak her nipples. He adored them with his hands and his mouth.

He finally backed her up against the bed and let her tumble down onto it. She stared up at him as he pulled his golf shirt over his head, exposing a well-toned chest with a sprinkling of dark hair between his nipples. Wow, she was surprised at how muscular he was. He looked like he spent time in the gym.

"Nice chest," she said.

He gave her a wicked smile. "I took up aikido this spring."

"Really? You don't strike me as a martial arts kind of guy."

"Aikido isn't about fighting. It's about keeping the peace."

Andrew definitely played peacekeeper on many occasions. That thought might have sidetracked her, but thinking was hard to do, especially with him standing there naked, aroused, and incredibly handsome.

He crawled up onto the bed, winked, and said, "You may regard me as your personal sex slave for the evening. Your every wish is my command."

Oh yeah. Thinking was definitely overrated at a time like this.

About a half hour after Laurie left with Andrew, Juni Petersen, the manager of the Jay Bird Café, placed another Manhattan in front of Courtney and spoke in a low-pitched voice directly into Courtney's ear so no one else could hear. "Andrew Lyndon and Laurie Wilson make a really cute couple, don't you think?"

Courtney looked up. Juni was wearing a long East India print dress with a little beading along the neckline. Her thick brown hair flowed down her back in waves. Her almost black eyes sparked with amusement.

What was Juni up to? She claimed to have the ability to read auras, and Courtney wanted to believe that was true, but she was also skeptical enough not to take everything Juni said as gospel. Juni might have some kind of ability, but she was also the quintessential sympathetic bartender who loved happy endings. Which was kind of funny because she'd yet to find her own.

And didn't Courtney know exactly how that felt? She met Juni's stare. "You're out of your mind. Andrew and Laurie are friends."

"Uh-huh, they weren't looking at each other like friends, not to mention the fact that their auras were smoking hot. I'm pretty sure they're going to hook up tonight."

"What? No. Wait. How did I miss this?"

Juni gave her a smile that didn't show any teeth. "Because that's your third Manhattan and you know what happens when you have more than two drinks." Juni's eyes rolled toward Brandon, Ryan, and Matt.

"Boy, honey, it looks like you have three tigers by the tail."

Courtney straightened in her chair. Ryan, Brandon, and Matt were all super hunky guys but she wasn't going to hook up with any of them. Ryan was the quintessential wounded man who was emotionally unavailable.

Brandon might have a pair of heavy-lidded blue eyes that could turn a girl to mush in five seconds flat, but he was the Nice Guy, Not, who'd left one woman at the altar already.

And Matt? He was the Player. Although she had to admit he was probably the best looking of the three. But really, he had to be ten years younger, and Courtney was not desperate enough to be a cougar.

"Wake up and smell the perfume, Court. Everyone is hooking up tonight. Trust me on this. Lust is in the air." Juni winked, and then turned away to deliver margaritas to Jessica and Madison, neither of whom really needed another drink any more than Courtney did.

In fact, now that she focused on it, she realized she was too buzzed to drive home. Maybe she should throw herself at Mr. Dudley Do-Right Pierce, but at the moment, the guy seemed to be giving Juni Petersen the once-over.

Wait, what was up with that? A moment ago, he'd been mooning over Laurie. She shook her head and took a sip of her drink and watched Ryan for a long moment. Damn. His gaze followed Juni as she worked her way across the room, greeting customers and delivering drinks.

Why had she not noticed this before? Did Dudley Do-Right have a thing for the hippy-dippy manager of the Jay Bird? Wow. They would be like the weirdest couple ever. Although now that she thought about it, Juni was a bartender, and Ryan was a wounded soul. Yeah, that kind of fit, didn't it?

Emma and Nabil stood up. "We hate to be party poopers," Emma said, "but it's a big day tomorrow. We'll see you all around lunchtime." She gave Courtney a long stare. "And I'll see you much earlier than that."

Nabil put some cash on the table to cover Emma's drinks, and the two of them left the bar arm in arm with sappy, happy looks on their faces. Courtney heaved a big sigh. Her next bride had just told her to go home and get some rest.

And while brides were always bossy, in this case Emma was right. She should go home. She had to be at the inn bright and early in the morning. Unfortunately, she was in no shape to drive herself. The excitement of almost going to jail, followed by too many Manhattans, had done her in.

Just then, Jessica and Madison picked up their chairs and moved to the adjacent table to join a couple of guys who looked like military types. Courtney didn't recognize them, but that wasn't a surprise since this weekend was the opening of the Shenandoah Valley Harvest Festival. People came from all over the landscape for a week of craft fairs, vineyard tours, the annual Harvest Festival Ball, and of course, the incredible fall foliage along the Skyline Drive. Eagle Hill Manor's busiest season was between September and

New Year's, although the spring Apple Blossom Festival brought in tourists as well.

"Looks like the party's breaking up," Brandon said, leaning in to her in a way that was not entirely comfortable.

"Yeah, it does. And I should go too... But I—"

"I'm happy to give you a lift home," Brandon said, but in Courtney's opinion, Brandon was too wasted to drive, and besides, who wanted to spend time with an idiot like Brandon Kopp?

"Not so fast," Ryan said. "I'll drive everyone home. I have a van."

"No, I can walk. I don't live very far away." She picked up her purse.

"Courtney, I don't—"

"Ryan, keep your thoughts to yourself. I'm fine. A little buzzed, but I don't think I'll be mugged on the street. You guys at the SFPD run a pretty quiet town."

He smiled. "I'd feel better—"

"Dammit, Ryan, I can take care of myself."

She stood up, feeling a little woozy but certainly capable of making it home on foot. She paid her tab and headed for the door. She'd traveled about a block before she realized someone was following her.

She stopped. "You know, Ryan, I'm not some delicate wallflower that needs protection."

"No truer words were ever spoken."

She turned. "Wait, you're not Ryan, are you?"

Matt strolled up to her, the streetlight gleaming darkly off his hair. "Nope."

"Jeeze, what part of *no* do you not understand?"

His mouth curled up on one corner in a devilish smile. "Oh, I understand *no*. But to me it's like a come-on."

"Oh brother, you aren't even ashamed of being a player."

She turned and continued walking toward her house. Matt matched her stride for stride.

"Why should I be ashamed? In fact, I'm thinking about starting a blog to help Clueless Guys like Brandon learn how to find dates for themselves."

"And you think you're helping Brandon by teaching him crap like that?"

He laughed as they walked along. "Come on, be honest. He was hitting on you tonight. You tell me if his technique was any good."

"Okay, you have a point, but it's an unfair test because I already know that Brandon is a Nice Guy, Not, who left his girlfriend of ten years at the altar. I'd never be impressed with a guy like that, even if he was as smooth as Casanova."

"Really? You'd turn down a chance to spend the night with Casanova?"

"You know that is the lamest thing I've ever heard any guy say to me, ever."

"What's lame about it? Casanova was supposed to be an incredible lover. You wouldn't want to spend a night of pleasure with him?"

Damn, he had her there. "Depends," she said.

"On what?"

"Whether I was in love with someone else."

He snorted. "Love. See, that's your problem right there. You're looking for love."

"What's wrong with that?"

"Nothing. But it's just my experience that, when a woman decides to look for love, all she ever finds is heart-break. Seems to me that looking for pleasure is way easier."

"You are such a guy."

"Thanks."

"Why are you following me?"

"Because I'm curious about you."

"In what way?"

"Well, for starters, I find it amusing that you're a wedding planner who has a side gig of helping women get revenge on the men who dump them."

"Amusing? Really? You think it's funny what Brandon did to Laurie? In my book, he's an asshole who deserves to be punished." She turned toward him, the streetlamp painting the planes and angles of his face with a golden light. Damnit all, Matt Lyndon was unbelievably handsome. It irked her to no end that she was attracted to him. There had been a moment when she'd been staring down the barrel of that rifle when she'd stopped fearing for her life and started fearing for her sanity. The man excited her in ways she knew for certain were unhealthy.

"I guess you have a point," Matt said. "Brandon was stupid to let his relationship with Laurie go on for as long as it did. He should have dumped her a long time ago."

"You're an asshole too."

"I am. I freely admit it. But I have to say, Courtney, I'm really blown away by the racket you've got going."

"What does that mean?"

"You help these women get married in the most elaborate and expensive ways possible, and when that doesn't work out, as it inevitably doesn't, you plan the retribution phase as well. It's brilliant, even if it's slightly amoral," He gave her a devilish smile. "Without assholes like me, you'd be looking for a job."

She didn't have a chance to respond to his provocation because she stumbled. Her ankle rolled, and she started to go down.

But before she hit the pavement, Matt caught her. And damned if he didn't have some really hard biceps going on underneath his blue blazer. But then he was still in his twenties. He hadn't gotten old enough to develop love handles or a beer belly.

"You okay?" he asked with something like real concern in his voice.

"I'm fine. I just stepped funny."

They stood there for a long moment, waiting each other out. Would he kiss her? Would she push him away?

He didn't kiss her. And for some reason she couldn't quite fathom, it disappointed her. Instead he set her back on her feet, And hovered there until he made sure she was steady. It was the kind of thing a girl didn't really expect from a Player.

"Thanks," she said under her breath. "My house is just up the street."

She continued to walk, and he remained by her side. When they arrived at the old Victorian that had been turned into a duplex apartment, she stopped. "This is my house. And I'm going up alone."

His mouth quirked at the corner. "Of course you are."

He turned then and started back up the street in the direction of the Jay Bird. He walked with his shoulders back and the cool September breeze riffling his hair.

What had just happened? Had Matt paid her back for the way she'd played him on Laurie's wedding day? Or had he followed her to make certain she got home safe?

She honestly didn't know.

Chapter Fourteen

Andrew left Laurie's bed at five in the morning with several long, sweet apologies. She wasn't sad when he left. She'd fully expected him to leave much earlier.

Plus it was hard to feel sad when he left her feeling deliciously well used and delightfully exhausted. Never, in her wildest imagination, had she realized that orgasms could be so incredible.

She'd been in search of the big O for most of her adult life. Brandon had managed to give her a few, but never while they were actually making love. Andrew had no problems in that department.

Wow. There really was a difference, wasn't there? For years she'd been fooling herself about this essential fact of life. The realization was nothing short of mind-altering. As she lay in bed replaying the night in her head, she unexpectedly appreciated the truth. If she'd married Brandon, last night would never have happened.

She drifted off to sleep on that thought, utterly content and at peace until she bolted awake again shortly after eleven. Oh God, she'd forgotten. How could she forget? Emma's wedding was scheduled for high noon, and Laurie had a date…with someone other than Andrew. Which seemed wrong somehow. But it wasn't. Not really. She'd been honest last night when she'd told him she was looking for an experience and not emotional ties.

Ha, what a joke. As she stood in the shower, washing away the night before, she understood how dangerous it could be to have sex with a friend. She liked Andrew. She admired him. He'd rescued her a couple of times. How could she not have feelings about him?

Damn. Was she being stupid? Was she falling in love with him?

It was too soon to tell, and she refused to make the fatal mistake of confusing good sex with love. Courtney had drilled that one into her head, and she understood it now. Also, great sex did not necessarily make a great relationship, especially when everyone she knew would be thoroughly shocked if they ever found out that she and Andrew had slept together. So she would go to the wedding with Tobin and enjoy herself. There was no reason to feel guilty.

She hurried through her shower, slapped on makeup, and was a tiny bit damp when her date arrived to pick her up twenty minutes later.

Tobin was eye candy in every sense of the word. Tall, dark, and handsome was just the starting point. He also had the requisite blue eyes, cleft chin, and killer bone structure. To top it off, he had a law degree from Harvard and a brilliant future ahead of him as a litigator. He was already pulling down a comfortable salary, and his chances for a partnership in her father's law firm were practically a done deal. In short, Tobin Grant was a dream date.

He rang her doorbell precisely on time, and when Laurie came to the door, his eyes raked over her conservative navy blue georgette sheath dress. He smiled and said, "You look beautiful today." Then he moved in like a shark and kissed her cheek.

The kiss didn't unlock her heart or knock her on her butt, but it didn't leave her cold either. Okay, she could do this. She could be a new, modern woman in touch with her sexuality, experiencing life before she made any more permanent commitments.

Tobin took her by the arm and guided her to a bright red Porsche Boxster with its top down. She flashed on long country drives in Brandon's Camaro with the wind doing serious damage to her hair. Not once, in all their years together, had Laurie ever insisted that her hairdo came before Brandon's car. How could she have been so submissive? Where was her grit, her fortitude?

"Uh, Tobin," she said in her most authoritative tone, "I know it's a lovely fall day, but we're going to a wedding, and I would appreciate it if you could put the top up for the drive to the inn. I don't want my hair messed up."

She braced for an argument, but Tobin flashed his pearly whites and said, "Sure, okay, no problem."

Whoa. What was up with that? Had one night of mind-blowing sex turned her into a take-charge woman? Maybe she should use the same tone of voice with Michael Altimari, her department chair. Or better yet, just go around Michael and apply for the Jephson Foundation grant on her own.

She made a mental note to get working on that first thing Monday as she gave Tobin a wide smile. "Thank you. I really appreciate it. Maybe next time, when we're not going to a wedding, we can ride with the top down."

He gave her another winning smile. "I'd like that," he said.

Had she just suggested a second date? Probably. Wow. A girl could get used to this feeling. She settled back in the bucket seat, thoroughly enjoying her ride in Tobin's sports car, especially since he had an amazing sound system and he'd tuned his XM satellite radio to the Symphony Hall station. An all-brass arrangement of "Promenade" from Mussorgsky's *Pictures at an Exhibition* filled the cabin with the resonant timbre of the trumpets and French horns.

"Nice sound system," she said, leaning back. "I love Mussorgsky."

He gave her a wide smile. "I do too."

Oh boy. Her life was suddenly looking up. Guys who enjoyed classical music were incredibly rare and wonderful.

Tobin didn't disappoint her at the wedding either. During the reception, he entertained everyone at their table with polished and polite conversation. He was well read and could talk intelligently about movies and popular culture with the women and sports with the guys. In short, he was Mr. Perfect.

When the reception was winding down, he offered to drive Laurie home, but she'd left her car at the inn the night before. So instead she walked him out to his sports car, which he'd parked in only *one* spot, proving that he was not at all like Brandon, and kissed him good-bye. The kiss was more than friendly but less than passionate.

"I'd like to see you again," he said.

"I'd like that too," she found herself saying. And she really meant it. Tobin was good company. She'd had a good time with him, even if he didn't make her burn the way Andrew did. There was something to be said for spending time with someone who shared her interests. She had no idea what kind of music Andrew liked.

Tobin gave her another kiss on the cheek and promised to call her. Who knew if that would really happen? Nevertheless, she stood in the inn's parking lot watching him drive away and congratulating herself for being a modern, grown-up woman who could make choices for herself. Maybe she wouldn't wait for him to call. Maybe she'd call him first.

Just then, Jessica shouted from the steps of the portico, "Okay, we need the details on *that* guy." Madison stood beside her with an avid look on her face.

"I told you, he's one of Dad's associates. I hate to say it, but my father set me up with him as a semi-blind date."

"Does your dad have any more associates who look like that?" Madison asked.

Jessica rolled her eyes. "Down, Maddy, you're just a little too boy-crazy. And speaking of which"—Jessica pinned Laurie with a probing stare—"what gives with you and Andrew Lyndon? I was sure you would go home with that cute cop last night."

Had she and Andrew been that obvious? Damn. Laurie didn't want anyone to know about her one night of orgasmic sex with Andrew. It was her secret, and for now, she wanted to keep it close. Besides, what they'd done last night could become incendiary. It could end Brandon and Andrew's friendship.

"Come on, guys, I'm not that into Ryan. And besides, Andrew offered me a ride."

"Yeah, but you asked him to bring you here to pick up your car. But your car was here all night."

Shoot. She'd just been caught in a lie. "Well, I decided

it made more sense for him to drop me off at home because I knew Tobin would be picking me up in the morning. And I wanted the ability to send Tobin home at the end of the wedding." She glanced from one face to another. The girls seemed to be buying her story, but it was time to change the subject.

"So how late did you guys stay at the bar last night?" Laurie asked.

Madison gave Jessica a guilty look.

"You know," Jessica said with a long sigh, "last night was probably best forgotten by everyone. And I swear, I am never going to try to kill a car again...or drink that many margaritas. Honestly." She rubbed her forehead.

"Just how late *did* you guys stay at the Jay Bird?" Laurie asked.

"It wasn't how late we stayed, it's where we ended up," Jessica said. "I swear those guys looked way cuter when I was buzzed."

"Yeah, I'm afraid we're doing the walk of shame this morning." Madison put her arms around Laurie. "You were the smart one, leaving the party with boring old Andrew Lyndon." She paused for a moment. "Do you think Andrew is gay? I mean, he's never with anyone, you know? And last night he wasn't even remotely interested in flirting."

Oh my God. "No, I don't think so. He had a girlfriend for a long time."

"Where is she now?"

"She dumped him about two years ago."

"Two years?" Jessica's eyes grew round. "I bet he is gay, which is too bad because he's kind of cute, you know?"

Laurie didn't know what to say. The idea of Andrew being gay was absurd. Her mind flashed on some of the stuff he'd done to her last night, and her core melted at the memory.

"Oh, look, she's blushing," Jessica said. "I think she really *liiiikes* Andrew."

"And Tobin too. It would appear," Madison added.

"Who has a killer sound system, a red sports car, and likes classical music," Laurie said. Better to keep the girls guessing.

Her friends laughed and patted her back. "It's good to see you getting over Brandon," Madison said.

"So, it's still early. And my hangover is craving a glass of wine," Jessica said. "Why don't we see what's up at Bella Vista Vineyards. I've been told they've got some kind of party going on up there for the Harvest Festival."

Madison turned and scanned the portico, where Emma's wedding lunch had been served. Staff was already tearing down the tables. "Maybe we should see if Courtney wants to join us."

"I already checked. She said she had to work. Plus she's really hungover," Jessica said.

"Courtney hungover?"

"Well, if you want my opinion," Jessica said, "I think she hooked up with Matt Lyndon last night."

"Really? I don't believe it. Matt's a total jerk." Laurie was shocked.

"Yeah, but he's cute," Jessica said.

"But Courtney is smarter than that. I mean, Matt is a player. Even I can recognize that."

"Of course he is, but you know, Laurie, it's not always about lifelong commitment. Sometimes a girl just wants to have fun. And Matt looks like a real fun guy to me."

"Yeah, he's the fun guy who took Brandon to Bermuda on *my* honeymoon and who leveled a rifle at Courtney last night."

"Yeah, well, there is that," Madison said. Then she patted

Laurie's back. "Come on. Let's not worry about Courtney. I rented a Mustang, and I want to get the full use of it before I have to turn it back in. Let's go tour a winery. I hate dry weddings, don't you?"

The Shenandoah Valley Harvest Festival was a big deal for Bella Vista Vineyards and many of the other wineries in the valley. On Saturday, more than a hundred guests would descend on the vineyard for wine tastings and other activities. The vineyard hosted live music, barbecue, hayrides, winery tours, and the traditional grape stomp in the afternoon.

With all that activity, Andrew's father needed help, and the family was expected to provide it. Andrew had never missed a Harvest Festival, except for his undergrad years at Yale. Even Andrew's spoiled sister, Amy, showed up for the grape harvest, as did his younger brother and many of his cousins.

So Andrew left Laurie's bed in the wee hours of the morning, not because he wanted to, but because Dad expected him to show up at the vineyard at six in the morning, bright-eyed and wearing his burgundy Bella Vista Vineyards golf shirt. He made it on time, but maybe not so bright-eyed—a fact Dad noticed.

"Where were you last night?" Dad asked in a gruff voice as he pressed a Styrofoam coffee cup into his hand.

"I'm not going to answer that question."

His father gave him an oh-so-sober look. "Does this mean you're finally over Valerie?"

Boy, that was a good question. "Maybe," he answered.

His father gave him a long, searching look. "So, I hear on the family grapevine that you were seen dancing with Laurie Wilson."

What was it about Dad? Andrew could fool a lot of people but he couldn't fool his father. So he didn't try to. He just nodded his head and said, "Yeah."

"Be careful with your heart," Dad said. "I'm not sure Laurie knows what she wants."

Andrew locked gazes with his father, but Dad didn't say another word about Laurie. He just nodded his head to indicate that the father-son conversation was closed. A moment later, he slapped Andrew on the back. "So where is your brother, Edward?"

"He said he would drive down this morning. He had some kind of big meeting last night about the Higgins campaign."

"Well, that's a lost cause. Come on, it's going to be a busy day. And this year, your sister can't help because she has a job." Dad didn't even roll his eyes at that statement, proving that he'd come a long way over the summer. There had been a time last spring when Dad had been uber confused over Amy. He'd wanted her to grow up and be responsible, but when she decided to take a job working on the landscape crew at Eagle Hill Manor, Dad had kind of lost it.

Amy had worked her way up to assistant wedding planner, but she'd surprised everyone when she'd married Dusty, the chief landscaper. Although Dusty wasn't a landscaper now. He was in the thick of building an eco-tourism business. The Liberty Run Fishing Lodge was under construction and would open its doors sometime next year.

"You up for managing the wine tasting?" Dad said.

"Sure, but don't you want to schmooze the customers?"

"No. I just bought a brand-new Massey Ferguson tractor, and I'm itching to drive it." Dad's eyes lit up like it was Christmas Day. "So I'm handling the hayrides and leaving Ozzie to do the tours and supervise the grape stomp.

Camilla will handle the caterers, the live music, and all the other craziness."

Ozzie Casano had been Dad's viticulturist for decades, and his wife, Camilla, was the winery's business manager. Ozzie and Camilla shared a three-bedroom apartment above the winery's business office and had been part of Andrew's life for as long as he could remember.

Andrew got to work, helping with the final decorations in the tasting room and toting bales of hay to various strategic locations. He kept very busy until 10:00 a.m., when the doors opened. But at that hour the trickle of customers wasn't enough to keep his mind from wandering back to the events of the night before.

Laurie had been... He didn't have the words to explain his feelings. Sex wasn't love, of course, but it was easy to make that mistake with a woman he'd known for years. He genuinely cared about her. She was his best friend's fiancée; his boss's daughter. She didn't fit as one-night-stand material, no matter what she said last night. And bottom line: The sex had blown him away.

He'd be lying to himself if he said he didn't want to make love with her again. But doing that would be fraught with complications.

Luckily, the crowd grew through the morning, and the winery got too busy for Andrew to brood about what had happened. He threw himself into the task at hand and didn't come up for air until almost two in the afternoon.

He was standing behind one of the tall counters pouring wine samples when he caught the unmistakable spark of red hair in his peripheral vision. He turned, almost out of reflex.

For the last two years, Andrew had never stopped looking for that precise shade of deep auburn. Every time a woman with that particular hair color crossed his path, his heart would skip a beat, his step would quicken, and a fleeting moment of hope would slam through him. He'd search out the woman's face, only to be disappointed one more time. It was never Val, until today.

He turned toward the woman who had just taken a seat at the bar and knew a moment of utter surprise.

"Hi," Val said, the skin between her freckles darkening with a blush. "I knew you'd be here today. You're dependable, Andrew Lyndon, you know that? It's what I love most about you."

She leaned her elbows on the bar as if she planned to stay awhile. His heart twisted in his chest. Val certainly had a catastrophic sense of timing. The day she walked out on him was the day he had planned to propose. And now, here she turns up like a bright copper penny on the day after he thought he'd finally let go of her bittersweet memory.

Apparently he hadn't yet excised her from his heart because right now it was thumping against his rib cage like a drum line. Val. Beautiful, mercurial, wild, impetuous Val. He'd fantasized about this moment hundreds of times. He'd been so sure that he could forgive her. After all, she'd been the color in his life. When she'd left, he'd become a dull gray person.

But now, standing there looking into her witchy green eyes, he remembered the crazy ups and downs of living with her, and he wondered if he truly wanted that much drama in his life.

He should go. He should run. He should get out of this tight space where it was suddenly hard to breathe. But he remembered what Laurie had said last night. Moving on wasn't the same as running away.

So instead of running, he leaned in close to Val and asked, "What are you doing here?"

Chapter Fifteen—————————

The parking lot at Bella Vista Vineyards was full, so Jessica had to park her Mustang in the grassy field next to Jamie Lyndon's million-dollar home, and the three of them had to hike up the road a quarter mile to the tasting room.

It was one of those beautiful, warm September days in the valley with a deep blue sky, lots of sunshine, and temperatures in the mid-seventies. The vineyard's guests availed themselves of the sunshine by sitting at the wrought iron tables scattered over the patio. They sipped wine and ate barbecue while enjoying traditional bluegrass music compliments of Joker's Wild, a local roots music band.

As Laurie and her friends headed toward the tasting room—a building that looked like a restored barn with weathered wood and big sliding doors—they had to move to one side to make way for a tractor pulling a trailer piled with hay and laughing families. The tractor came to a stop near the platform where the grape stomping competition would soon begin, and the driver, who wore a wide-brimmed brown felt fedora, tipped his hat back and said, "Laurie Wilson, is that you? How are you doing?"

Laurie almost jumped out of her skin because the man's voice was so much like his son's. She turned to find Andrew's father, Jamie Lyndon, the owner of Bella Vista Vineyards, staring down at her. She had never realized, until this moment, how much Andrew looked like his dad. Andrew was taller, slimmer, and obviously younger, but Jamie Lyndon had the same serious brown eyes.

Mr. Lyndon set the brake on the tractor, hopped down, and covered the ground between them in a couple of strides. He took her hands and pulled her into a fatherly hug. "I never had the chance to say how sorry I was about you and Brandon," he said, pulling back.

Damn. Another pitiful moment. "It's okay, Mr. Lyndon. I'm doing fine."

"So I've heard," he said, giving her a dark probing stare.

Damn. He had probably heard Matt's story about seeing her dancing with Andrew. She forced a smile. "Andrew has been a good friend."

He nodded, but the intensity of his stare didn't waver for one moment. "I'm glad to hear that. You tell whoever is manning the bar, that you and your girlfriends are welcome to drinks on the house."

"Thank you, Mr. Lyndon."

He turned with a wave and headed back toward the tractor, directing the next batch of kids lining up for hayrides.

"So what did you mean about Andrew being a good friend?" Jessica asked.

"He's been nice to me, which is more than I can say for the rest of Brandon's friends." Laurie bit her lip to stop from blurting out the rest of the truth. Instead, she hastened her pace through the doors and into the tasting room, which wasn't nearly as crowded as the tables outside.

But the moment she entered the room, she became instantly aware of Andrew. His presence tugged at her as if he were a magnet and she were made of iron. But the attraction pulled in only one direction, because he seemed utterly unaware of her arrival. Instead his gaze was riveted to a willowy woman with auburn hair who sat at the bar. He leaned in her direction, smiling that flirty smile that sometimes escaped his emotional control.

Laurie came to an abrupt stop. No. This was not actually happening. Was it?

"What's the matter?" Jessica turned with a concerned expression.

"Val," Laurie breathed.

"Who?" Jessica asked.

"Andrew's old girlfriend. The one I told you about. The one who dumped him."

"The redhead?" Jessica asked.

"Oh, wow, maybe you were right. He's not gay," Madison said. "Oh, Laurie, I'm so sorry. You kind of like him, don't you?"

Laurie nodded as her composure unraveled. For an instant, she was teleported back to that moment when Brandon told her he didn't want to get married. She couldn't breathe, and down deep the betrayal was like a knife plunged right into her heart.

She had no right to feel this way. She had no claim on Andrew. Last night had been about experience and no-strings sex, right? God, she was such a ninny.

"She's not much to look at," Madison said.

"Now you're just being catty," Jessica replied. "C'mon,

let's get our free wine and stop worrying about the Lyndons. I think they can take care of themselves."

Jessica, always the trailblazer, made a beeline for the empty bar stools beside Val. She claimed three of them and planted her fanny on the one nearest to Val. "So what's the best wine here?" she asked, leaning toward Val and Andrew.

"The Chardonnay," Andrew said before he glanced in Jessica's direction.

On the other hand, Val turned on her stool, her eyes widening as her gaze met Laurie's. "Oh my God, Laurie, it's so good to see you." Val jumped down from her perch and threw her arms around Laurie as if they were long-lost BFFs. In truth, they had never been very close even though their respective boyfriends were best friends. "How's Brandon? Did you guys finally tie the knot?"

Laurie glanced at Andrew, hoping to read his reaction, but his mild-mannered Clark Kent mask of steel was back in place. His eyes looked vacant, as if he'd just been knocked on the head with a two-by-four.

Laurie turned her attention back to Val. "No, Brandon and I are not together anymore."

"Oh." Val backed away a step, and the dreaded moment of awkward silence descended.

"All water under the bridge," Madison chimed in, ever the helpful one in a difficult social situation. "Andrew, we'd like three glasses of the Chardonnay. Your dad told us the wine is on the house."

Apparently happy to have something to do, Andrew pulled down three white wine glasses from the overhead rack and concentrated on pouring. When he finished, he slid the glasses in Jessica's direction. "There you go," he said, never once making full eye contact with Laurie.

"Why don't we see if there's a table outside?" Laurie

said. She snagged her wine from the counter and didn't wait for her friends to respond. She turned and strode toward the patio.

What the hell had she said last night about running away and moving on? Yeah. She was an idiot. There were times, like this one, when the only sane option available was running like hell.

Val occupied her barstool until the wine-tasting event came to a close. And even then, she didn't leave her perch. She behaved as if the last two years hadn't happened. As if she were entitled to stay after the doors had closed.

Andrew's father made it clear he wanted her gone. Everyone had been invited to dinner up at Charlotte's Grove, and Val was most definitely not on the invitee list. Andrew waited until everyone had left for Aunt Pam's house, and then he walked her to the door.

"Why does your family always come first?" she asked, reminding him of the many fights they'd had over his family.

"Because they do."

"But I need to talk to you. I need to apologize."

"Yeah, okay, I get it. But this isn't the time or place."

Val's lower lip quivered, and he suddenly remembered just how good Val could be at manipulating his emotions. "Could we meet somewhere for drinks? Just to talk."

Damn. He didn't want to talk to her. He had moved on, much to his own surprise. "Yeah, sure," he found himself saying. "I'll call you."

That promise, insincere as it was, had been enough to get her out of the tasting room and back on the road to D.C. Thank God, because he didn't want a heart-to-heart with Val.

He wanted to call Laurie and explain about what she'd seen today. He even pulled his iPhone out of his pocket, his finger hovering over her number.

No. He shouldn't. He couldn't. Last night had been a one-time thing. She'd been very specific about that. And really, did he want to get involved with someone on the rebound? Someone who had the power to screw up his career and his relationships with his friends and family? He shook his head and tucked his phone back into his pocket.

By the time Andrew arrived at Charlotte's Grove, the buffet of barbecued pork loin, potatoes, and salad was already picked over. The family had gathered on the mansion's back terrace, where propane heaters dispelled the autumn chill and party lights twinkled from the pergola.

He hadn't taken more than three steps onto the patio before Aunt Pam descended on him. "Oh, darling, I'm so happy to see you. I heard all about Val's reappearance from your father. I was afraid she'd waylaid you."

Living in a large family was annoying as hell. Everyone gossiped about everyone else. He gave his aunt a kiss and ignored her reference to his ex. "I try never to miss your barbecues, Aunt Pam."

"I hope you told that woman to back off."

"I think I can manage to—"

"Don't you let that woman jack you around. You can do better. Andrew, honestly, I've been working so hard to find you the perfect woman. And I keep coming up against blind alleys and roadblocks. Well, don't you worry. I know everyone is upset about you and Laurie going out together, but we can just put that in the past. In fact, I have the perfect girl for you. You remember Lindsay Mayfield, Connie's daughter? Well, she graduated from Mary Washington College last May, and since Connie is such a stalwart on the

Jefferson County Historic Society, I convinced your uncle Mark to give Lindsay a job as a receptionist up on the Capitol Hill. You should give her a call."

Was his aunt taking credit for his assignation with Laurie? What the hell was she up to? He thought about cross-examining her but he jettisoned the idea. He had learned long ago not to fight Aunt Pam's matchmaking suggestions. Ignoring them was the far better response. He gave his aunt his most charming smile and said, "I'll think about it." Then he looked away, scanning the crowded terrace for his uncle Charles.

"You do that. She'd be so happy to hear from you. Maybe you can bring her to the Harvest Festival Ball. I have two extra tickets."

He didn't respond to that suggestion. Instead, he extricated himself from Pam and crossed the patio without stopping for food. His uncles, Mark and Charles, were standing together deep in conversation. Uncle Mark looked up as he approached. "You made it. I hear Val has returned."

Andrew ground his teeth. "Unfortunately yes. And even though I told her to get lost, I have no intention of dating Lindsay Mayfield."

Mark grinned that big, toothy smile that had helped him maintain his senate seat for the last two decades. "That's what you think."

"What's that supposed to mean?"

"It means that, now that Amy is married, David is settled, and Heather has a seat in Congress, your aunt has entered the we-must-find-Andrew-a-bride phase. I'm afraid she's given up on Daniel for the moment. And, of course, everyone's in an uproar because you went dancing with Laurie Wilson."

Andrew groaned.

"Sorry. And by the way, you *are* taking Lindsay to the Harvest Festival Ball. I'm afraid there's some sort of *quid pro quo* involved. The vote swapping on the Jefferson County Historical Society is more vicious than in the U.S. Senate. I gather Pam needed Connie's vote on something important. Plus, for the sake of family harmony, it might be a good idea. You wouldn't want people to think that you and Laurie were anything other than old friends, would you?"

Mark Lyndon was frequently called the bulldog of the U.S. Senate precisely because of the look he gave Andrew in that moment. "No sir," Andrew said, and then turned to glare at Aunt Pam. She smiled back, like the cat who'd just swallowed the canary.

"I know, she likes to spring these things on us at the last minute. You weren't planning to bring someone else, were you?" Mark asked, suddenly back to his friendly, avuncular self.

Andrew shook his head. "I wasn't planning to go."

"Well, now you are. Can I get you a drink? You look like a man who needs one," Mark said.

"No. Actually, I was wondering if I could have a private word with Uncle Charles." He turned toward Charles, who looked utterly surprised.

"What is it, son?"

"Well, I, um..." He gave Mark a look.

"I think it's something serious and personal," Mark said. "Don't worry, I need to chat with Heather about something." Mark turned and headed toward his daughter, the congresswoman who represented Shenandoah Falls.

Charles's face grew solemn as Mark left. "What is it?"

"I'd rather not talk about it here."

"Of course. Let's go in the house."

A few minutes later, they arrived in the formal parlor just

off the front center hall, a room used only during special occasions, which meant their privacy was virtually assured.

"What's the matter?" Charles asked as he took a seat on one of the centuries-old side chairs.

Andrew sat down and leaned forward. "I don't know. To be honest. I'm..." Suddenly Andrew's situation seemed utterly ridiculous. How could he explain to his often solemn and down-to-earth uncle?

"Mark was right. You do look like a man who needs a drink," Charles said.

Andrew shook his head. "No, I think this is better discussed sober. And this is confidential, Charles. Privileged. If I have to, I'll pay you a dollar."

Charles chuckled. "Let me hear what's on your mind, and then I'll decide if I need a retainer."

Andrew nodded, pulled in a deep breath, and told Uncle Charles all about Noah Wilson's odd behavior and the way he'd enlisted Andrew's help to set up Laurie on dates.

Uncle Charles didn't seem overly concerned. "Well, you can't really blame Noah for being ticked off at Brandon, can you?"

"No, but there are times when I get the feeling that Noah is trying to force Laurie and Brandon into a reconciliation. And I can't understand why."

"You really think he wants them to get back together?"

"I do. I mean, Noah is a master at effecting reconciliations and he's going through all the motions. I just can't figure out why. I mean, I don't see that Laurie wants Brandon back, and I'm not sure it would even be good for her to reconcile with Brandon."

"Really? You feel that strongly?"

He nodded.

"Well, I'm sure there's no way Noah can force his daughter to marry someone she doesn't want."

Andrew nodded. "Yeah, I guess so. But here's the thing—I did a little research that has unsettled me. Based on publicly available information, it looks like the profits per partner at Wilson Kavanaugh have been declining. The firm has taken on a lot of new partners recently because of the number of acquisitions. I'm starting to worry that the mediation practice might be jettisoned at the upcoming partners meeting. And that led me to wonder if Noah wants Laurie and Brandon to marry in order to create a better negotiating position for a merger with LL&K."

Charles frowned. "This is a bit concerning," he said, "but you have no evidence aside from some conjecture based on public information that may not be entirely accurate."

Andrew nodded. "I know. Call it a hunch or something. Do you know if Noah and August have had any conversations along these lines?"

Charles finished his drink and put the glass down on the coffee table. "Andrew, I always thought you were too level-headed to give credence to conspiracy theories. I think Noah's behavior can be explained by the fact that he's angry as hell. In fact, your father and Mark and I had to physically pull the man off Brandon the day of the wedding."

"Okay. But what if he was angry because Brandon had messed up his plans for some kind of merger?"

"Well, I guess that's plausible. But it's not the truth. The truth is, he loves his daughter and wants the best for her. And he's pissed off at Brandon."

"So he decides to use me as a weapon? Is that it? I guess one way or another, my prospects for making partner are looking slim."

"Is that your main concern? Making partner?"

Was his partnership his main concern? Maybe. And maybe he was also concerned about the future of Wilson Kavanaugh's mediation practice. He was proud of what he'd accomplished as a mediator working with Noah. For all his faults, Noah Wilson was superb at making peace between litigants.

But even as he parsed through these thoughts, he knew, without question, that Laurie was at the top of his list of worries.

"I'm concerned about Laurie," he said and looked away. "I don't want to see her manipulated into making a bad decision and going back to Brandon. And I completely hate the idea of her being a bargaining chip in some law firm merger. And please don't give me a lecture about how I'm supposed to be standing with Brandon on this. I've already heard it. Everyone in the family is ticked off that I was seen dancing with her."

"I'm not." Charles's eyebrow arched.

"You're not?"

He shook his head. "The problem with this world is that we don't dance enough, Andrew."

Andrew stared at his uncle, speechless.

Charles laughed. "For what it's worth, I don't think you or Laurie are trying to stir up trouble. I think you've been doing what you always do—being a good friend."

Charles leaned forward and gave Andrew a friendly knee slap. "Your uncertainty about Noah Wilson will pass, son. As for your theory about mergers and acquisitions, as far as I know, Noah and August haven't had any discussions along that line. If I were you, I'd operate on the theory that Noah's only motive is the same as yours—to make his daughter happy."

Chapter Sixteen

Courtney sat at the Jay Bird Café on Sunday evening after a long day at the inn managing a big fat, two-hundred-guest Jewish wedding. Her feet throbbed, but her heart hurt even more. She sat at the bar stirring a Manhattan with its cherry-tipped toothpick. Her life was crap.

Matt Lyndon had called her bluff on Friday night. He'd offered her a real good time, and she'd blown him off. Now she wondered why.

What was wrong with enjoying a Player every once in a while? As long as she knew what she was getting into, what was the downside risk? Matt had one saving grace: He was totally up-front about who he was and what he wanted. Why had she said no?

She heaved a ginormous sigh and popped the cherry into her mouth.

"Rough day?"

She pulled herself out of her self-pity just as Ryan

Pierce, wearing a body-hugging Under Armor T-shirt, claimed the vacant stool next to her.

Courtney looked up into his bright blue eyes and read something that might have been real concern in them. She cocked her head and studied him for a long moment, just to make sure she hadn't misread him.

He was not drop-dead gorgeous like Matt Lyndon. He was more of the all-American, battle-hardened, ex-military type. A tiny scar marred his square jaw, prompting Courtney to wonder if it was a war injury. His nose meandered a little, as if it had been broken once or twice. She saw duty and honor in his gaze.

No question about it, Ryan Pierce was a born do-gooder. He'd even risked his life once by running into a burning building to save the town drunk. He took his job seriously. He cared about everyone. Equally.

She finally answered his question. "No, it was just another Sunday at the inn. We're kind of crazy this time of year what with the autumn tourist crowd and the Harvest Festival Ball coming up next weekend. The truth is, even when it's not so busy, I like coming down here and schmoozing with Juni on Sundays. It's quiet, and I usually need a drink after a long, busy weekend."

Ryan's gaze shifted toward Juni. "Yeah, Juni's pretty cool," he said in a suddenly dopey voice that set off all kinds of alarms.

Juni turned away from a customer farther down the bar. She gave them a smile, and strolled in their direction. She stopped in front of Ryan. "The usual?" she asked.

"Yeah, sure," he said, giving her a tiny, almost shy, smile that bounced right off Juni like bullets off Supergirl.

So Courtney hadn't been imagining things on Friday. Ryan had a thing for Juni. That was interesting because Juni was as emotionally unavailable as Ryan. The manager of the Jay Bird was almost thirty years old, and as far as Courtney knew, Juni had never had a boyfriend.

Or a girlfriend either.

In fact, now that Courtney thought about it, Juni lived the life of a nun, always reading everyone's auras and handing out advice to the lovelorn, but never actually jumping into the pond herself.

Ryan's interest in Juni underscored the fact that he was a bad risk all the way around. He clearly had a thing for unavailable women, didn't he? Juni. Laurie. She paused a moment in thought. Oh shit. Ryan had taken a seat right next to hers.

Well, the shoe fit, didn't it? She was the woman who had said no to Matt Lyndon on Friday just because he was a Player.

Juni returned a moment later and set a draft beer in front of Ryan, then she turned toward Courtney and leaned into the bar. "So what's up?"

"Nothing much," Courtney said, looking down into her drink.

"Ain't that the truth," Juni said in an ironic tone that compelled Courtney to look up.

"What does that mean?"

Juni gave her a tiny half smile. "It means that your muddy aura is almost the same as it's always been. You really need to let go of the past and move on."

Ryan audibly snorted back a laugh, and Juni turned in his direction. "If you can't be helpful, you can be quiet. I am well aware of your opinions about chakras, but Courtney has a far more open mind."

"You're kidding, right? You think Courtney has an open mind?"

Juni's eye's sparkled. "About some things."

"Oh, about some things. Like chakras. The rest of the time she's pigeonholing the male gender. Very open-minded of her."

"Good point," Juni said.

"I'm right here, you know," Courtney said in a flat voice. "You don't have to talk about me as if I'm invisible."

"Now you know how it feels," Ryan said.

Courtney looked back down at her drink. "Thank you, Ryan, for making me feel so much better about myself."

"You're welcome. And since you're listening, I suggest that you stop going around expecting the worst from people. It's true, people will disappoint you most of the time, but sometimes they can surprise you. You know?"

"I am not a—"

Juni interrupted the argument by reaching across the bar and tapping Courtney's hand. "Ryan is entitled to his opinion. And for what it's worth, your aura has changed just a tiny bit. Hardly noticeable, but significant nonetheless."

"Oh, really?"

Juni nodded. "There's a tiny spark of yellow in it now. Which is a good sign."

"What does yellow mean?"

"It's the color most associated with learning. I think maybe you're beginning a new quest for self-knowledge."

"Oh, great. That sounds like so much fun." She drained her Manhattan and slid the empty martini glass toward Juni. "I think I need another one. Learning can be a bitch sometimes."

Ryan cocked his head. "Did you drive or did you walk tonight?"

"Dammit, Ryan, you're not my keeper, you know."

"No, but I am an officer of the law. That gives me wide discretion. I could haul you in for drunk and disorderly even if you don't get behind the wheel of a car. Or I could be a nice guy and drive you home."

"It's okay. I walked. And please don't offer to walk me home, okay? I don't like company on my walks home."

Ryan and Juni exchanged a look.

"What?"

"So," Juni said. "Did you let him in?"

"Let who in?"

"Matthew Lyndon."

She blinked a couple of times but said nothing.

"I told you last Friday night that lust was in the air," Juni said. "And I certainly noticed when Matt left the bar just seconds after you did. So did he walk you home?"

"You know," Ryan said, "I take back what I just said. Guys like him probably deserve to be pigeonholed."

"Shh," Juni said. "Your opinion was not asked for."

Ryan looked a little taken aback, as if Juni's words had wounded him in some way. Him, the big strong alpha dude wounded by little Juni. Courtney filed this away. Maybe it was time for Juni to come out of her shell.

Juni turned her dark, compassionate eyes on Courtney. "So did he?"

"What? Walk me home? Yeah, he followed me. But in answer to your question, I did not invite him in. And to be honest, he was kind of a jerk to me. He said some pretty unkind things. Not unlike someone else." She gave Ryan one of her acid looks.

"Well," Juni said as one of her enigmatic smiles brightened her face, "sometimes unkind words need to be spoken in order to open up new pathways of thought."

"What does that mean?"

"It means the thread of yellow in your aura wasn't there on Friday night when you left the bar. But it's there now."

Laurie entered the Jay Bird Café and was pleased to see Courtney and Ryan sitting at the bar. This was exactly what she'd hoped for when she'd decided not to sit at home watching Netflix, breathing in the paint fumes from the freshly painted bedroom and upstairs hallway, and obsessing over Andrew Lyndon and their encounter on Friday night.

She was determined to be a grown-up, modern woman who could sleep with a guy and not get all hung up about him. She was determined to take the pleasurable lessons learned from Andrew and move on. She would be forever grateful to him for showing her how to enjoy sex. So really, she had nothing to be sad about.

Except, of course, that having sex with him could never happen again.

"Hey," she said, climbing up onto the barstool next to Courtney and ordering a margarita. She came in on the tail end of a conversation about Courtney's aura. Laurie could tell by the tense set of Courtney's shoulders that Juni's comments had annoyed her.

So Laurie came to Courtney's rescue. She turned toward Juni and asked. "So what do you see in my aura?" Juni was sure to find plenty of bad stuff to talk about, and Laurie had gotten used to people talking about how screwed up her life had become.

Juni cocked her head. "Actually your aura is surprisingly balanced, all things considered."

"Really?"

Juni tucked an errant lock of dark hair behind one ear. "Yeah. I'd say you're moving on well."

"See?" Courtney said. "Getting rid of Brandon has been good for you."

"I'll drink to that," Ryan said, lifting his beer and giving Laurie a grin.

She flashed on Ryan's behavior Friday night. She cocked her head and let fly. "Are you flirting with me?" she asked, utterly surprised by her courage.

Ryan's mouth quirked a little at the corner. "No. What gave you that idea?" But he cocked his head in the same direction, which was supposed to be some kind of body language cue. She knew this because she'd frantically read everything she could about dating and body language right before her disastrous date with Connor.

"Really, you guys?" Courtney said as her gaze bounced from Ryan to Laurie and back again. "Maybe I should change places with Laurie so you can be closer together."

Ryan gave Courtney an equally flirtatious look, and Laurie realized that Ryan was an equal opportunity flirt. "Aren't you going to warn her about me?" he asked. "You know, about how I'm emotionally not available?"

Courtney shook her head. "Laurie already knows that. She's flirting back at her own peril."

Ryan put his hands over his heart. "You're cruel, you know that?"

"Yeah, I guess I am. I'm also sadder but wiser." Courtney turned to face Laurie. "So, how are you doing, honey? And who was that guy you were with at Emma's wedding?"

Laurie filled Courtney in on Tobin's particulars and finished with, "I haven't figured out if Tobin fits into your list yet. I'm trying to decide if I should call him up and invite him to the Harvest Festival Ball."

Although really, if she were honest with herself, the only guy she wanted to dance with was Andrew. But she couldn't call him. Ever again. Especially not after all her brave talk on Friday about how she wanted no-strings-attached sex.

"I wouldn't call Tobin," Courtney said.

"Why not?"

"Because he promised to call you."

"Yeah."

"So you should let him do that. Sort of like a test."

"Oh, brother," Ryan said, rolling his eyes.

"What?" Courtney said, turning toward Ryan. "You think she should call him and let him know that she's super-interested?"

"Yeah. Why not?"

"Because then he has all the leverage."

"Boy, you have it all figured out, don't you?"

"Yes I do." Courtney turned toward Laurie. "If I were you, I'd find someone else to take me to the ball. That way when Tobin calls and asks you out, if he calls, you can legitimately tell him that you're busy on Saturday."

Ryan put his elbow on the bar and propped his head. "This is fascinating. So who do you think Laurie should ask?"

Courtney turned back toward Ryan. "How about you?"

Ryan straightened. "Me?"

"Sure. Why not?"

Ryan turned toward Laurie with a surprised, almost panicked expression. For a moment Laurie thought about telling Courtney to back off, but then she changed her mind. She wasn't all that interested in Ryan Pierce, but if she had to pick a guy to be her plus-one for the Harvest Ball, she could do a whole lot worse. Ryan would never get drunk, act like an ass, or otherwise embarrass her. His presence would also annoy the crap out of Brandon, who was sure to be there because Roxy's children's charity was one of the beneficiaries.

She gave Ryan a big smile. "I would be honored if you would accompany me to the ball," she said.

He blinked a few times and gave the impression of a deer staring right into the headlights of an oncoming truck. "Do I have to wear a tuxedo?"

Laurie laughed. "Is that your biggest problem?"

"I hate wearing monkey suits."

"Well, if you don't want to wear a tux, I believe it's acceptable for retired military to wear their service dress uniform. And you know, Ryan, I'd like to see you dress up like a Marine."

He smiled at that. "Would you?"

"Yeah, I would, actually." Plus that uniform would intimidate the crap out of Brandon.

A little blush crawled up Ryan's cheeks. "Well, in that case, I'd love to go with you to the ball."

Chapter Seventeen

Lindsay Mayfield wore the ugliest evening gown Andrew had ever seen. It was dark purple with black lace around the deep V of the neck. The lace did nothing to hide the ample curve of Lindsay's breasts, which bounced every time she moved or laughed.

She laughed a lot, at all the wrong times, and her laugh sounded like a cross between an adolescent giggle and a braying donkey. The drive from D.C. to Shenandoah Falls was interminable, made even longer by an unexplained traffic delay through Tyson's Corner. And while the traffic crawled, Andrew tried to keep a conversation going.

But he and Lindsay had absolutely nothing in common. Not movies, books, music. Nothing.

Thank God they weren't making the return trip to D.C. together. She was home to visit her folks for a few days. And he would spend the night at Dad's house and then go back in the morning. Alone.

Unfortunately, in addition to a two-hour drive, he had a three-hour dinner dance to endure. The only saving grace was the fact that August Kopp would be at this party, and Andrew hoped to escape Lindsay's clutches for long enough to corner Brandon's father and ask him a few pointed questions about law firm mergers and acquisitions.

Andrew wasn't at all convinced that Uncle Charles knew everything that was happening at Lyndon, Lyndon & Kopp. And if by some chance Andrew's theory was correct, then August was the man who could solve Noah's unspoken partnership problems and save Laurie from tumbling into a bad marriage.

Eagle Hill Manor was awash in light when Andrew finally escorted Lindsay into the large banquet hall, which had once been a carriage house. The ballroom's post and beam construction had been exploited to give the venue the feel of an old barn. Twinkle lights swayed from beam to beam, lanterns in various sizes lit the tables in a warm, friendly glow, and the floral arrangements included grapes on the vine. That last touch, an homage to the grape harvest that was so important to the regional economy, had Amy's fingerprints all over it. Andrew's sister, it turned out, had mad skills at floral arranging and decor.

"Oh my goodness," Lindsay said on a puff of air, "it's like an autumn garden party." She gave his arm a squeeze.

They were late, of course, and the room was already crowded with guys in tuxes and women in long gowns. "Let's get a drink," he said, pulling Lindsay in the direction of the bar. He got halfway across the room before he saw Laurie.

Everything faded to gray except the guy standing next to her.

Ryan Pierce was the only man in the room not wearing

black. And damnit all, that blue jacket with all those brass buttons marching up his chest, not to mention the medals and ribbons, was pretty damn impressive. But not nearly as impressive as Laurie's dress, which was the color of champagne with lacy sleeves, a neckline that showed off her long neck and collarbones, and a big skirt. She looked drop-dead gorgeous with her hair pulled back. He stopped moving and lost the ability to breathe.

"Who is she?" Lindsay asked, a little breathless herself. "She looks like that movie star who married the prince. What's her name?"

"Grace Kelly."

"Whatever. Who is she?"

"Her name is Laurie Wilson."

"You know her?"

"Yeah. She's my boss's daughter."

"Introduce me. I need to know where she got that dress. It's gorgeous."

Resistance was futile. He allowed himself to be dragged in Laurie's direction, but when she turned her head and their gazes met, his heart twisted in his chest. What an idiot he was. He should have known that getting intimate with Laurie Wilson would mess with his mind.

She was on the rebound. Experiencing life. Not ready for anything steady.

And, of course, she was off limits as long as he worked for Noah.

But his emotions weren't swayed by any of this logic. Right now, he wanted to call Ryan Pierce out and tell the guy to take his hands off her.

Instead he buried those feelings deep, plastered his best mild-mannered smile on his face, and said, "Hi, guys. I wasn't expecting to see you here. Let me introduce my date."

He made the introductions, and only Lindsay missed the awkward undercurrent. She invaded Laurie's personal space. "I just love your dress. Where did you get it?"

Tacky, tacky, tacky.

But Laurie grinned and leaned in with a sparkle in her eye. "At the Haggle Shop."

"Where is that? Downtown D.C.?"

"No, it's here in Shenandoah Falls. It's one step up from the Salvation Army. I'm redoing a house, and I went in there day before yesterday looking for decor and furniture. And this dress caught my eye. I think it might be a Carolina Herrera. But the label is torn out."

"No kidding?"

Laurie shook her head. "I won't tell you how much I paid for it. I'm an untenured college professor so I can't afford couture. The store owner had no idea how much it was actually worth, and I didn't tell her." She frowned for a moment and glanced at Ryan. "Was that wrong?"

His mouth quirked. "Absolutely not," he said, looking down at her with a gaze that irritated the crap out of Andrew.

"Well," Andrew said in a sterner voice than absolutely necessary, "it was nice seeing you guys. Now, if you'll excuse us, we were just heading toward the bar." He yanked Lindsay away from Laurie and her secondhand dress.

"That was kind of rude. We'd just started talking with them," Lindsay said.

"Look, let me make myself clear. I don't want to spend any time with the boss's daughter or her Marine boy, okay?"

"She seems really nice and down-to-earth."

Yeah, that was Laurie. He flashed on an image of her wearing GW sweats and bunny slippers. She'd been just as beautiful that day too. Hell, Laurie was more than nice and down-to-earth. She was smart, adorable, and sexy. "I need a drink," he said.

Laurie watched Andrew walk away, her heart in tatters. What was up with him anyway? He sleeps with her, and then the next day she sees him hovering around his ex-girlfriend. And a week later, he's got his hands all over a much younger woman with a chest out to there.

Well, at least she hadn't come to the party solo. That would have been humiliating in the extreme. Instead, she was on the arm of the only man in military dress. And Ryan was certainly causing a stir. Unfortunately, Brandon didn't seem to be here tonight. So Ryan was causing a stir with all the wrong people.

Still it was kind of nice being on his arm for the evening. His presence immediately banished the pity talk that she hated. Obviously she was getting over Brandon, and she had Ryan by her side looking rather regal with his medals and ribbons.

"Remind me to thank Courtney for backing you into a corner," she said as the cocktail hour wound down and they began searching for their table.

"Why's that?" he asked in a low voice.

"Because you look fabulous in your uniform, and everyone is staring at you."

"Me? Laurie, they are not staring at me. Believe me."

She smiled at him. "You are a good guy, you know that, Ryan?"

"I try my best. Besides, I'm having fun. I never knew what it was like to be the guy escorting the best-looking woman in the room. It kind of rocks, actually."

She gave him a long, earnest stare. "You do realize that I'm not taking you home tonight, right?"

He snorted a laugh. "It's all right, Laurie. I'm happy to be your friend. And I'm well aware of the fact that you've been waiting for Brandon all evening."

"Am I that obvious?"

He pointed toward the front of the room, near the podium. "Oh, look, there's our table. Hey, it's right up front. You clearly have some pull with the organizers."

It suddenly occurred to Laurie that she'd been placed at this table back when everyone expected her to come with Brandon. Her worst fear materialized when Roxy showed up solo, wearing a slinky black dress and looking gorgeous as always.

Her eyes widened. "You're here," she said.

"I am. I bought tickets, remember?"

"Yeah. I just..."

Laurie launched herself into the silence by introducing Ryan.

A moment later, Andrew and his date arrived, followed by Daniel, Matt, Jason, and Edward Lyndon. All of the Lyndon men, aside from Andrew, appeared to be traveling solo, and they made an incredible statement in their matching tuxes. Good thing Ryan was perfectly capable of holding his own with any of them, especially with all that polished brass on his uniform.

Ryan leaned over and whispered in Laurie's ear, a gesture that was probably misread by everyone assembled there. "Mission accomplished," Ryan murmured. "Brandon may not be here but I think he's going to hear all about it."

With that, Ryan stood at attention and pulled out a chair for her. She made a big show of thanking him, and he smiled down at her with the sappiest smile she'd ever seen in her life. Thank God for Ryan. Without him, Brandon's friends would have battered her self-esteem.

It was clear they didn't want her at their table. They made her feel unwelcome the moment she took her seat. Matt and Jason periodically stared at her as if they wanted her to fall through the floor directly into hell. Daniel pointedly ignored her while surreptitiously glancing at Roxy with a sad, puppy-dog look. Yet Roxy seemed utterly unaware of Daniel's regard. Instead she tried to be nice to everyone, and failed. Andrew stared down at his plate while his date for the night chattered on about one banal subject after another.

It was painful. And the more Lindsay talked, the more Laurie wondered why on earth Andrew had asked her out. She was too young, too brash, too opinionated, and too socially inept for him. Plus she drank way too much wine, while Andrew nursed a single beer.

Oh, how she wished she could get up and rescue him from that woman. But she couldn't. And as much as she longed for Andrew's touch, the barriers between them were so clear. All she had to do was look around the table.

Roxy and these Lyndon men were loyal to Brandon. They'd known him longer. They loved him like a brother. They didn't want her around because Brandon had dumped her. What truly stung though was the realization that, if she were to stand up and tell them that she'd slept with Andrew last weekend, no one at this table would believe her. Hell, Andrew would probably deny it, which was enough to make Laurie's heart wrench in her chest.

Even so, it wasn't Andrew's fault. She'd made the choice. She'd been honest and clear with him about what she wanted. She hadn't asked for commitment. She didn't even want commitment. What she wanted was to sleep with him again.

But that was out of the question.

Her throat unexpectedly knotted up. She needed to leave. Now. She leaned toward Ryan, "I need to powder my nose," she said. Then she stood and made her escape.

Laurie almost knocked over her chair in her haste to leave the table, and Andrew didn't blame her for escaping. If he hadn't been chained to Lindsay, he might have chased after her, which wouldn't have defused the situation but would have made him feel useful.

He was about to rebuke everyone at the table about their manners when Matt heaved a big sigh and said, "Good riddance," in a loud enough voice for everyone to hear.

"What was that you said?" Ryan asked. He stood, and he was really quite impressive as he looked down his slightly crooked nose at Matt. Ryan was at least two inches taller than Andrew's idiotic cousin.

"Um, I . . ." Matt stammered.

"Stop," Roxy said, standing up. "I'm disgusted with all of you. Thank you for supporting my brother, but you all seem to have forgotten that Laurie was the one who was left at the altar. Brandon is the one who did all the hurting that day. The breakup wasn't Laurie's fault. And it sure wasn't Laurie's fault that she ended up at this table. That was my bad. I guess I just didn't think she would come, you know?" Roxy's voice wavered, and tears formed in her eyes.

"The thing is . . . I adore Laurie. I wanted her as my sister. And that's not going to happen, and it really steams me to see you people being so cold to her. Especially you, Matt. Grow up, okay?"

She turned and fled in the direction of the ladies' room, and to Andrew's astonishment, Daniel got up and ran after her.

"Way to go, Matt," Andrew said.

Matt's eyes rounded in surprise. "What? You gotta admit she doesn't belong at this table."

"Why not?" Lindsay asked. "She seems like a really nice person."

"It's a long story," Andrew said.

"Okay, I'm listening."

Christ on a crutch. How had he ended up with this clueless, rude, idiotic woman? "Not here," he said.

"But why?"

Matt pushed up from the table. "It's a very long story," he said. "Why don't we take a little stroll out onto the terrace, and I'll fill you in. I need a smoke."

Lindsay gave Matt a wide smile and then looked up at Andrew. "You don't mind if I go with Matt? The truth is, I could use a cigarette myself."

"No, not at all."

Matt and Lindsay exited the scene, and everyone breathed a sigh of relief. "Why do I have the feeling that Aunt Pam set you up with that woman?" Edward said.

Andrew nodded. "Because she is the last person on earth I would ever be attracted to?"

"Well, I think you're off the hook. Matt was very impressed with her," Edward said in a snarky tone.

Jason turned toward Ryan, who remained standing. "Look, I know what my brother just said was kind of stupid, but hey, you need to understand that we've known Brandon since we all wore Pampers together." That was Jason, all right, always defending his brother no matter what.

Ryan, who had assumed a chest-out military position with a stone face, said nothing.

Andrew locked gazes with him for a long moment. "Take care of her," he said.

Ryan gave a tiny nod. "I intend to."

Andrew had no doubt that Ryan Pierce was a man of his word. Andrew hated the idea of Laurie and Ryan together, especially since Ryan was so clearly worthy of her. In any event, he wasn't about to sit there and watch the two of them. It was time to escape.

"I'll see you guys," he said, and then headed off across the room. Andrew had been watching a table on the other side of the dance floor for the duration of the uncomfortable dinner. A moment ago, just as Laurie had escaped to the ladies' room, August Kopp had gotten up from his assigned table and headed in the direction of the bar.

But as Andrew headed in August's direction, Aunt Pam intercepted him, threaded her arm through his, and pulled him in the opposite direction. "Darlin', I'm wondering how you like Lindsay."

"She can carry on a conversation without much problem," he said, trying to find something nice to say about her.

Pam gave him a steely, blue-eyed stare. Sometimes it was easy to dismiss his aunt, but as the daughter of a governor and the wife of the United States senator, she was no pushover. "I see you've let Matt take Lindsay out to the terrace, so I'm thinking you prefer someone a little less talkative. Someone more like Laurie perhaps? I must say she looks spectacular with that Marine."

Boy, Pam must be furious with him or something. There was no other explanation for the way she kept throwing Laurie in his face. "Okay, Aunt Pam, I apologize. I know I shouldn't have gone out dancing with Laurie. It's made everyone so unhappy. But honestly, it's not what you think, okay? We're just friends. And the Marine's name is Ryan. He's a member of the SFPD."

"Oh, so she's serious about him?" Pam asked with a gleam in her eye.

"God, I hope not." Andrew almost spat the words. Then he bit the inside of his cheek to stop himself from saying more.

"He's quite handsome."

"Look, Aunt Pam, I hate to run, but I need to talk to August Kopp about something. I promise I'll make sure Lindsay gets home in one piece."

"Of course you will. You're such a good boy." She paused a moment. "Sometimes I think you're just a little too good."

"Thanks, Aunt Pam. Now, really, I need to run before the program starts."

She finally let go of his arm, and he hurried toward the bar, where he finally caught up with August Kopp, just as he reached the front of the bar line. "Hello August, you have a moment?"

Brandon's father had lost much of his hair, and he'd put on a little weight since his wife's death a few years ago. But he still had a likable face with a ready smile and keen gray eyes. "Andrew," he said, "what are you drinking?"

"I'm good, but I was wondering if I could speak with you for a moment."

August accepted his scotch on the rocks and stepped away from the bar. "From your tone, I get the feeling you don't want to chat about the weather."

"No. And I'd prefer speaking privately."

"The terrace calls, then," August said with a smile. They crossed the ballroom and emerged on the terrace, where propane heaters were running full blast to take the chill out of the late September air.

Luckily Matt and Lindsay had gone elsewhere to smoke ... or whatever.

"So," August said, "did Brandon send you to negotiate? I

should tell you before you start that it nearly broke my heart when I told him he couldn't join the firm. But the thing is, Brandon doesn't really know the meaning of hard work. Or commitment. I was so ashamed of him when he walked away from Laurie. And my God, did you see her tonight? Such a vision. What an idiot my son is."

August waved his drink around and continued. "I've been way too easy on him. And I really think that working on Capitol Hill will teach him something. The hours are long, and the pay is terrible. And your cousin has a reputation for being hard on her staff." August grinned and winked.

"Um, actually," Andrew said, "I didn't come here to negotiate on Brandon's behalf."

"Oh?" August took a sip of his drink. "What then? I can tell by the set of your shoulders that something has gotten under your skin."

Damn. August was pretty good at reading body language himself.

Andrew forced himself to relax before he spoke again. "Are you and Noah Wilson negotiating some kind of merger that depends on Laurie and Brandon's marriage?"

August laughed. "What? Are you crazy?"

Andrew took a deep gulp of air. "No, I'm not crazy. But I am concerned."

"About what?"

"About Noah's recent behavior."

"Tell me."

Andrew jammed his hands into his pockets and proceeded to tell August exactly what he'd laid out for his uncle Charles last weekend.

When Andrew had finished, August shook his head. "Andrew," he said in a fatherly tone, "I don't blame you for trying to connect the dots. And I'll be utterly honest with you, Noah and I have spoken about a merger. But all that is off."

"Because of the wedding?"

He smiled. "Because Noah wanted me to leave Lyndon, Lyndon & Kopp and set up a new firm with him. He's not at all interested in your uncle's small country practice. And that was a complete nonstarter for me."

"But it might not be if Laurie and Brandon were married."

August shook his head. "Maybe Noah thinks that way, but he would be wrong about that. Son, if it weren't for your uncle Charles, I would never have met or married Sally. Charles is like the brother I never had. Now, the truth is, Charles would do just fine if I took my D.C. practice elsewhere. But I don't think I would do as well. Having a partner who cares about providing services to regular people keeps me balanced somehow. Besides, I know Sally's watching me from up there." He pointed upward toward a sky spangled with stars.

"What if you could bring the mediation practice into Lyndon, Lyndon & Kopp, without jettisoning the work Uncle Charles does here in Shenandoah Falls?"

"I might be interested in that. Especially if it meant bringing you into the family firm. That would please Charles too. But I have to tell you that I'm not entirely sure I'd like working with Noah. He's too secretive in his dealings with clients, and he's used to a large firm. LL&K is not big. He might not like our culture. And he might not fit in."

"Look, August, you should know that sometimes Noah seems to really want to see Laurie and Brandon back together. The other day he even told Brandon he wanted the two of them to sit down and work things out. But the thing is, I don't think Laurie wants Brandon back, if you'll pardon my saying so."

August cocked his head. "You really care about Laurie, don't you? I've heard some rumors about you two."

Damn. August was a wily old fox.

"I do care about her," Andrew said honestly. "And if she were my daughter, I'd want to..."

"Murder him?" August said this with a smile. The smile was a surprise.

"Look, I'm sorry. Brandon's a friend but he—"

"Disappointed you. I understand, Andrew. He disappointed me too. That's why I told Brandon he wasn't ready to join Lyndon, Lyndon & Kopp. Would it surprise you to know that I adore Laurie and want to see her happy?"

"I guess not."

"So here's the thing. I'm one hundred percent confident that Noah wants to see Laurie happy too. He adores his daughter. He would do anything for her."

Chapter Eighteen————

Roxy found Laurie in the ladies' room. "I'm so sorry about what happened," she said. "Honestly, I didn't think you were coming tonight, and I didn't even think about making changes to the seating chart."

Laurie stood in front of the mirror taking deep breaths. She was not going to cry over Andrew Lyndon. Good thing Roxy didn't know the truth.

"It's fine," she said.

"No, it's not. But I don't know if I can do anything about it, except to say that I'm heartbroken that you're not my sister." There were tears in Roxy's eyes.

They embraced, and the knot in Laurie's throat swelled. "Damn," she said on a hard breath. "I'm going to ruin my makeup."

Roxy held her by the shoulders. "Even if your mascara runs, you'll still be the most beautiful woman in the room tonight. Honestly, I almost wish my brother was here to see you. Especially with that Marine. Wow. Where did you find him?"

"He's a member of the police force. He came around to check on me. I had stopped answering Mom's texts, and she was sure I was lying dead in a pool of blood."

"No, really?"

"Really."

"Well, that just shows that you never know where you might bump into Mr. Right."

Laurie bit her tongue. She wanted to confide in Roxy, but she didn't dare. Her one-nighter with Andrew would remain a secret forever. No one would understand how they had ended up in bed together. And no one would ever forgive them for it.

"Can we be friends?" Roxy asked.

"Of course we can."

Roxy pulled a tissue from the box on the counter. "Here, you need this."

Laurie stared into the mirror and tried to fix the damage.

"You know," Roxy said, "I've been thinking about what you said the other day at the coffee shop."

Laurie stopped dabbing at her eyes. "Oh?"

Roxy sighed and leaned against the counter. "It occurred to me as I endured the last hour listening to Lindsay Mayfield, that Pam Lyndon, as much as I love her, has no sense when it comes to matching people up. I mean, Lindsay and Andrew? Really?"

"Pam set Andrew up on that date?"

"Yeah. You didn't think Andrew picked that girl on his own, did you?"

That was exactly what she thought.

"No. Pam knows Lindsay's mother from the Jefferson County Historic Society, or something. I'm sure they cooked this up between them. But you know Andrew; at least Lindsay will make it home safe, right?" Roxy smiled.

"Yeah," Laurie said. And until last Saturday she would have shared that view. But now she realized that Andrew wasn't nearly as safe as some people thought.

"So anyway, I realized that Pam has spent an incredible amount of time reminding me that Danny and I used to squabble all the time as kids. And I've been listening to her."

"And not noticing the way Daniel was looking at you tonight."

"How was he looking at me?"

"One part lost puppy and another part hungry wolf."

"Really?" A smile played on her lips.

"Really."

They looked at each other through the mirror's reflection.

"Damn," Roxy said. "Maybe I should go after him?"

"Maybe you should."

Roxy turned. "I'll let you know what happens," she said as she hurried from the restroom.

When Laurie finally emerged, the program had started. Pam Lyndon was introducing the members of the steering committee, and the lights had been dimmed a little.

She should go back to the table and find Ryan, but going back there was the last thing on her mind. So instead she skirted the back wall and slipped through one of the French doors out onto the terrace.

And ran right into Brandon's father.

Damn.

"Hello," she said, hoping the ground would open up and swallow her. She had nothing to say to him.

"Laurie," he said in a kind voice, "you look beautiful this evening."

"Thank you. I—"

He held up his hand. "I will not impede your progress. If you're looking for a friend, I think Andrew is over there lurking in the dark."

She turned to look over her shoulder, and August escaped.

"Hi," Andrew said from across the patio. "It's a little warmer here under the heater."

She crossed the flagstones, drawn by the heater's purple-blue flame. "Where's Lindsay?" she asked.

"I think she went off with Matt. And before you—"

"Roxy told me that your aunt set you up with her."

He said nothing, but the twinkle lights strung over the patio sparkled in his dark eyes. "So, how's Val?" she asked, and almost kicked herself. She was behaving like a jealous woman.

"Back from South Carolina. I gather things didn't work out for her and her Marine. The big alpha-male fantasy turned into a nightmare."

Ouch. He could give as well as take. And for the moment she didn't want him to know how Courtney had maneuvered Ryan into this date. "Ryan isn't an alpha dude."

"No?"

She shook her head.

"Then what is he?"

She almost blurted out the words "emotionally not available," but she held her tongue. "He's a hero who served his country and continues to serve."

Andrew let go of a very long breath. "Yeah, I guess you're right. He's pretty okay."

Silence welled up between them before she turned toward him and said, "Yeah he is, but he's not you."

Andrew blinked, and Laurie walked right up to him

and pulled his head down into a kiss. Oh yes. This. This was what she wanted. And she had this terrible feeling that her want was specific. It couldn't be satisfied by anyone else.

Andrew's hand slid down her back, and he pulled her hard against him as the kiss deepened. She wrapped her arms around his neck, reveling in his hard male body. She couldn't get close enough; she couldn't breathe; her whole body ached for him.

And just when she was about to suggest that they run off together for a long weekend of sex, a familiar voice called Andrew's name.

Andrew pushed her away just as Brandon came around the corner of the carriage house. He wasn't wearing a tuxedo, and by his uneven gait, he appeared to be drunk.

"Hey, Andrew, are you out here? Dad said—whoa. Laurie? Great dress, babe."

"You're drunk," Laurie said, stating the obvious.

"Yeah, I guess. I had a few at the Jay Bird before the party. And then I kind of forgot about the party. You know." He stumbled sideways. "Jeeze, you look terrific."

Just then Ryan came through the French doors. "Thank God," he said, coming up to Laurie's side in full-out hero mode. "I was worried about you. Are you okay?"

"I'm fine."

"Whoa, nice suit, dude," Brandon said.

"It's a uniform," Ryan said.

"Whatever." Brandon frowned. "Hey, wait a sec, is he your *date?*"

Laurie didn't have a chance to answer this because Ryan drew all six feet three inches of himself up and said, "Yes. And I came to find her because the dancing is starting. Let's go, Laurie. There isn't anyone out here you want to talk to."

And with that, Ryan swept her back into the ballroom, where it was impossible to escape.

Half an hour later, after making a statement on the dance floor, Ryan said he needed a restroom break. Laurie returned to her assigned table, where she found Roxy and Daniel looking deeply into each other's eyes.

"Hey," she said, interrupting, "have you seen Andrew?"

Roxy rolled her eyes. "He's gone. My idiot brother showed up three sheets to the wind and made a scene at Dad's table. Andrew offered to drive him back to D.C." Roxy lowered her voice. "If you ask me, Andrew was looking for an excuse to run away from Lindsay, although she seems to be having a great time with Matt. So...whatever. Where's Ryan?"

"He's taking a break."

Roxy grinned. "He's a great guy, Laurie. Way to go, girl."

Yeah, way to go.

Courtney had been too busy most of the evening to pay much attention to anything but making sure the bar was stocked, the food got served, and the PA system worked. So it was late in the evening when she finally took a break and stepped out onto the terrace for a breath of fresh air.

It was cold, and all but one of the propane heaters had run out of gas. Since the party was all but over, she didn't use her walkie-talkie to communicate with the facilities staff to get more propane canisters brought up. It was dark out there, since the timer automatically shut off the twinkle lights at midnight.

She took a couple of steps in the direction of the one working heater and then halted. A couple stood in the circle of its warmth, locked in a kiss that was definitely X-rated.

Damn, these people needed to leave the party and get a room so she could go home and soak her tired feet.

She was about to say something when the woman giggled and then guffawed. But the kiss went on. Man, she had one goofy-sounding laugh, but at least she seemed to be having a good time, which was more than Courtney could say about her life.

She'd been busy all night, but not too busy to notice Laurie and Ryan dancing the night away. They'd looked fabulous together, like a royal couple or something. And Laurie seemed to be enjoying herself.

The whole thing left a sour note.

Courtney hated this grumpy feeling in the middle of her chest. It seemed so petty.

Laurie deserved to have a fun time. And who knew Ryan was capable of dancing that well? Courtney should pat herself on the back instead of feeling grumpy. Laurie and Ryan looked like they were made for each other, and Courtney had certainly goaded Ryan into coming tonight, so she could take credit for what had happened.

She tried feeling happy about it, and she failed.

Just then the guy under the propane heater came up for air and said, "So, why don't we take this to your place?"

What the...? Courtney recognized that velvet voice. Matt Lyndon. Damn. Just what she needed.

"No, we can't," the woman said. "I mean, I'm staying at my folks' place over the weekend."

"Oh."

"Yeah, Andrew was supposed to drop me there. We could go to your place."

"No, that won't work."

"Why?"

There was a long pause. "I'm staying at my dad's house."

It was comical, really. They sounded like teenagers. And now that Courtney thought about it, Matt was way closer to his teen years than she was. But still.

She crossed her arms over her chest and assumed a bad-ass position. "It's time to go home, children," she said.

They turned toward her. The light spilling through the French doors must have been enough for Matt to recognize Courtney. "Well, well, it's the ice queen, isn't it?" he said.

She probably deserved that, but she wasn't letting him get away with it. "Ice queen, really?"

"You know this woman?" the girl asked.

"Yeah. She's the party planner."

"Oh, really? It was a great party. I especially loved the floral arrangements."

"Thanks. I didn't do the flowers." Amy did the flowers because she rocked when it came to all things botanical. Courtney was just good at making lists.

"Oh." The woman's voice sounded confused.

"Time to go," Courtney said.

"Oh. I wonder where Andrew is?" the girl said in a querulous voice.

"Andrew Lyndon?" Courtney asked.

"Yeah, he was my date."

Courtney refrained from asking the girl why she was kissing Matt. "Uh, honey, Andrew left hours ago."

"Oh. Well, I guess that's okay. I kind of ignored him after dinner."

"Yeah, I'll bet."

"No worries," Matt said. "I'll drive you home."

"You will?"

Honestly, this girl had like half the brains a normal woman should. Which was kind of sad because she was going to get played.

"Honey, where do you live?" Courtney asked.

"Oh, my parents live ten minutes away. I'm fine."

Courtney took a few steps in the girl's direction. "What's your name, honey?"

"Lindsay."

"Okay, Lindsay, here's the deal. I know the guy you've been kissing is a Lyndon, and they are all kind of good looking, but trust me, they all have serious personality flaws. Matt here is a consummate player."

"A player?"

What planet did this girl come from? "Yeah, he seduces unsuspecting women like you. Since Andrew, who is too selfless to be true, left you in Matt's clutches, it seems to me that your best option is to let me drive you home."

"Don't I get to say something?" Matt asked.

"No, you don't. I'm not letting you talk this girl into a one-nighter at some no-tell motel. Or worse yet, a quickie in the backseat of your car."

"I don't do quickies," he said in a voice that did something wicked and unwanted to Courtney's insides. "I like to take my time."

"That sounds like fun," Lindsay said.

"See? She doesn't need your help," Matt said.

And Lindsay, fool that she was, piped up and said, "You know, there's a motel about ten miles from here, not far from Winchester."

"I know that place," Matt said. "Why don't we check it out?"

Lindsay giggled, and Matt looked in Courtney's direction with that infernal Lyndon eyebrow arched just so.

She turned her back on him and stalked into the ballroom. Damn Matt Lyndon and every guy like him.

Chapter Nineteen —

On Sunday evening, Laurie sat at her desk in her small campus office with the paperwork for the Walter Jephson Foundation grant spread out before her. She'd read and reread the foundation's mission statement and its guidelines for grant submissions.

Her research project on party identification fit the foundation's research guidelines to a T, and since the topic was relevant and had practical polling applications, she felt confident she could win the grant. But if she proceeded on her own, Michael would make her life miserable.

Well, hell, she could let her fears stop her from moving forward or she could just cross the bridge and see what happened. She'd come to understand that no one was going to fix her life for her. Not her friends, or Andrew, or Mom, or Dad. If she wanted to move on, she would have to fix it herself.

And doing the hard work for this grant money would help her gain control of her life again.

She was deeply involved in drafting the outline for the grant proposal when her cell phone buzzed. She checked the caller ID. Damn. Brandon had the ability to pop up like a bad nightmare every time she started feeling good about herself. Like last night, when he'd ruined her moment with Andrew.

Of course, Andrew had run away last night like a scared rabbit. And that was all she really needed to know. She stared at Brandon's name for a couple of rings and finally decided it was time to face her problems. She pressed talk and said, "Hello, Brandon."

"Laurie." The sound of her name in his voice made her heart pound.

"What is it, Brandon?" She barked the words into the phone. Damn. She shouldn't have picked up. Just hearing his voice had shaken her confidence.

"I...uh...look, I want to apologize for last night. Apparently I behaved like a jerk."

"You don't know that you behaved like a jerk?"

"I was drunk. But trust me, Andrew spared no words in conveying just what a jerk I was."

"Good old Andrew."

"Yeah. He's a good friend. Look, Laurie, I...well, I need to talk to you."

She drummed her fingers on the desktop. "About the finances?"

The silence on the other end deepened for an interminable moment. "Look, I know I hurt you on our wedding day. But I had serious doubts about us. I mean, I thought we might be making a big mistake. I needed to make sure, you know, that..." He heaved a sigh and didn't continue.

"Make sure of what?"

"I just needed to have a few more experiences."

"You mean like going to Bermuda with Matt and picking up women? That sort of thing?" She cringed when the words popped out of her mouth. She sounded just like Mom when one of her boyfriends inevitably cheated on her. Mom had a talent for choosing men who cheated.

Of course, Laurie was one to talk. He may have gone to Bermuda with Matt, but she's the one who'd had earth-moving sex with Brandon's best friend.

"I get why you're pissed at me," Brandon said. "But the truth is, I didn't have much fun in Bermuda. I certainly didn't meet anyone worth dating. And in the meantime, you've been dating the world."

"No. Not really. And if you're trying to shame me for going out, it's not going to work."

"Laurie, come on. I saw you out with Danny. Matt saw you out with Andrew. Someone told me you took some other guy to Emma's wedding. And then you show up at the ball with that cop, which kind of pissed me off because he should have arrested Courtney for what she did to my car. The milk she purposefully spilled on the carpet is starting to stink."

What the hell? A surge of fury coursed through her, and the tips of her drumming fingers were starting to hurt. "Sorry," she said, her tone sarcastic.

Brandon's breathing got lower and deeper over the connection. "Look, Laurie, the thing is, I love you. This last month has been...well, it's been lonely as hell, to tell you the truth. I miss you."

She stopped drumming her fingers as her brain short-circuited. This was precisely what she'd wanted four weeks ago. And yet, it occurred to her that she'd stopped missing Brandon somewhere along the line.

That wasn't to say she was happy with her life. She

definitely missed the collegiality of the political science department at George Washington University. She missed the wide circle of friends that she and Brandon had hung out with. She missed the equilibrium of that life, where everyone was happy.

But she hadn't been all that obsessed with Brandon the last couple of weeks. She'd been having fun. Dating guys like Tobin Grant. And…lusting after Andrew.

In a totally unrequited way. But still.

She squared her shoulders and spoke carefully. "Look, Brandon, I'm happy to keep the door open for a while, just as you suggested on our wedding day. But I think we need to talk about finances. Maybe we can schedule a meeting at Andrew's office or something."

"What?"

"I'm serious. To be honest, I'm coming to see that you were right. I need to experiment a little more."

"Come on, Laurie. Don't be that way, okay? You've won. I've received your message loud and clear."

"What message is that?"

"You know. You've made your point."

Holy crap. Andrew's stupid plan appeared to have worked. Sort of. Brandon wanted her back. But did she want Brandon? That was the question.

"What point have I made?" she asked.

"That my idea for an open relationship was dumb."

"Did you suggest an open relationship? Because I missed that. As I recall it, you told me to go experience life. I think you should take your own advice and do the same."

On Monday morning, Noah Wilson stepped into Andrew's office and shut the door behind him. Out in the bullpen, Kim's head popped up over her cubicle's divider like a prairie dog on the alert. In five minutes, the whole office would know about this encounter. Andrew was so tired of this.

"So?" Noah said as he took command of the single side chair, his face a study in neutrality. "I gather there was quite a scene at the Harvest Festival Ball on Saturday."

Damn. How did he know what had happened? Was he still talking to Aunt Pam? "I don't know what you mean, Noah."

"Don't play dumb with me. I know all about how Laurie showed up with a Marine. And if your aunt is to be believed, this guy is handsome as the devil. Who is he? And why did you set her up with him? I thought we were going to let Tobin take her out a few times."

Shit, shit, shit. Noah was still talking to Aunt Pam. That couldn't be good. What was Pam up to? Andrew took a deep breath and reached for calm. "His name is Ryan Pierce. He's retired military who now works for the Shenandoah Falls Police Force. And for the record, I didn't set Laurie up on this date. She did that all on her own."

Noah's neutral expression evaporated. His eyes almost bugged out of his head. "She set herself up on a date?"

"She's a grown woman, and a beautiful one. She isn't going to have any problems finding boyfriends."

"How does she know this guy?"

"I think she met him when your ex-wife called the SFPD and asked them to check on Laurie. This would have been a couple of days after the wedding."

"Oh my God. My *wife* set them up?"

"Uh, no. Your wife called the police, and that's how Ryan met Laurie. I think they've become friends."

Noah squirmed in his chair. "This isn't going well, Andrew. Do you think this is going well?"

"I'm not sure. Brandon showed up at the ball on Saturday. He was drunk as a skunk. I drove him home, and he spent the entire drive talking about your daughter. So maybe it—"

"He's jealous?"

"I don't know. Maybe. Or maybe he's beginning to regret his actions."

"Yeah, well, he should—" Noah bit off the rest of what he had planned to say, took a deep breath, and continued, "So how do you feel about these developments?"

What the hell? Andrew was tempted to get right up into Noah's face and tell him just how much he resented being pushed around and lied to. And while he was at it, he could tell Noah just how much he hated the idea of Laurie being with Ryan. Or Brandon. Or anyone for that matter.

But of course, he couldn't say any of that.

"I don't have any feelings," he said in a calm voice.

"What?" Noah exploded out of his chair. "What's wrong with you? Why don't you have any feelings?"

"Um, well, I like Ryan," he said.

"You do? Why?"

"He's a grown-up. And Laurie needs someone like that. Not because she's immature, don't get me wrong. But because she's—I don't know—classy and reserved and smart. And Ryan is a good guy."

As much as he hated to admit it.

"As good as Brandon?"

"Yes, I think so. Look, Noah, the thing is, Brandon broke your daughter's heart. He put her in a bad financial situation. And he messed up her career. So yeah, I think Ryan might be a better bet for her. I mean, any fool can see she's better off without Brandon."

He stopped speaking the moment he realized he'd more or less called his boss a fool.

"Does Brandon know you feel this way?" Noah's voice had lowered. He'd reined in his emotions and sat back down.

"I don't give a rat's ass what Brandon knows or thinks."

"Really?"

"Yeah, really. He's an idiot for letting her go. And if you want my opinion about Laurie's happiness, you should just back off and let her figure it out on her own. Ryan's an okay guy."

"What about Tobin?"

"What about him?" Andrew wanted to break Noah's head.

"Do you think he'd be good for her? Tobin told me they had a wonderful time at the wedding they went to."

That would have been the day after Andrew slept with Laurie. And the idea of her going out with Tobin made his skin itch. He couldn't say that out loud. So instead he took a breath, and said, "Yeah, sure. Tobin's a great guy."

Noah stood up. "Yes, you're absolutely right. Tobin would make an excellent husband for my daughter. He's smarter than Brandon and better looking. And I'm sure, with all his education, he could blow away that Ryan guy."

"Right," Andrew said in a weak voice. After all these weeks of insisting that nothing short of a reconciliation would please him, now Noah was on a mission to find Laurie an alternate husband—in Tobin no less. There was something seriously wrong with Noah. He needed to see a psychologist or something.

Or maybe he'd just been listening to Aunt Pam, who had clearly decided that it was her duty to get Laurie back on her feet and safely married off to someone. Anyone. That's exactly what Pam had tried to do with Andrew's sister Amy too. Damn.

"Good work, Andrew," Noah said, pulling Andrew from his disquieting thoughts.

Andrew looked up just as Noah was leaving his office. "Tobin, there you are. Do you have a minute?" he said, just as Tobin strolled through the common area in the direction of the break room.

"Sure, Noah." Tobin smiled his oily, obsequious smile.

"Have you called my daughter yet?"

"Uh, no. But I was planning to."

Andrew groaned and banged his head on his desk. He hated Tobin Grant. And he hated Noah Wilson.

"Perfect," Noah said in a big voice that carried all the way into Andrew's office. "I've got a couple of box seats for *Madame Butterfly* at the Kennedy Center for this coming Saturday evening. You can have them."

"Thanks, Noah. I'll call her right away and see if she's available."

"Oh, she'll be available. My daughter never misses a chance to go to the opera. Just don't tell her I bought the tickets, okay?"

Chapter Twenty

Laurie's cell buzzed on Monday evening as she was stirring the eggshell-white paint she planned to roll onto the living room's walls. It was Tobin.

"Hi," he said in a low, sexy voice. She waited for the hormonal rush, but it didn't come. Like Ryan, Tobin was handsome and smart and accomplished, but for some reason, he just didn't push all her buttons. It didn't matter though because she didn't need a man in her life.

She'd come to this conclusion directly after hanging up on Brandon last night. She was going to be the opposite of her mother. She would land her own research grant, tell Brandon to take a hike, and live like a nun for a while, occasionally hanging with her friends at the Jay Bird.

And if she needed help with home improvement, she could always call Ryan. He was exactly the kind of guy who would help out and never make any demands. So really, what else did she need?

Besides Andrew Lyndon's kisses.

"I've got a surprise for you," Tobin said, pulling her away from her daily fantasy.

"Oh?" Laurie wasn't sure she liked surprises anymore.

He chuckled. "I've got two box-seat tickets for the National Opera Company's performance on Saturday evening."

Was Tobin for real? This had to be the first time in her life that anyone, other than Dad or Mom, had invited her out to the opera. Tobin scored major points for this, even if he didn't make her heart go pitty-pat.

"Wow," she said.

He chuckled. "I remembered what you said at Emma's wedding, about how you loved Puccini. When I found out the National Opera was performing *Madame Butterfly*, I had to get the tickets."

Tobin really was a great guy. She grinned like a fool. "Yes, I'll go."

"I'll pick you up at four, and we'll have dinner someplace in Georgetown."

"Oh no, that's silly. I'll meet you in town."

"Don't be ridiculous, Laurie. I'll pick you up."

"But it's sixty miles one way give or take."

"I like to drive." He paused a moment before continuing. "Laurie, I assure you I'm a complete gentleman. I'm not working on a nefarious plan to convince you to spend the night with me in D.C. I will happily drive you home after the show."

Laurie didn't exactly know how to read the hint of amusement in his voice. Was he so sure that she'd succumb to his charms? Tobin Grant had a healthy ego, and she had to admit there was something attractive about a confident man.

So she capitulated. And then spent the next few days

wondering if she'd made a mistake. Did she want to be in control? Or did she want to experiment with Tobin the way she'd experimented with Andrew?

She honestly didn't know. But just in case, she scheduled an appointment at the local salon Saturday morning. When Tobin showed up promptly at 4:00 p.m., she was blow-dried, hot waxed, manicured, pedicured, and dressed once again in her new black dress and high heels. Tobin hadn't seen the dress before so she figured she could get her money's worth.

And, bless the man, he openly admired what the dress exposed and then kissed her—quite thoroughly. Although his kiss didn't ignite any fireworks.

She found herself comparing his kiss to Andrew's. And then she felt guilty for not even thinking about Brandon.

Damn. It looked as if she would need to experiment with a lot of guys before she found someone who could match Andrew Lyndon's kisses. Clearly experimentation could be lots of fun, especially if it included occasional trips to the opera.

Tobin took her to Fiola Mare, a pricey Mediterranean seafood restaurant on the Georgetown waterfront. Their table commanded a fabulous view of the Potomac, and the menu was nothing short of amazing. It included three different varieties of clams on the half shell as well as caviar and calamari. Tobin seemed ready to wine and dine her in grand style. He offered to buy the $180-per-ounce caviar if she wanted it, but she'd never been a big fan. Instead, she opted for the simply grilled Spanish branzino, which, at $40, was one of the cheapest items on the menu.

Her natural frugality didn't matter because Tobin bought a $100 bottle of white wine, which was so crisp and tart that she had trouble remembering to sip it. And since they were early for the 7:30 p.m. curtain, he ordered after-dinner drinks that tasted like licorice.

She was definitely feeling a little glow when they arrived at the Kennedy Center, where Tobin added to the alcoholic haze by pressing a flute of champagne into her hands. Maybe it was a good thing she hadn't driven herself. She seemed to be making the same mistake with Tobin that she'd made with Connor Strickland. Only she didn't have a wingman tonight.

Which became an issue after the first act, when the alcoholic haze morphed into a punishing headache above her right eye. Damn. Just her luck. A migraine on opera night seemed like a really bad omen.

When the first intermission arrived, she excused herself and headed for the restroom, where she bypassed the ridiculous line for the toilets in order to gulp down some water and a couple of Excedrin. She never left home without her migraine pills, and if taken early enough, they could knock out a headache in about ten minutes. Unfortunately, this one was fueled by too much wine and had been developing for more than an hour.

She loitered near the restroom until the dimming lights and chimes announced the intermission's end. The Excedrin had taken a tiny edge off the pounding in her brain, but she still wasn't feeling very well when she entered the door to the private box. The box seats had a small anteroom separated from the seats by a curtain. She heard Tobin's voice just as she was ready to walk through the draperies. He was obviously speaking on his cell phone.

"Stop calling me," he said in a low voice. "I'll give you a full report tomorrow, okay?"

He paused a moment. "It's going great. Honestly."

Laurie stopped in her tracks, the ache in her head morphing into tiny, prickling needles stabbing her right eye.

"No, of course I'm not planning to sleep with her," Tobin continued. "I get the feeling she's not into that sort of thing. She's kind of a nerdy ice maiden, you know? I mean, who likes opera? But I figure that's a bonus, really. I just have to sit through this opera and pretend I'm enjoying it."

Another pause, and then he said, "Of course I didn't buy the tickets. Her father did."

He stopped talking again and then said, "Look, I have to go. The first intermission is almost over, and she'll be back any minute. Just remember that I wouldn't be doing this if she wasn't the boss's daughter."

Laurie backed out of the room. Her head felt about three sizes too big, and her stomach was reacting badly to the wine, fish, and Excedrin. She managed to make it back to the powder room, where she heaved up the $150 dinner Tobin had bought for her. By then, the second act had started, and even though she would miss the famous aria, "*Un bel di vedremo*," she had no desire to sit next to Tobin Grant.

She should have known Dad had bought the tickets. And she suddenly wondered if Tobin was going to put the dinner on his expense report.

She'd be furious if she wasn't so woozy. But all she really wanted right at the moment was a glass of sparkling water and a place to lie down. She headed down a flight of stairs to the grand foyer and then through the Hall of Nations to the street entrance. The taxi stand was deserted this early in the evening. In another couple of hours, there would be dozens of cabs lined all the way back up onto Twenty-Fifth Street.

She walked toward the steps that would take her to New

Hampshire Avenue and dug in her purse for her cell phone. Maybe it was time to give Dad a piece of her mind.

She tried his number but got no answer.

She tried Roxy Kopp and got voice mail.

Emma and Nabil were still out of town on their honeymoon so there was no point in calling them.

Ryan and Courtney were sixty miles away.

Damn, she needed a place to crash. Maybe she should just book herself into a hotel or something. But her head was pounding so hard, she could barely think. She stared down at her contacts list. There were two more options left: Brandon and Andrew.

She chose Andrew.

On Saturday evening, Andrew met his brother and cousins at the sports bar on Eighteenth Street to watch the nationally televised football game between the University of Virginia and the University of Oregon. They had just finished off their second plate of wings when the Virginia Cavaliers gave up their third interception of the first quarter. It looked as if the Ducks were going to slaughter the hapless Cavs.

UVA was not particularly known for its prowess on the gridiron. On the other hand, its law school, created by Thomas Jefferson himself, had produced such notable alums as Robert Kennedy, Woodrow Wilson, and David Baldacci, not to mention countless members of the Lyndon family, including Senator Mark Lyndon; his son, David; and his nephews, Andrew, Edward, Matthew, and Jason.

Matt finished off his Sam Adams and waggled his empty glass at the passing waitress. "I think we need to make an intervention," he said, leaning back in his seat.

"For who, the Cavs' quarterback?" Edward asked.

"For Brandon. I hate the fact that he's stopped hanging

out with us." Matt scowled in Andrew's direction. "I think he's really ticked off at you for taking Laurie's side. You know, for hanging out with her at The Park, and for bugging him about the mortgage."

"Well, that's his problem," Andrew said, trying to invest his voice with all the innocence he could muster. But Matt had a point this time. The moment Andrew had taken Laurie to bed, he'd done irreparable damage to the fabric of relationships that defined this group. And yet, he didn't regret doing it. That was the weird part.

"Look, dude," Matt said. "Brandon may have said that he wanted a break from Laurie so they could both see other people. But he sure didn't mean for Laurie to follow through on that, you know?"

"Matt, you're an idiot," Edward said. "Just shut up and watch the game."

"Come on. No guy wants his girlfriend to really date other guys."

Andrew let go of a long-suffering sigh. "Matt, are you completely blind to the fact that you have a double standard? If Brandon is going to go off to Bermuda to pick up women, shouldn't Laurie be allowed to do the same?"

"Hell no. It's different for women."

Just then Andrew's cell phone buzzed, and Laurie's number and name flashed big as life. The guys saw it.

"Damn," Jason said. "She calls you on Saturday nights? What's going on, Andrew?"

A deep uneasiness swept through him. Laurie was supposed to be at the opera with Tobin, and the performance of *Madame Butterfly* lasted three hours at least. It was just after 9:00 p.m., too early for the show to be over. He snatched the phone from the table and hit the talk button.

"Laurie, what's the matter?" he asked.

"I need your help." Her voice wobbled, and every one of Andrew's senses went on alert.

"Where are you?"

"I'm here at the Kennedy Center, and I'm sick."

"Where's Tobin?" he asked.

"I don't give two shits where Tobin is. He's a jerk and an asshole. Oh God, my head is about to explode."

"Migraine?" he asked, and then wondered how he knew Laurie suffered from debilitating headaches. Probably because he'd known her for years and years.

"Yeah. I'm on New Hampshire Avenue trying to find a cab, but even if I find one, I don't even know where I can go. I don't have a key to Dad's apartment, and he isn't answering his phone."

"Stay right there. I'm on my way. Don't hang up."

He stood. "Hey, guys, cover the bill and let me know how much I owe you. Laurie's in trouble."

"Since when are you her keeper?" Matt asked. "Where's that big Marine she was with the other night?"

"I don't know where Ryan is. Probably back in Shenandoah Falls. But Laurie is in town right now, and she's in trouble."

"Yeah, well, you should tell her to call Brandon. This is exactly the problem we've been trying to talk to you about."

"Laurie isn't a problem, Matt. She's my friend. She's in trouble and needs my help. What do you want me to do? Stand here and tell her to go screw herself? Because telling her to call Brandon after what he did to her would be the same thing. Just because Brandon dumped her doesn't give us permission to treat her like crap."

Laurie had never been so grateful to see anyone in her life. She took one look at Andrew, casually dressed in a navy and orange Cavs sweatshirt, his dark hair curling down over his forehead and a look of real concern deep in his brown eyes, and started to cry. She sank back into his bucket seats and let the tears roll down her face. In the meantime, her phone kept buzzing with one message after another from Tobin.

"Where do you want to go?" he asked.

She rocked her head back and forth, each movement excruciating. "I just want to lie down somewhere until my head stops hurting. And I probably need to tell Tobin I've gone home, but I can't really focus."

Andrew took the phone out of her hand. "I'm going to tell Tobin you didn't feel well and took a taxi home, okay?"

She managed a nod.

When he'd finished sending the message, he put the car in gear and started driving back up Rock Creek Parkway to his apartment. He drove like a sedate old lady, taking each turn in the curvy road at a ridiculously slow rate of speed. She wondered if he always drove like that until she realized that he was just being careful not to jar her head.

Wow. Brandon always had to be reminded to slow down, and even then, he always took turns too fast in his Camaro. Brandon also had no patience for her headaches. Sometimes he acted as if she should be able to control them.

But Andrew wasn't like that at all. He seemed to understand what was needed in a moment of crisis. Just like he'd known what to do on that horrible day when Brandon had walked away from her. She could remember the feel of Andrew's hand in hers, leading her away from the altar and the disturbing murmur of the wedding guests. He'd taken her to safety that day. He'd done the same thing when Connor Strickland got the wrong idea.

He was a terrific wingman.

But wasn't he more than that? A wingman was a side-kick, and she'd stopped thinking of Andrew that way.

When they arrived at his place, he helped her up the stairs of his walk-up apartment and right into his bedroom, which had a gigantic picture window overlooking a shared courtyard. He quickly drew the curtains to shut out the light from the streetlamps.

"Lie down," he said as he guided her to the bed.

He slept on one of those memory foam mattresses, and when she sank down into his bed, she felt cradled. He retreated to the hallway and turned off the light. A moment later, he returned with a cool washcloth.

"Which eye?" he asked as if he knew something about migraines.

"The right one."

He pressed the cloth to her head above her right eye. The cold soothed as nothing could.

"Do you feel sick?"

"No. I threw up already in one of the Opera House bathrooms."

"Did you take anything?"

"A couple of Excedrin, but then I threw up."

He left again but returned shortly with two Excedrin and a cup of strong, black coffee. "Here, take the pills and drink the coffee."

She did as directed. "How do you know about the coffee?"

"My mother had migraines," he said. "I guess I learned by watching my dad."

She sank back into the mattress, insanely glad to know that Andrew hadn't learned about migraines by taking care of a girlfriend. She pressed the washcloth to her forehead and curled up on her side, waiting for the caffeine in the Excedrin and the coffee to kick in.

Andrew sat next to her, his weight shifting the mattress slightly. He didn't talk, but his presence was like an unmovable rock in the middle of a raging stream. He'd be there for her to cling to if she needed him.

Andrew didn't leave Laurie's side until she drifted off to sleep about thirty minutes after she'd taken the Excedrin. He strolled into the living room and turned on the big-screen television.

He'd recently redecorated, and he truly loved his living space once he'd given the final heave-ho to Val and her shabby chic style. The decorator Aunt Pam recommended had done a terrific job of capturing his clean, modern, no-nonsense style.

The living room featured a comfortable sectional sofa and glass-topped end tables with steel frames. His kitchen was nothing short of a stainless steel temple dedicated to gourmet cooking, which was kind of funny because he didn't cook unless it involved heating something in the microwave or making coffee in his expensive, pod-style coffeemaker.

He employed the coffeemaker for a second time that evening and settled on his couch with his cup to watch the last quarter of the football game. Virginia was down by twenty-eight points but making a heroic effort at a comeback. Unfortunately, less than ten minutes remained on the clock so it was doubtful they would prevail.

He sipped his coffee and focused on the game in a vain attempt to forget about the woman sleeping in his bedroom. He was utterly unsuccessful, but that didn't change the situation. Laurie was a pipe dream. A fantasy that he would never have.

Five minutes later, the buzz of his cell phone called him back from his thoughts. But when he glanced at the caller ID, he swore out loud and pressed the ignore button. He did not want to talk to Brandon.

A moment later, his message app lit up.

C'mon Andrew, I know u r home. I'm outside ur door & I can see the TV is on.

His doorbell rang.

Damn. There was no escaping this awkward situation, was there? Maybe the time had come to tell the unvarnished truth. But how could he do that to Laurie? How could he do that to his friends and family? The truth would not set Andrew or Laurie free; it would embroil them in a big, messy, emotional morass.

But he couldn't avoid Brandon forever so he buzzed him in.

"What gives?" Brandon asked a moment later as he strolled into the apartment. "I'm starting to think you've been avoiding me."

Which was the truth. But Andrew could hardly admit that. "I'm not in a talkative mood tonight," Andrew said.

Brandon gazed at the football game. Two minutes remained in the fourth quarter, and Virginia had closed the scoring gap to fourteen points. "Hey, why didn't you and the guys meet up at the sports bar on Eighteenth to watch the game? I dropped by the place a little while ago. I was kind of surprised that none of you were there. I know I'm late, but I got hung up at the Capitol, working overtime. Heather is a tough boss."

So the guys had left shortly after Andrew had gone to

rescue Laurie. And Brandon had intended to meet them there after all. Damn.

"We were there, but Virginia was losing and we left early. Sorry. You want a beer?"

"Yeah, sure." Brandon dropped onto the sofa and made himself comfortable.

Andrew escaped to the kitchen and snagged a beer from his outrageously expensive drawer-style beverage cooler.

There were no two ways about it. Andrew was trapped in an ethical quagmire. He needed to get Brandon out of the apartment as fast as possible before he discovered that Laurie was there.

He returned to the living room and handed Brandon his beer. "So, what's up?" he asked, trying for nonchalance and failing miserably.

"I've been thinking," Brandon said, just as time ran out for the Cavaliers.

"About what?"

He took a long pull on his beer. "About Laurie."

Oh, crap. This was *not* happening. "What about her?"

Brandon threw his head back onto the couch and let go of the longest, most mournful sigh possible. "I really messed up."

"Are you saying that you want to get back together with her?"

He nodded his head. "I've been thinking about this since that night when her girlfriends tried to trash the Camaro and we all ended up together at the Jay Bird. It drove me crazy watching that cop flirt with her. And then she takes him to the Harvest Ball and now everyone is talking about how great they looked together."

"It was the Marine dress uniform," Andrew said. He

could totally empathize with Brandon's feelings on the subject of Ryan Pierce.

Brandon took another sip of beer and nodded. "I guess I didn't expect her to just get on with her life like that. A couple of weeks and she's fine. I guess I didn't think guys would come on to her like that."

"Uh, buddy, I hate to point this out but Laurie is a beautiful woman."

"Yes, she is."

"And you're the one who walked away from her and told her to go experiment."

"Yeah, I did. I thought I'd...I don't know what I was thinking. I guess I thought I would feel free once we split. That it would be fun, you know, going out. But I haven't found a single woman who was half as interesting as Laurie. And freedom is highly overrated."

Brandon drained his beer. Andrew said nothing. Anything he might say would be held against him when the crap hit the fan. As it would...inevitably.

"So the last laugh is on me," Brandon said. "I thought I could be free, and she would just wait for me, you know. But it hasn't worked out that way."

"Being a single guy is nothing to write home about," Andrew said.

"Yeah, I guess. I mean, there are always women who are happy to hook up for a night, but they aren't interested in relationships. And after a while, that sort of thing is kind of...sad, really. No matter what Matt says."

"Matt's an idiot."

"Yeah, he is. A lovable idiot, and I hope one day some woman turns his head and makes him realize the truth."

"And you're saying you realize the truth now?"

He nodded and sat forward, bracing his elbows on his

knees. "I called Laurie last Monday and asked her to meet with me so we could talk things over. She refused. She told me to go find a life."

"Really?" Something wonderful took flight in Andrew's heart. And then it crashed and burned. Even if Laurie had fully ended her relationship with Brandon, there was no hope for the two of them together. How would he explain that to Brandon? Or his brother and cousins? They would see it as a betrayal or something. Especially now that Brandon wanted her back.

"Yeah, that's what she told me. But the only life that means anything to me is with her."

"So what are you going to do?" Andrew asked.

"I need your help."

Adrenaline almost jolted Andrew right out of his chair. "Why on earth do you need me?"

"Because you're a whiz at patching things up for people, you know, for making peace. I need you to do this for me. Laurie admires you. She'll listen to you if you tell her she should cool her jewels and rethink."

"No," Andrew said firmly, folding his arms even though he knew the body language was way too aggressive for the moment.

"Why not?"

"Because a good mediator needs to be impartial."

"Yeah, but it's not like you're automatically on my side either. Look, I know what Matt, Jason, and Edward are saying—that you're siding with Laurie. But they're wrong. I mean, they seem to think that this is some kind of battle. But it isn't. You're the only one who's realized how important it is to keep the lines of communication going. Plus you've done me a favor or two, like that night at the Jay Bird when you whisked Laurie away from that annoying cop."

Oh, if Brandon only knew what he'd done that night, he wouldn't be very appreciative. "Yeah, but she went to the ball with that cop anyway."

Brandon shrugged. "Doesn't matter. You're still the best friend anyone could ever hope to have," Brandon said, looking up at Andrew with a totally open expression on his face. "I'm asking, Andrew. No, I'm begging you. I need you to carry my brief to Laurie and make her listen. All I want is a meeting where we can talk things out. Is that too much to ask?"

"No, it's not," Andrew said, feeling as if Brandon had just dropped a gigantic lead weight on his shoulders.

Chapter Twenty-One

Laurie dozed for an indeterminate period of time before her buzzing cell phone awakened her. She cracked an eye and found the device on the bedside table. Tobin had sent another message, to know if she'd gotten home. He seemed a little frantic. And with good reason since he didn't want to piss off Daddy.

She sent another text telling him she was fine and then lay back in the bed, her headache still throbbing but not totally out of control. The Excedrin had helped. She closed her eyes and became aware of voices coming from the living room.

Uh-oh. She recognized one of those voices. Brandon was there.

She got up and tiptoed to the bedroom door and cracked it open. Andrew's one-bedroom was pricey and beautiful, but also tiny. She could hear everything they said, and when Brandon asked Andrew to "carry his brief," her stomach roiled. Did lawyers talk to each other this way in real life? She waited for Andrew to refuse, but instead of telling Brandon no, he agreed to do it.

What the hell? Had he been playing her all this time? Telling her one thing, while telling Brandon something else, and all the while dancing to Daddy's jig? She slammed the door open, intent on giving both of them a piece of her mind.

Unfortunately, her stomach and her head were still coming to terms with the alcohol she'd consumed earlier in the evening. She took one step into the hallway and knew she was in trouble. There would be no dressing down or bawling out. In fact, she nearly didn't make it to the bathroom in time, as her stomach heaved up the rest of its contents, leaving her hugging the commode while Brandon and Andrew argued outside the bathroom door.

"What the hell is she doing here?" Brandon shouted.

"Look, I can explain," Andrew said in a tone that annoyed the crap out of Laurie because it sounded as if Andrew was embarrassed by her presence.

"Okay, but it better be good. I've been here for more than half an hour. When were you going to tell me that Laurie was in your bedroom?" Brandon's voice was so laden with angry testosterone that Laurie feared for Andrew's handsome face. A fistfight seemed like it might break out at any minute.

"Oh, for chrissake, Brandon, shut up. Laurie went out with Tobin Grant tonight," Andrew said in that low, controlled, rational tone he always used to defuse every emotional situation.

"Tobin Grant? The asshole you hate so much from Wilson Kavanaugh?"

"Yeah. Tobin took her to the opera, but he must have fed

her a lot of wine beforehand. She called me about nine this evening, before the show was finished. She had a migraine."

"Why didn't Tobin take her home?"

"I honestly don't know. All I know is that she called me distraught. So I picked her up and brought her here. She was sleeping it off when you arrived."

"Why didn't you tell me she was here?" Brandon raged.

"I didn't tell you about Laurie because I knew you'd react badly."

At that moment, both men tried to enter the tiny bathroom and render aid. Laurie, who was feeling more sober and less sick by the moment, snagged a wad of toilet paper to wipe her mouth. She looked up at them. "Don't," she said in a raspy voice. "I don't need either of you, okay? I can handle this on my own." She threw the toilet paper in the commode and flushed.

She stood up and glared at Andrew, her eye sockets aching and her head still feeling far, far away. "If you want to know why I called you tonight, it was because I heard Tobin talking on the phone to someone bragging about how he was advancing his career by dating the boss's daughter. And then he admitted that he hated opera, after spending the whole evening bullshitting me about how much he was looking forward to it." She hauled in a breath, her outrage growing by the minute.

"Asshole," Brandon said.

She ignored her ex-fiancé and looked Andrew right in the eye. "I'm thinking the very same thing can be said of you."

Andrew said nothing, and she couldn't look into those deep, dark eyes of his a moment longer. She shifted her gaze to Brandon. "My father has been pushing Andrew around, using him to get his revenge on you. All those dates I've been going on—Andrew set them up because Dad wanted you to realize your mistake. Andrew has been sucking up to me. Making me think he was my best friend and didn't really agree with what Dad was doing. The thing is, it was obvious from the start that this was all about Andrew advancing his career. I don't even know why I thought it was about something else." Her throat closed up.

"Asshole," Brandon said, looking at Andrew.

"Oh, shut up, Brandon," Laurie said, right up in Brandon's face. "You're just as big an asshole. Maybe an even bigger one because you're the guy who left me at the altar."

"Look, baby, I'm really sorry about that. I don't know what came over me. But I'm sure we can work it out. And honestly, I don't care that you've been dating all these guys because—"

"Stop!" She put up her hand. "I don't want to hear it. And if you're only saying it because you didn't like seeing me go out on dates, then you should know you've been manipulated. Andrew came to me a few days after the wedding with a plan to make you reevaluate your options."

"What?" Brandon turned toward Andrew.

"Laurie's telling the truth," Andrew said in that infernally calm voice of his. "The plan was to make you jealous. At least that's what Noah wanted. And Laurie is also correct when she says that I went along with it because I was worried about my job and was more interested in making partner than just about anything else."

Laurie elbowed her way between the two men and stalked back into the bedroom, where she started searching for her shoes. To her surprise, both Andrew and Brandon behaved like civilized men and refrained from punching each other out. Instead they followed her into the bedroom.

"What are you doing?" Andrew asked.

"I'm leaving. I'll find a cab to take me home."

Brandon, always a man of action, snagged her by the arm. "You'll do no such thing. I'll take you home."

She looked up into his blue eyes, prepared to yank her arm away. But the concern on his face was so familiar. Dammit, it made her feel safe. Sort of. But then the look in Andrew's eyes made her feel the same way.

Safety was nice. But it wasn't everything, was it?

Andrew also had the ability to make her burn. But there was no need to let Brandon know that. No need at all, especially since she'd invited Andrew in and she, herself, had insisted on no strings. Which made her wonder what might have happened if she hadn't set those ground rules.

Nothing would have happened, and she would never have had that many orgasms in a row. So who was she to complain about the way things turned out?

"Look," Brandon, said pulling her away from her confusion and regret, "I know I made a mistake on our wedding day. But I never lied to you, and I never cheated on you. In fact, I haven't really gone on any dates since the wedding, to be totally honest."

Well, that was a surprising turn of events. Poor Brandon. At least she'd had one night of unforgettable sex and had enjoyed a Cinderella moment at the Harvest Ball with a handsome man she didn't love. It could be worse. Maybe Brandon deserved another chance.

"Okay," she said, looking him in the eye. "I'm going to let you drive me home, but it's just so I can save the cab fare. It doesn't mean I'm taking you back."

Brandon nodded. "Okay. I understand. I realize that I've got a lot of work to do in order to get you back."

She pulled her arm away from him and waited for a long moment, hoping against hope that Andrew would do something or say something—anything—to stop her from leaving with her ex-fiancé.

But he didn't say a word, and his silence was as eloquent as any speech.

And just to punctuate the point, the doorbell buzzed right as they were heading for the front door. Brandon opened it, and there stood Val with a big grin on her face and a bottle of wine in her hand.

"Hi," she said, "did I miss the party?"

"So, just like old times, huh?" Val said as she entered Andrew's apartment. She took three steps into the living room and stopped. "What the hell happened here?" she asked. "The place looks like one of those furniture showroom vignettes. Where's the rocking chair we found by the road that day we went down to Fredericksburg?"

"It went into the trash the day you left. I was so angry, I smashed it to pieces. Truth is, I never liked that thing."

"You smashed something? Really?" She seemed surprised.

He made no reply to this. On the day Val dumped him, Andrew had gone a little crazy, breaking the chair she loved as well as every single plate of the rosebud china she'd bought at some antique place. Getting that angry had not made him feel better. But it had begun the process of cleansing his apartment of Val's decorating choices.

"I always thought you loved that rocking chair," Val said into his silence.

"I lied. You should know that I have a hidden talent for prevarication." He crossed the room and picked up his coffee cup and Brandon's empty beer bottle.

"What's the matter with you?"

He turned. "Why are you here?"

She shrugged. "Because I love you."

How many lonely months had he waited to hear those words? He turned his back on her and walked into the kitchen, where he put his cup in the sink and the bottle in the recycling bin.

"Holy crap," Val said from behind. "This is like one of those kitchens you see on *House Hunters Renovation*. Oh boy, I can't wait to cook you a meal. How about lasagna? You always loved my lasagna. Do you have a casserole dish?" She started opening cabinets and drawers, exclaiming over the storage space, the small appliances, and the double ovens.

Andrew leaned on the quartz countertop and ground his teeth, angry that he'd let Laurie leave with Brandon without saying one word to discourage her. And then there was what she said. In the end, Andrew was really no better than Tobin.

Still, the idea of her getting back with Brandon disturbed him, even though he knew that their reconciliation would restore everything. His relationship with the guys, with his family, would all go back to the way it was.

No, it wouldn't, he realized. If Laurie married Brandon, he'd have to play the role of best friend while he watched Brandon take Laurie for granted. He'd have to stop falling in love with her. How could he do that? There was no way back from this precipice.

"Oh, good, I found the corkscrew," Val said, pulling him from his regrets. "Where are the wineglasses? I think we should celebrate."

He spun around to face her. "Get out."

"What?"

"It's the absolute height of arrogance for you to come here tonight without calling or even asking if I want you here. I didn't wait around for you to come back." This was not technically the truth, but it was true as of this moment.

"Andrew, please. I made a—"

"Oh yeah, you made a mistake. You were lured by the myth of the big, strong man. Well, I'm sorry it didn't work out for you. But as you can see, I've redecorated my apartment and my life. I've moved on, and I don't want to go back to the way things were."

"But I love you."

"Well, if that's what you call love, then I want nothing to do with it."

"But—"

He put up his hand. "Stop. I need to make this clear, Val. I'm not your fallback guy. Just because your fantasy alpha dude turned into a nightmare doesn't mean you can come back here and pretend you respected and loved me. You did no such thing."

"Of course I—"

"No, you didn't. You cheated on me, and then you dumped me."

"But, Andrew, you know people can forgive and get back together. You tell people this all the time."

"Yeah, I do. And most of the time it's not possible. And when it does work, it's because people have decided to meet in the middle. But here's the thing—I'm not interested in meeting in the middle. To be honest, although I loved you deeply at one time, there's someone else I care about now. And besides, I don't think I could ever trust you again."

"There's someone else? Who?"

"That's none of your business. Right now, I'd like you to leave. Please."

Val started to cry right on cue, and Andrew had to stifle his usual reaction. Why was it that crying women and children always called him to action? He stood firm in the middle of his kitchen and reminded himself that Val had often manipulated him with her tears. Val's sobs were nothing but a big, fake act.

He folded his arms and waited for her to compose herself. It didn't take long before the tears dried up, and Val scowled at him like a petulant child. "You'll be sorry," she said.

"I'm already sorry," he said. But he wasn't thinking about Val.

Brandon was repentant during the drive from D.C. to Shenandoah Falls. He apologized every few minutes—for his behavior on their wedding day, and for going to Bermuda without Laurie, and for not being honest about his fears and the way the over-the-top wedding plans had fed them.

He professed his love and stupidity in alternating speeches that did nothing but inflame Laurie's already pounding head.

When he pulled the Camaro to the curb in front of their house on Rice Street, he came to a jarring and abrupt stop and said, "Let's elope. We could fly out to Vegas next week and surprise everyone." He set the brake, turned in his seat, took Laurie's hand, and kissed it. "Say yes, please."

She studied him. He was a nice guy. Forget what Courtney said about Nice Guys, Not. Courtney was wrong. There were no perfect guys. Marriage was an exercise in compromise—something neither of her parents had ever been able to accomplish. Marriage was give, and take, and accepting your partner's foibles and imperfections. She loved Brandon. Why shouldn't she marry him?

He was a good man. He hadn't cheated on her. And

really, they'd been together for so many years, during which they'd fought and made up countless times. Not taking a man back after he apologized was something Mom did. Over and over again.

Besides, marrying Brandon would solve so many problems. The house would get renovated without her having to do it all. She could concentrate on her career and not have to worry about dating. She wouldn't ever end up lonely and jaded like Courtney.

"Okay," she found herself saying.

"You mean it? You'll marry me?"

To her surprise, the idea of marrying Brandon wasn't repulsive at all. In fact, her neck and shoulder muscles eased. "Yeah. But not in Vegas," she said.

"Why not?"

Really? She'd capitulated to him and he wanted to argue? She rolled her head in his direction. "Look, I've got a headache, okay? Why don't we just let things settle tonight, and you can call me tomorrow? We can go out for brunch at the Red Fern or something. We can talk, instead of yell."

"Yes, okay, that sounds great, Laurie, really. I'll call you tomorrow." And then, instead of getting out of the Camaro and walking her to her door, he just sat there waiting for her to leave. But then, when had he ever opened doors for her? Just because Tobin and Andrew had done stuff like that didn't make them better men. Neither one of them had stuck with her over the years like Brandon had.

She opened the car door. "Good night," she said and hurried inside to her own bed, where she collapsed. Her head hurt too much for her to cry over Andrew. What was there to cry over anyway? One night together with no strings attached. And clearly he wasn't ready or even able to settle down with someone. And Laurie knew one thing—she didn't want to spend the next five or ten years out there dating one guy after another. She did not want to become Courtney Wallace.

With that settled in her mind, she finally fell asleep and didn't wake up until Brandon called at 9:00 a.m. It was nice to have him back. It was comforting. It was definitely safe. She agreed to meet him at the tavern, where she ordered the Benedict Cumberbatch for a second time, and they talked for two hours, settling their dispute face-to-face like a couple of adults.

They agreed not to elope. Instead, Laurie called Courtney and discovered that the inn could accommodate a small afternoon wedding reception in the solarium the following Sunday. Laurie booked the chapel and the reception space. Courtney was curt and professional as ever, but disapproval dripped from every word she said.

Chapter Twenty-Two————

Edward called Andrew on Monday afternoon and invited him out to dinner at an East Indian restaurant near the White House. Andrew didn't think twice about the invitation because neither he nor Edward could cook. It wasn't uncommon for him to meet up with his younger brother for dinner.

But dinner at the Bombay Club was a little over-the-top for an average weeknight. It was one of those places that catered to the K Street lobby crowd and featured raj-era decor, potted palms, and turbaned waiters. Andrew often brought clients here for business lunches because of the wide spaces between tables and the quiet, restrained atmosphere. People didn't have to shout to have a conversation at the Bombay Club.

Which was probably why Edward had selected the place. In all likelihood, Andrew was about to be taken to the woodshed by his little brother. The guys were probably upset by what had happened on Saturday night when he'd stormed off to rescue Laurie. No doubt, Brandon had also filled them all in on the scene that had ensued.

He didn't want to have the inevitable conversation. He wasn't sure how he could navigate through the suddenly treacherous currents and shoals of his personal relationships. It was stunning how screwed up his world had become since Brandon jilted Laurie.

He expected Edward to be sitting at one of the two-person tables that ringed the dining room, but the moment Andrew stepped through the restaurant's front door, he knew he'd been sabotaged. Everyone was there—Jason, Matt, Edward, and Brandon—plus they'd brought along Daniel and Roxy for good measure. All six of his closest friends sat at a big, round table right in the middle of the dining room.

As Andrew approached the table, Brandon stood up, a big smile on his face as he raised a glass of wine. "The man of the hour has arrived."

"What's going on?" Andrew stopped when he reached the table and cast his gaze over the group of friends and family. He loved them all. He couldn't imagine losing them. And he'd been skating so close to that possibility the last few weeks.

"We're celebrating," Roxy said.

"What are we celebrating?" He came around the table to stand behind the one unoccupied seat, right beside Brandon.

"What are you doing this coming Sunday?" Brandon asked.

"Watching the Redskins?"

"Sorry, buddy, but you'll have to give that up," Brandon said with a big grin, "I need you to be my best man."

A surge of adrenaline hit Andrew's bloodstream, making

every one of his nerve endings ache and buzz. "Who are you marrying?" Andrew asked.

His family roared with laughter. "Laurie, you dumbass. Who else?" Brandon said, slapping Andrew on the back.

The adrenaline evaporated, leaving Andrew feeling shaky.

"Hey, man, don't look so surprised. After all, you're the guy who wouldn't give up on getting us back together. You and your plan helped me see the light. I'm really sorry I didn't believe you on Saturday, but Laurie told me the whole thing. And then Roxy confirmed everything, especially about Laurie's fake date with Danny, which convinced Laurie to have a heart-to-heart with Roxy, and now look at them."

Andrew shifted his gaze toward Danny. He had his arm draped around Roxy's shoulders, and he looked happier than he had in months.

"So in a way, you even helped take care of my sister. You're a great guy, Andrew."

"By the way," Danny said, "Roxy and I have decided to get married too. I'm trying to convince her to elope."

Roxy gave Danny a long, sober look. "That's not going to happen."

"I was afraid you'd say that."

"Thank you, man," Brandon said, interrupting the love-birds. He pulled Andrew into a big man-hug. "You're the best friend a guy could ever have."

When Brandon let go, Andrew scanned the table a second time. "Where is she?" he asked.

"Oh, she couldn't make it tonight. She's got some teaching thing, and since the wedding is next Sunday, she's pretty busy."

"But we thought we'd surprise you," Edward said.

A moment later, Andrew found himself sitting at a table surrounded by joyous friends and family. The wine flowed. Toasts were made. Dinner was ordered and consumed. But Andrew was too numb to connect with the reality unfolding around him. Was he the only one at the table who missed Laurie?

She should have been there.

He sipped his wine and realized that the idea of Laurie marrying Brandon was so repulsive to him that he could hardly contain himself. How could she tie herself to a man who had taken her for granted? How could she forgive a man who had humiliated her in public? Maybe it was a good thing she hadn't come. Because if she'd been there, Andrew might have spoiled the evening by asking her difficult questions. By second-guessing her. And that would be wrong.

Because he'd seen couples reconcile all the time, even when the facts of their relationship seemed starkly negative. So it wasn't his place to judge Laurie. But he was certainly entitled to his feelings. He recognized that tight, cramped feeling in his chest as the worst kind of jealousy.

The next morning, Andrew awakened with the headache to end all headaches. So much for his plan to drown his sorrows. He'd had more than one glass of wine at the restaurant, and then he'd come home and polished off a bottle of bourbon. Drinking alone was a bad sign.

At least he hadn't broken any furniture or dishes this time around, probably because his current situation was so different from Val's betrayal. Laurie had never promised him anything. She'd never lived with him. She'd never imposed her rosebud china on him.

Which was sort of the point, because Laurie wasn't the

rosebud china type, although he couldn't say for certain what her china looked like.

Not that he cared about china. It was just that . . .

Hell.

Laurie was a lot like him. She was neat. She made hospital corners on her bed. She picked up her clothes. When she fell apart, she didn't blubber or resort to fake tears. In fact, when Laurie fell apart, she shut down or she retreated into herself. And when she cried, it was heart wrenching.

Hell.

He made it to work and sat in his office, his head pounding, his mouth dry, his body aching as he stared at his cell phone weighing the pros and cons of calling her. He was locked in a battle between his good and evil angels when Noah came bursting into his office with such fanfare that Andrew's head almost exploded.

"You're being hailed as the hero of the hour," he said. "If I'm to believe Brandon, you are the main reason my daughter is going to be married next Sunday."

Andrew stared at Noah. For some reason, his boss didn't seem all that pleased. But what the hell, Andrew had given up trying to figure out what Noah wanted. A tight ball of anger formed in his chest.

"What's the matter?" Noah said. "We've brought young lovers back together. Aren't you happy?"

What the hell was Noah's game anyway? It was almost as if he were goading Andrew or something. It worked because Andrew's anger exploded. He stood up, leaned over his desk, and spoke in a hard voice. "Yeah, I'm ecstatic. When should I start packing my stuff up for the move to Lyndon, Lyndon & Kopp? Before or after the partners' meeting?"

Noah's face went still as stone. "What are you talking about?"

"I'm talking about the crap storm that's coming when the partners meet at the end of October. You took me off the AVIEN negotiations, and I had a lot of time on my hands. So I did some research. Wilson Kavanaugh's profits per partner have been taking a beating the last few years. I'm thinking the partners in New York and Chicago want to shut down the D.C. office and give all of us pink slips. So naturally you've been looking for somewhere to take the mediation practice. I get it. But it's not fair to Laurie, making her marry someone she no longer wants just to advance your career. And furthermore, it's not necessary. If you hadn't wanted August to jettison Charles, he would have been happy to entertain a merger discussion. He told me that last Saturday."

Noah sat there with his mouth half open. "How did you know about the declining PPP?"

"I looked up the gross receipts figures that are publicly reported, and I did a little back-of-the-envelope math."

Noah nodded and looked away for a moment. "I'm sorry about that. There won't be any partnerships handed out this year. Not to anyone. But if you think I've been using my daughter as a way to worm my way into Lyndon, Lyndon & Kopp, then you're out of your mind."

"I don't believe you, Noah. You've lied to me for weeks about this. You've made me do things I never should have done. These last few weeks have made me see what my future would be like if I worked here. You're a master at helping people compromise, but I swear, sometimes you bully them into it. And I don't want any part of that anymore. You'll have my letter of resignation by midmorning."

"What? No. I won't accept your resignation. And besides, you'll regret—"

"I already regret the stuff I've done. It would have been better if we had refrained from manipulating Brandon and Laurie. It would have been better if they'd taken time to figure out what each of them truly wants in life."

"So you are concerned about this wedding then?"

"Of course I am. Laurie and Brandon don't know what they want because we manipulated them into thinking they wanted each other."

"Andrew, we didn't manipulate them into anything. Your job was simply to set my daughter up with some dates."

"Right, so Brandon would see the error of his ways. Look, Noah, I know how you operate. You push people around until they capitulate. And that's what we did."

Noah stared at him for a long moment. "It wasn't my intent to push Laurie or Brandon around."

"Of course not. It's never your intent. But it's what you do. You don't always listen. You don't always try to help people get what they want. You push them into accepting a deal."

Noah stroked his chin, as if in thought. "So tell me, Andrew, what do *you* want?"

Laurie. But that was impossible. "What I want is not the issue."

"No? It seems to me that what you want is the *only* issue."

"Okay, what I want is for Laurie to marry someone who respects her career, who stands by her, who takes care of her, who listens to her, and who loves her with every fiber of his being. I don't think Brandon's that guy."

"Why do you feel that way?"

"Because he doesn't respect her career. Brandon has

taken a job working on the Hill, so now Laurie is being pressured to give up her job at Winchester University. First it was the job offer in Michigan. And now it's the job in Winchester. Noah, wake up. Brandon is jacking your daughter around, and you're facilitating it. Do you want her unhappiness on your hands? Or do you just not care?"

Noah's impassive face changed radically. A spark flared in his gray eyes. "Don't you dare impugn my integrity. And for the record, there is nothing I wouldn't do for my daughter's happiness."

"Okay, then you should talk to her. Right away. Before it's too late. And for once in your life, listen to what she says instead of trying to impose your will on her. Honestly, you're no better than Brandon. Someone needs to get up into her face and tell her not to give up her life just to be safe."

"Have you said this to her?"

"No. After what I've done, I have no right to speak with your daughter."

"What have you done?"

"I've taken advantage of her."

Noah's stood up, his face so red, Andrew was concerned for his health. He was clearly losing control of his rage. But when Noah spoke, his voice was measured and hard. "I think you should leave. Right now. I don't need your resignation. You're fired."

Chapter Twenty-Three

Planning a wedding in a week had its good points and bad points. There was no time to be OCD about anything, which was good. On the bad side of things, Emma, Jessica, and Madison were not able to make it on Sunday. Still, Laurie forced herself to look on the bright side. Her friends were of the unanimous opinion that any man who left his bride standing at the altar was a dickhead and a scumbag who could never be redeemed. Her girlfriends were, by and large, an unforgiving group.

Of course, Roxy would be there, and she was very excited about the wedding, but her charity group had a big fund-raiser event in D.C. on Saturday. So instead of a pre-wedding party with friends, Laurie ended up going to dinner with Mom and Dad at the Red Fern Inn. Dining with both parents at the same time and place was unusual. But this was, after all, a special occasion. Even if it didn't feel all that special.

"Sweetie," Mom said as they sipped their cocktails, "I

can't believe you didn't go to the salon today. What are we going to do with your hair?"

"Do we have to do anything with it? I mean, I will wash it tonight and put some hot rollers in it tomorrow."

"But you opted for the baby's breath and the crown braids instead of a veil, and the last time—"

"Let's not talk about the last time, shall we?" Dad said in a blunt voice.

"I wasn't talking about the last time, Noah. I was merely pointing out that—"

"Mom, please. Dad's right. Courtney will come up with something. She's resourceful."

"But—"

"Zip it, Susan," Dad said.

Mom zipped it but the tension at the table rose perceptibly. It was a sad fact that being with Mom and Dad together at the same time was always three times harder than being with either one of them alone.

They picked at each other constantly. And Dad, who was usually so self-contained, never managed to keep his temper around Mom. For a man who made a living seeing both sides of every argument, Dad had a huge blind spot when it came to Mom. And maybe that was because he loved her. And Mom was often so difficult to love.

As she watched her parents' tense body language, she realized she could have used someone like Andrew when she was nine years old. Andrew had a talent for smoothing over the angry words people hurled at each other. Laurie had never been able to defuse Mom and Dad. And in a lot of ways, she'd been the collateral damage when their relationship exploded.

"So," Dad said, playing with the olive in his martini, "I hear that Brandon has gone to work for Heather Lyndon as her chief of staff. Is he planning to commute from Shenandoah Falls to D.C.?"

"No. He'll be staying in D.C. for a while and coming home on weekends. We need to flip the house and resell it."

"But what about your job?" Dad asked.

Yeah, what about her job? Good question. "I'm thinking about resigning."

"What?" Dad's voice rose, and several other patrons turned to look at him.

"Keep your voice down, Noah, really," Mom said.

"You can't resign."

"Why can't she?" Mom asked.

Dad rolled his eyes. "Susan, I realize that you have never had any ambitions in life, but Laurie—"

"That's not true, Noah, and you know it. I was an editor once. And when we moved to D.C., I did my best to raise our daughter. You were absent most of the time."

"Yeah, well, when you moved back to New York, all you did was find ways to spend my money."

"Guys, please, can we not argue?" Laurie asked in a small voice.

Her parents retreated to their corners of the table, where they sipped their cocktails in silence for several moments.

Finally Dad cleared his throat and asked, "Honey, I'm starting to think that I've missed something important. Someone recently told me that I need to listen to you better. So I'm listening now. Why on earth are you thinking about resigning?"

"Because it's a sixty-mile commute to D.C., and to be honest, I hate my department chair."

"You do?"

"He's a misogynist of the worst kind. He's as much as told me that if I want the department's help to get research money, I'll have to share the credit with him, even if he does none of the work."

"I had no idea," Dad said gently.

"That's not fair. You should tell him to screw off," Mom said.

It was nice to have them both on her side. And really, it would be terrific if Dad would spend more time listening to her. For a man who made a living listening to people, he sure had tuned her out for much of her life. So she offered up a small slice of her thinking.

"I've decided to go for the grant on my own. And I think I have a shot at getting the money. That would be better than telling him to screw off."

"That sounds like a good plan," Dad said. "Which begs the question. Why walk away now?"

She shrugged. She didn't have a very good answer. And Dad was listening well enough to know it.

"Honey," Dad said, "I guess what I'm asking is why Brandon gets to work for Heather and you have to give up your job?"

"Oh, for God's sake, Noah, don't go messing things up again. You've been manipulating everyone for weeks, and it's only Laurie's cool head that has salvaged this situation. Honestly, I'm dying to know how you managed to get on Pam Lyndon's wrong side."

"What?" Laurie sat up straighter in her chair.

"She's furious with Dad for firing her nephew."

Laurie glared at her father. "You fired Andrew?"

"He resigned first." But Dad's voice sounded strained. "To be honest, honey, I got mad at him when he suggested that he'd taken advantage of you. Did he do that?"

"What? No. He didn't take advantage of me." God, did Andrew really think that?

"Then why does he believe he did?"

"I have no clue. Andrew and I are good friends."

"And he's the reason you and Brandon have decided to reconcile."

She nodded. "Yes. But, Dad, I can't believe he resigned. He wanted a partnership so badly."

"He's very clever, you know. He figured out that the mediation practice is in trouble and there won't be any partnerships handed out this year. So he probably figured he didn't have much to lose."

"The mediation practice is in trouble?"

"Honey, it's a sad fact of life that litigators make more money than mediators. And Wilson Kavanaugh has gobbled up a bunch of litigators recently. They seem to think that the mediation practice is deadweight. I'm in negotiations with several smaller firms to see if I can find a landing spot. I expect to be handed my walking papers the first week of November."

She looked down at her drink but didn't say a word. Poor Andrew.

"Laurie, look at me, please," Dad said.

She reluctantly looked up.

"Why have you made all the compromises in your relationship with Brandon?" he asked.

Tears suddenly filled her eyes. "Because I have to."

"She's got that right," Mom said sourly.

"No, you don't. For instance, I'm suddenly wondering why you didn't take that professorship at the University of Michigan."

"Come on, Dad. Do you think Brandon would ever have moved to Ann Arbor?"

"I don't know. Ann Arbor is a very nice town. It's bigger than Shenandoah Falls. The country's largest university is right there. It's probably on some list of great American university towns. Why wouldn't Brandon move there in order to support your career?"

"Oh, for God's sake, Noah. Men don't do that. It's a fact of life. Women have been compromising themselves for eons."

"Okay, I suppose that's true on a macro level. But in my experience, it's not healthy when one party makes all the concessions and the other party doesn't make any. Are you sure marrying Brandon is what you want? Or are you just taking the easy way out instead of going after what you really want?" His voice sounded oddly gruff.

Mom threw back her head and laughed. "You're joking, right?"

"Why would I joke?"

"Oh, no reason, except that I distinctly recall your view about my editing job all those years ago. I didn't make much money, of course, so in your view, my job was not terribly important. While your job, setting up Wilson Kavanaugh's Washington office, was way more important. Honestly, Noah, I don't think you even consulted me. I turned around, and it was a done deal."

Dad sat there blinking at Mom as if he were seeing her for the first time in years. "Is that why you left me?"

Laurie waited for the moment when Mom trotted out the usual accusations of Dad having an affair with his secretary. But they didn't come. Instead, Mom's eyes teared up. "I followed you because I loved you, Noah. But it's hard to love someone who tells you you're not worth anything. After a while, you start believing it." She pushed up from the table. "Excuse me. I need to powder my nose." She fled.

And to Laurie's utter surprise, Dad stood up and ran after Mom, leaving Laurie alone. Again.

*   *   *

Andrew joined Brandon for a couple of beers at the Jay Bird Café on Saturday night but he left early in the evening, after assigning the groom's care and feeding to Matt. No doubt Brandon would show up tomorrow morning hungover, but Andrew refused to feel sorry for the guy.

Instead he went home to his father's house. It was after 10:00 p.m., but Dad was still in his office peering into his computer screen through a pair of half-moon glasses. Andrew knocked on the door frame of the open door and said, "Hey."

Dad looked away from the computer. "Hi. You're home early." He pushed his glasses up onto his forehead, where they rested against his eyebrows. He looked a little comical.

Andrew strolled into the room and collapsed into the big leather chair by Dad's desk.

"What's the matter?" Dad asked, as if he could sense Andrew's deep disquiet.

Andrew drew in a breath and let it out slowly. "I need your advice."

Dad leaned back in his chair, a smile curving his lips. "That's music to every father's ear."

"What would you say if I told you I was thinking about calling Uncle Charles and asking for a job in the Virginia office of LL&K?"

Dad huffed out a breath. "Son, I'm pretty sure that Noah Wilson would take you back if you asked him."

"What makes you say that? I said some pretty over-the-top things to him when I quit."

"Because I happen to know that he has very high regard for you."

"Well, maybe not anymore. Besides, Wilson Kavanaugh is in financial distress. So it might be better for me to look for something else. Like, for instance, that open associate position at Lyndon, Lyndon & Kopp."

"So you don't want to be a mediator anymore?" Dad leaned back in his swivel seat and took off his eyeglasses.

"I do. But I feel as if I've broken the basic tenet of mediation. I allowed myself to get involved in a dispute where I was not impartial. And I did it for wholly selfish reasons."

Dad didn't say anything for a very long moment while he played with his glasses. His mouth curved downward in a thoughtful frown. "This wouldn't happen to have something to do with Brandon and Laurie, would it?" he finally asked.

"It might have something to do with that."

"Might? Son, you stepped in to save the bride the instant Brandon abandoned her. But, of course, she is your boss's daughter, after all. So maybe I'm wrong about you. Maybe all that kindness you showed to Laurie on her first wedding day was just your way of sucking up to Noah."

"No," he said. "That was before—" He bit off the rest of his sentence.

"Before what?"

He let go of a long sigh. "Before Noah asked me to do whatever I could to get Laurie and Brandon back together."

"And this was a problem because . . . ?"

Andrew leaned forward in his chair and braced his elbows on his knees and studied the carpet. "Dad," he said, "if some guy left Amy at the altar, would you be all hell-bent to get her back together with the bastard?"

Dad chuckled, and Andrew looked up. "Okay, I see what you mean. I have to admit, if any guy dumped Amy at the altar, I would probably go after him with a baseball bat. But then keep in mind that I'm not a fount of wisdom when it comes to stuff like this. After all, I tried to break up Amy and Dusty, and I also tried to manipulate her into marrying that Carson jerk."

"Okay, I can almost understand that, Dad. I mean, you tried to keep Amy safe when she got involved with Dusty because you didn't think Dusty was right for her. But Noah wanted Laurie married to Brandon even after Brandon dumped her and humiliated her."

Dad squinted at him. "Are you entirely sure that's what Noah wanted? I mean, on the day of the wedding, Noah didn't have a baseball bat but he went after Brandon with his fists. Uncle Mark and I intervened."

"So I heard."

Dad leaned forward on his desk. "Okay, so where did you get the idea that Noah wanted Laurie and Brandon to reconcile?"

Andrew thought back to that day when Noah first broached the subject. "He told me that he wanted Laurie to get out and date people. I remember he asked me to set her up on dates with my friends. But he also said he thought it might make Brandon realize the error in his thinking. Noah really seemed to believe that Brandon's cold feet stemmed from the stress of planning a wedding, not because Brandon had fallen out of love with Laurie."

Dad stood up. "I think we need a drink," he said, getting out of his chair and crossing the carpet to the small bar hidden away in his bookshelf. "Bourbon?"

"Sure."

Dad poured the drinks and crossed the room, sitting in the second chair. "I think I can provide a little bit of clarity for you."

"About what?"

"About the situation you find yourself in." Dad leaned back in his chair. "First of all, let me assure you that Noah's only objective has been to see his daughter happy. But I'm afraid things got a bit muddled when your aunt Pam interjected herself into things."

Andrew sat up straight. "What?"

"Come on, Andrew, surely you realized that Aunt Pam has been skulking around creating chaos behind the scenes."

Andrew frowned. He did know this, but he'd discounted it. Pam had certainly suggested that Laurie go out with Danny. And on two separate occasions, Noah had mentioned speaking with Pam. Damn. Why hadn't he connected the dots?

Dad chuckled. "I know. It's so easy to ignore her. But you do that at your peril. The truth is, after the wedding debacle, Pam happily volunteered to take charge of Laurie and find her a suitable husband."

"Okay. That sounds exactly like her."

"Well, of course your uncle Mark wasn't about to let Pam do that. So he suggested that Laurie didn't need a husband; she just needed to go out on a few dates. He's the one who suggested that Noah rely on you to find dates for Laurie. His theory was that you would make sure Laurie remained safe at all times because that's the kind of man you are." Dad gave him a proud smile.

"Uncle Mark set me up?"

"Yes, I'm afraid so. But his motives were pure."

At a loss for words, Andrew drained his drink.

"Good thinking. Let's have another." Dad headed to the bar and returned with the bottle of bourbon.

He refreshed their drinks and then said, "I'm afraid it gets worse."

"Worse? How long have you know about this?"

Dad's face reddened. "I'm afraid I've known for quite

some time. But it seemed like the plan was working. Laurie was getting out and having some fun, and Brandon was losing his mind. But then everything changed. I should have put a stop to it then, but..." He let go of a long sigh.

"How did it change?"

"When Matt saw you dancing with Laurie, Pam started to wonder if you and Laurie were becoming more than friends. And then I gather she ran into Laurie at the coffee shop one day and became convinced that you and Laurie were falling in love because Laurie insisted that you were just friends." Dad rolled his eyes. "I'm sorry. Sometimes your aunt makes no sense at all. It seems to me if a person says she's just friends with someone, it ought to be taken at face value." Dad finished his drink.

"Wait," Andrew said. "If Pam thought I had a thing for Laurie, why did she set me up with Lindsay?"

"That, my dear boy, was part of what became known as Plan B."

"Plan B?" Andrew poured himself another glass of bourbon. Something told him that he didn't want to remain sober.

"Plan B began with an effort to ascertain if you and Laurie were more than merely friends," Dad said. "When neither Noah nor Pam were able to determine this, they decided to see how you'd react if each of you were set up with someone else."

"Tobin Grant," Andrew said, his face growing warm.

"Exactly. Noah sent Laurie on a date with Tobin because Tobin is your rival. He expected you to react. But you didn't."

"And then Pam set me up with Lindsay."

"Yes. But Laurie showed up to the ball with that Marine. It became obvious that Plan B was a figment of your aunt's imagination. This should have surprised no one, given Pam's matchmaking track record."

"Right." Andrew poured another drink and downed it. He was starting to feel numb, which, all things considered, wasn't a bad way to feel.

"Laurie really surprised us all the night of the ball showing up with that Marine. I'm sure that was entirely for Brandon's benefit. But, wow, she looked quite beautiful that night, didn't she?"

"Yes, she did."

"So you see, there wasn't any reason for you to resign from Wilson Kavanaugh. And it's no wonder that Noah finally lost his temper on the day he fired you, if you accused him of manipulating his daughter. But I'm sure you and Noah can mediate this dispute if you go to him and tell him the mistake you made."

"What mistake?"

"Andrew, you assumed that Noah wanted you to manipulate Laurie into taking Brandon back because of a law firm merger. Charles told me about that one. Honestly, Andrew, you need to take a vacation or something."

"But Noah did have conversations with August about a merger."

"So what? He wasn't using his daughter as a bargaining chip. But in any event, everything worked out just fine, despite Pam's silly Plan B, and your mistaken assumptions about Noah's motives. Brandon and Laurie managed to reconcile without anyone's help. And now everything will be back the way it's supposed to be."

"You think so?"

"Of course. Brandon and Laurie are getting married tomorrow. The only loose end is what happens to you."

"I'm not a loose end." Andrew stood up, taking the bottle with him as he left the room.

Chapter Twenty-Four

Courtney had seen a lot of crap in the two years she'd been managing events and weddings at Eagle Hill Manor. But this was the first time the parents of the bride had gone missing. Noah Wilson and his estranged wife had been seen last at the Red Fern Inn, where they had apparently quarreled and left Laurie alone to pick up the bill.

"I don't know where they could be," the bride said as she paced the little room just off the Laurel Chapel's vestibule. "I'm really worried. They haven't responded to any text messages."

Laurie wore her wedding dress, which fit a little too snugly around her boobs. She'd definitely put on a little weight since the first wedding day. And the skin around her eyes looked puffy, as if she might have cried herself to sleep last night. She'd tried to cover up the damage with concealer, but all that had done was give her a reverse raccoon look.

In short, Laurie was a mess.

Courtney wrapped her arm around the bride. "Relax. Take a few deep breaths."

"I can't. The dress is too tight. I knew I shouldn't have binged on ice cream and pizza."

"Yeah, well, it's all going to be okay. I've called Ryan, and he's done me a favor and put out a BOLO on your parents. The SFPD is searching for them right now. Normally they'd have to be missing longer than overnight for a search like that."

"Thanks," Laurie said with a shaky breath.

Her phone buzzed. "Oh, thank God," she said, snatching it from her purse. "Damn, it's not Mom. It's Roxy."

Courtney watched as Laurie answered the phone. She couldn't hear what Roxy was saying but the look that marched across Laurie's features was practically heart-breaking. Courtney had to hand it to her though; Laurie didn't cry. A lot of other brides would be sobbing by now.

"What is it?" Courtney asked when Laurie ended the call.

"It's Roxy. She's been in an accident."

"Oh my God, is she all right?"

"She's fine, but her car has been totaled. She's going to be at least an hour late."

"Damn. We can't wait."

"Why?"

"The JP is booked solid today. She squeezed you guys in as a favor. She doesn't have an hour to wait around."

"But I need a bridesmaid."

"I'll do it. Or you could ask Amy. I'm sure she'd stand up for you."

"No, it's okay. I think I'd rather have you."

"Okay. I've got to go check on some things, and I'll be

right back. Do you want me to send Amy in to sit with you?"

Laurie shook her head. "No. I'm fine."

Courtney left the bride's waiting area and headed to the little room behind the altar where the groom and best man were staged. Unlike Laurie, Brandon had plenty of friends supporting him in his last hours as a single man. It looked as if the entire Lyndon clan had come out for the occasion.

"Okay, guys, are you ready?"

They turned as one. "No," Brandon said. "Andrew's not here."

Courtney scanned the group. Brandon was right. Andrew was conspicuously missing. "Well, where the hell is he?" she asked.

"We don't know. He's not answering his texts or phone calls. The last time I saw him was last night at the Jay Bird around nine," Matt said.

"What the . . ." She refrained from saying the f-word out loud. "We don't have a father of the bride, or a bridesmaid, or a best man. This is great."

"What do you mean? Where's Roxy?" Brandon asked.

"She got into an accident. Don't worry, she's fine, but she's not going to make it in time."

Brandon started pacing. "I can get married without my sister, but not without Andrew."

"Well, you're going to have to, if you want to get married today," Courtney said. "The JP has to leave in the next thirty minutes."

"I knew we should have eloped to Vegas," Brandon said.

"It's too late for that now. You don't get to call off a wedding twice."

"Don't get snarky, Courtney," Matt said.

Courtney zeroed in on the man she'd been fantasizing

about. He looked as gorgeous as ever in a gray business suit with his dark hair curling over his forehead. She was every kind of idiot for not availing herself of all that male goodness when she'd had the chance. Chalk one up for stupidity.

"Hey, you," she said, grabbing Matt by the worsted of his suit sleeve. "You're nominated to be the best man."

Matt pulled his arm out of Courtney's grasp. "You know I really don't feel comfortable—"

"Shut up," Courtney said. "This is your penance for luring Brandon on a trip to Bermuda to pick up women, not to mention the fact that you took Lindsay to a no-tell motel."

"You are a man-hater, aren't you?"

"Yup. That's me. Okay, does someone here have the rings?"

"I've got them," Brandon said. "Good thing I didn't give them to Andrew last night." He handed the rings to Matt.

"Okay, you guys, it's show time. Get your butts out there. Right now." She literally pushed Matt and Brandon out the door into the sanctuary, following after them. She cued the organist and then hurried to the back of the church.

As she opened the door to the bride's waiting room, panic spiraled through her. Laurie looked like a zombie going through the motions. She was as white as her dress, with two ugly splotches of color on her cheeks. The universe had spent all morning throwing impediments at this wedding. Why the hell had Courtney been working so hard to make it happen?

Laurie studied herself in the full-length mirror. The cleaner had done an amazing job on her wedding dress. No one would ever know that she'd thrown up on it. The Alençon lace still dripped from the gown's bodice, and the Swarovski crystals still sent colorful sparks of light up the walls and ceilings. The tulle skirt still puffed out in true princess fashion.

But she didn't want to be a princess anymore. And really, the woman staring back at her didn't look like a princess.

The door opened, and Courtney stepped inside. "We can't wait for your parents anymore. The JP is already getting antsy. You'll have to give yourself away."

"Okay," she said in a small voice.

"And there's one other snafu."

"Oh?"

"The best man is missing too. Matt's standing in."

"Andrew's not here?" Laurie didn't know whether to laugh or cry. She'd lost a lot of sleep last night wondering how it would feel to walk down the aisle and have to see Andrew standing there while she married Brandon. So maybe it was a good thing.

Or maybe he'd had an accident too. "Do we know where he is?" she asked.

"Apparently not. Honestly, I'm starting to think that Shenandoah Falls has been invaded by body snatchers or aliens or something."

"I'm kind of worried about him. And Mom and Dad. At least we know where Roxy is."

"Look, we've now got fifteen minutes to make this happen before the JP turns into a pumpkin. So are you ready to rock and roll? Are you sure you want to go through with this?"

"Yes," Laurie said, squaring her shoulders. "I just want to get this over with. I just want to be married and settled, you know?"

Courtney shook her head. "No, I don't, really. But okay, whatever you say. Let me give the JP the high sign and cue the processional music."

Courtney left the room, and Amy came in bearing her bouquet.

"Have you heard from Andrew?" she asked.

Amy shook her head. "No one seems to know where he is. Dad saw him last night but he was gone this morning. Courtney pressed Matt into service," she said with a smile. "Everyone is amused by that."

From beyond the open door, the unmistakable strains of Pachelbel's Canon in D greeted her ears, although today's organist wasn't nearly the musician she'd had for her first wedding day.

"It's time," Amy said and helped Laurie with her train. Meanwhile Courtney grabbed Roxy's bouquet and hotfooted down the aisle in her black business suit.

"Okay, it's your turn," Amy whispered. And for the second time in six weeks, Laurie headed down the aisle toward her groom. She kept her gaze straight ahead, focused on Brandon, thankful that Andrew wasn't there to distract her.

Brandon looked so handsome standing there with a sheen of tears in his bright blue eyes. His mouth curled at the corner and exposed his adorable dimple. He winked at her.

Wait. Stop. Why did she resent the fact that Brandon was behaving exactly the way she'd fantasized a million times? Those fantasies had fallen apart six weeks ago.

With each step, her dress seemed to weigh her down. The bodice once again morphed into a tourniquet shutting off her air supply. By the time she reached the altar and the music faded, she felt just like a small creature caught in a very large trap.

Andrew drove all the way back to D.C. in the early hours of Sunday morning. His head pounded for all sixty miles from the bourbon he'd anesthetized himself with last night. His gut churned with anger.

He'd been used. By Noah. By Pam. By his own father.

And for what? To get Laurie and Brandon back together even though any fool could see they were wrong for each other. He would not, could not, stand there beside Brandon and watch it happen.

But coming home didn't make him feel any better. He paced, and then he got out a few dishes and threw them against the tile floor. Venting his anger didn't make him feel any better.

He had to stop the wedding. Not boycott it.

Dammit.

It was after ten o'clock when he fired up the Audi and headed west. There had been a four-car pileup on Route 7 just west of Tyson's Corner that backed up traffic for miles. He decided to backtrack and get on the Dulles Toll Road. And good thing too because he hit more traffic in Leesburg. It was after noon by the time he pulled the Audi into the parking lot at the Laurel Chapel.

He raced up the steps, busted through the doors, and tore down the aisle like a crazy man.

The moment he saw Laurie's beautiful face, something in his chest eased. It didn't look as if they'd exchanged rings yet.

"Am I too late?" he asked in a breathless voice.

"Not at all, dude," Matt said. "But hey, you could have dressed better."

It wasn't until that moment that Andrew realized he was wearing the same jeans and T-shirt from last night.

"Here, why don't you take the rings?" Matt said.

"I don't want the rings," Andrew replied. He looked at the officiant. "Have we gotten to the *speak now or forever hold your peace* part?" he asked.

"No," she said, "I was just getting to that. Did you wish to raise an objection?" An enigmatic smile played on her lips.

"Yeah, I do."

"What?" Brandon got all up in his face but Andrew ignored him. He was too busy looking at Laurie, where the strain of the last few weeks showed in the dark circles under her eyes and in the pallor of her face. She looked as if she was about to go down for the count.

Andrew stepped around Brandon and captured Laurie by the shoulders just as she started to collapse. He lifted her up into his arms and would have carried her off like a rogue pirate, but her dress had a gigantic train on it. So he ended up standing there staring at the congregation that was composed almost entirely of his family.

He noted, with some consternation, that the older generation of Lyndons—Charles, Mark, Pam, and his father—were smiling. Even Brandon's father seemed amused.

Andrew turned toward Brandon, who might have been the only person in the room who didn't have a smile on his face. His expression could only be called "thunderstruck." His mouth hung open, his brow knitted into a frown, and a slow spark of realization lit up his gaze.

"You lied to me," Brandon said. It wasn't a question.

"No, not entirely," Andrew said.

"What does that mean?"

Andrew didn't answer because the officiant said, "Excuse me, but I think we need to take the bride someplace where she can lie down and maybe get something to eat. I'll bet she didn't eat a thing this morning. Once we get her blood sugar up, she'll be good to go. I see this happen a lot."

"I'd be happy to take her someplace to recover," Andrew

said. "If someone would do something about the dress's train."

"No, I'll take her. She's *my* bride," Brandon declared.

Andrew glared at his best friend. "Yeah, but possession is nine-tenths of the law."

Just then, Amy came flying down the aisle. "Come on, I'll open up the Churchill Suite. It's empty right at the moment. Courtney, grab her train."

"Got it," Courtney said from behind.

"No, wait. You can't just whisk her away like that," Brandon said. "I mean, this is my wedding, for God's sake."

"Is it?" Courtney asked in a tight voice. "You're the guy who dumped her and then went off with Matt to pick up chicks. What happened, Brandon? Did you realize just how lonely Matt was?"

"Wait a sec," Matt said. "I'm not lonely."

"Maybe not yet. But I hope one day you are. Because, honestly, guys like you irritate the crap out of me. Come on, Andrew. Let's get out of here."

Andrew started up the aisle just as Ryan Pierce came through the open doors with Noah Wilson and his ex-wife following. Susan and Noah looked as if they'd slept in their clothes.

"I'm sorry, y'all," Ryan said with a little smile. "Courtney called me a while ago, frantic because the father of the bride had gone missing. She gave me a description of the man's car, and it turned out we had him and the missus in the county lockup."

"For what?" Andrew asked.

"For indecent—"

"Shut up," Noah said. "This is my daughter's wedding. Uh, I think?" Noah looked around, taking in the chaotic scene.

"Oh my God, what have you done to Laurie? Unhand her this minute," Laurie's mother said. Then she frowned. "Why are you carrying her and not Brandon?"

"Yes, Andrew," a voice came from somewhere behind him that he immediately recognized as his father's. "We're all wondering that."

Just then Laurie's eyes fluttered open. They were the most beautiful shade of hazel. "Andrew," she whispered.

"I'm here. I've got you. And when you hear the story I have to tell you, you won't believe it."

The corner of her lip curled up. "Oh, thank God. I had this awful dream that I married Brandon."

"What?" Brandon said. "It's not a dream. I mean, we're not married yet. But we will—"

"No," Andrew said.

"No, what?"

"No. I'm saying no. You and Laurie are not getting married."

"What are you saying? Did you and Laurie…" Brandon didn't finish the sentence, and Andrew wasn't inclined to finish it for him.

Instead he looked down at Laurie. Now that she was awake, she shifted a little and encircled his neck with her arms. Her head rested on his shoulder, and the weight felt perfect. She gazed into his eyes with her mouth slightly parted. He wanted to kiss her. To claim her. To make her his own.

"Oh, look at them," Aunt Pam said. "They are so darling together. Noah, I think our Plan B actually worked."

Laurie blinked. "What plan?"

"Ignore her," Andrew said. "Besides, I have something important I need to say. That night before Emma's wedding, I lied to you. The truth is, I'm just not very good at relationships without strings attached. After that night, you were constantly on my mind. I wanted to find a way to tell you how I felt. I started to call you dozens of times, but one thing after another got in the way. Val turned up, and Brandon changed his mind, and…and then I decided it would be best to keep my mouth shut.

"Everyone seemed so happy that you and Brandon were getting back together. And I knew if I said anything, I would make everyone angry or sad or something. Anyway…" He stopped talking, suddenly aware of the audience in the church, hanging on every word he said. He took a big breath. "Laurie, the truth is, I've fallen in love with you."

Laurie caressed his cheek with her cool, soft hand. "I have a confession to make too. I guess I'm not as modern and adult as I thought. I know what I said about no strings and experience and all that, but…I fell in love with you too. Last Saturday all I wanted was for you to tell Brandon to get lost, only…"

"Only I was trying to mediate when I should have been telling you how I felt. Is that it?"

She nodded.

"Okay, let me tell you exactly how I feel, Laurie. I think you deserve someone who will support your career, and respect you, and cherish you. And I've been sitting back, watching one guy after another fail on that score. Especially Brandon.

"So here's the thing. I've resigned from Wilson Kavanaugh, and I'm pretty sure that there's an open position at Lyndon, Lyndon & Kopp because August told me last week that if I ever left Wilson Kavanaugh, he wanted to recruit me. So we can be together, and you don't have to give up your job or your research career."

A few tears escaped her eyes. "Thank you. But you

know, even though I love you, I think I need time before I try getting married again."

"Of course you do. I'm patient. I'll wait. But one day you will marry me, consider that a promise right here and right now. And one day, I also promise that we'll find a way to laugh about how we were played."

"Played?"

"Yeah. Your father and my aunt played us like a pair of violins. How are you feeling? Do you need to lie down?"

She shook her head. "No. I kind of like it up here. Do you really love me?"

"I do. Do you love me?"

"I do."

"Well, in that case, since you've both said I do, I think you should kiss the bride," the justice of the peace said with humor dripping from her voice.

And Andrew did.

Privileged Amy Lyndon needs the one thing she has never had before—a job.

Her boss, Dusty McNeil, is going to give her the one thing she never expected—love.

A preview of *A Small-Town Bride* follows.

Eagle Hill Manor had been built in the late 1800s in the style of an antebellum mansion, with a massive portico held up by a dozen classical columns. David's wife, Willow, had recently refurbished and enlarged the place, adding a gazebo and a swimming pool on the west lawn, converting an old carriage house into a sizable reception hall, and restoring the manor's many outbuildings to create guest cottages with quaint porches and window boxes.

The December issue of *Brides* magazine had done a seven-page feature article on the manor house, with photos of the inn's sweeping half-circle staircase and guest rooms decorated for the holidays and images of the nearby Laurel Chapel all blinged out for a Christmas wedding. The magazine had also praised the inn's food and beverage operations, as well as its daily breakfast service.

That famous breakfast was still being served when Amy dashed up the steps onto the front portico and through the double doors into the lobby. She got as far as the dining room and stopped. Willow was there, making the rounds of the tables and chatting up her patrons.

Even though Willow had only married into the Lyndon family, she still managed to convey the air of power and authority that every Lyndon was supposed to have. She had a master's degree from Wharton and had single-handedly exposed a huge case of Medicare fraud, winning a million-dollar settlement from Restero Corporation. A lot of that money had gone into the inn's restoration, although Willow also had a silent partner in her business—Jeff Talbert, a bona fide billionaire and another one of Amy's exceptional first cousins.

David, yet another one of Amy's brilliant first cousins, had walked away from a career in politics in order to marry Willow.

Amy couldn't imagine any man giving up anything for her. Unlike Willow, she was an ordinary person. Not brilliant and not particularly stunning. She stood barely five feet tall with absolutely no breasts to speak of and standard-issue brown hair that went limp whenever it rained. She had a degree in English from a small, liberal arts college that catered to rich students with less-than-stellar SAT scores. She did not speak in full sentences or have an Ivy League education like Willow. She was, in a word, unremarkable.

In a family composed of smart, beautiful, well-educated people, Amy was a poser.

The moment Willow spied her lurking in the doorway, she concluded her conversation and proceeded across the dining room, surprise all over her face. "Wow, Amy, you're up early. Have you come to talk about the wedding?"

Damn. Damn. Damn. Had Grady posted lies about her on Facebook? With her phone out of commission, Amy had no way of finding out. She would kill him if he had. She met Willow's probing stare. "No. I'm here to apply for the job. And for the record, I'm *not* engaged."

Willow's eyes widened a moment as she gave Amy's outfit the once-over. Right. Bad move. Showing up for a job interview wearing sneakers probably ranked right up there on the things-not-to-do-during-a-job-interview list on *Gen Y Girl.*

"Which job are you talking about?" Willow asked.

"The event planner job. I don't have a lot of work experience, but I was the social secretary of my college sorority. And I've been a maid of honor seven times. I know a lot about weddings, believe me."

Willow's green eyes softened. "Oh, Amy, I'm sorry. I had no idea you were interested in a job. I filled the event planner job yesterday. Honestly, I thought you were—"

"No, I'm not marrying Grady." She balled her hands into fists. "Everyone needs to get that in their heads, okay?"

Willow took a step forward. "Are you all right?"

"Uh, yeah, I'm good. But I need a job," she said on a shaky sigh as a tear escaped from her right eye. She turned her back on Willow, forcing herself to walk slowly toward the door breathing normally even though her pulse had taken off like a runaway jet engine.

"I have another job opening, if you're interested. It's seasonal, and it only pays minimum wage," Willow said to her back.

Amy stopped. Did she want a minimum-wage job? No. But what other choice did she have? In the let's-face-reality department, she had no skills and no real experience, and with a résumé like that, she should probably expect to start at the absolute bottom.

She turned. "I'll take it," she said.

Willow cocked her head. "Don't you even want to know what the job is?"

"Whatever it is, I'll do it."

"It's on the grounds crew. We need extra hands in the summertime to keep up with the gardening chores and set-ups for weddings and other events. It's a lot of physical labor. You up for that?"

Amy nodded. Physical labor didn't sound like much fun, especially since it had been months since she'd visited the gym. But, on the other hand, becoming a laborer was exactly the kind of thing that would annoy the crap out of Daddy. And that thought warmed her through and through. He'd be so sorry he'd locked her out of the house, drained her bank account, and left her with only enough money to buy eggs Benedict at the Red Fern.

"Okay," Willow said with a nod. "The job is yours. You'll be reporting to the Eagle Hill facilities director, Dusty McNeil."

Dusty loved his little office with the big picture window and the view of the Blue Ridge Mountains. It occupied space in the new outbuilding everyone called "the barn," because it had replaced the old one that had been there for a century. This building was much more than a barn, however. It served as the state-of-the-art headquarters for Eagle Hill Manor's facility-management team. It had Internet, a workshop, garage space for a fleet of golf carts and utility vehicles, and storage for all manner of folding chairs, tables, trellises, tents, columns, pedestals, and fountains.

It also had a kennel for Sven, Natalie Lyndon's gigantic

labradoodle, a doggie obedience school dropout three times over. Right now the dog was being a good boy, sitting at Dusty's feet while Dusty enjoyed his second cup of coffee. In Dusty's opinion, Sven needed a firmer hand and a little more attention—something ten-year-old Natalie didn't quite get and her busy parents had no time for. That was Dusty's fault in some ways, because he'd been the one to give the dog to Natalie in the first place, the Christmas before last.

He gave Sven's head a little scratch as he reviewed the upcoming schedule for the day. The Chapman-Cuddy wedding would be taking place at one o'clock in the Laurel Chapel with a small reception under a tent on the terrace to follow. The Ganis-McQuade two-hundred-guest wedding reception was scheduled to begin at six o'clock in the Carriage House.

Dusty was jotting down notes for the day's activities when Sven suddenly sprang to his feet and started barking. "Hush," he directed, just as Willow knocked on the door frame of his always-open office door.

"Got a minute?" she asked as Sven jumped up on her, earning him a scolding. "Why is he here?" she asked.

"Because he gets lonely when Natalie's at school. He keeps me company in the mornings, and I return the favor."

Willow gave him the evil eye. "Maybe you should have kept him instead of giving him to Natalie."

Yeah, maybe he should have, but he didn't have room for Sven in his tiny house or his single life. "What's up?" he asked, ignoring the gibe.

Willow strolled into the office without answering his question, and that's when Dusty noticed Amy Lyndon hovering in the doorway, eyeing Sven like he was one of those dire wolves from *Game of Thrones*. Why was Amy here?

And why had she been having breakfast at oh dark thirty at Gracie's?

She looked like a windblown juvenile delinquent in those ragged jeans and that biker-girl jacket. 'Course that only proved that he knew nothing about fashion. If Amy Lyndon was wearing it, then it cost the moon. Dusty would never understand why rich folks spent good money for jeans with holes in them.

"Good news," Willow said in a falsely bright voice. "I've found you the helper you needed." Willow gestured toward Amy. "Come on in, Amy. Dusty doesn't bite."

"Does the dog?" Amy continued to eye the pooch as if Sven might attack at any moment.

"Sit," Dusty commanded, and Sven actually complied.

"How'd you get him to do that?" Willow asked.

"I don't have any trouble with him." He cast his glance from Willow to Amy and back again. This had April Fools' prank written all over it. Willow was notorious for her April Fools' pranks. Last year she'd wrapped his entire office in Bubble Wrap. This year he'd retaliated with toilet paper. Had she visited her office yet this morning? Was this her weird way of getting him back?

"Ha-ha. Funny. But the Bubble Wrap last year was better," he said.

Willow's cheeks pinked. "Um, Dusty, this isn't an April Fools' prank. I'm not joking. I've hired Amy to be your summer intern."

Amy took a cautious step into the office and shoved her hands into her back pockets. "Yeah. Like she said, I'm not a joke."

"What?"

"You heard me," Willow said, giving him a serious stare. "I'm sure Amy has a lot to learn from you."

"But—"

Willow turned her back on him and headed toward the exit like a coward running from a fight.

"Wait, Willow," he said to her retreating back, but she didn't stop.

"You, stay right there," Dusty said, pointing at Amy and Sven at the same time. He turned and scooted after Willow, catching up to her on the gravel walk that led to the manor house.

"I need a hand, not an...itty-bitty, spoiled rich girl who's scared of dogs."

Willow lifted her chin. "Dusty, you know better than to judge her that way."

Yes, he did. But it was hard not to. "Come on, Willow. She's not strong enough to haul stuff or dig holes. She probably doesn't even weigh a hundred pounds."

"I know, but here's the deal. I never in a million years expected Amy to ever even *think* about getting a job, much less a minimum-wage job. I don't know what's gotten into her, but I think her wanting a job—any job—is a good thing. And, to be honest, getting her hands dirty will be good for her. I can't think of anyone better than you to teach her what she needs to learn."

He held Willow's gaze. "So, just to be clear," he said, "you aren't expecting me to treat her with kid gloves?"

"Did I say I wanted you to do that? She's been hired to be a seasonal helper on the maintenance crew. Do I need to e-mail you the job description?"

"She won't last a day."

"So?"

"C'mon, Willow, you can't be serious."

"I am serious. And now I've gotta go. Courtney and Brianna, the new wedding planner, need help managing today's bridezillas and their equally scary mothers."

Dusty stood on the path for a solid minute watching his oldest friend rush back to the manor house. Well, didn't this beat all?

He was scratching his head as he returned to the office and found Amy backed up against the wall with Sven sitting right in front of her. The dog wasn't doing anything but giving her his adorable cocked-head puppy-dog appraisal.

Boy, she was a tiny thing. She'd be useless in the garden. And she was clearly scared of her own shadow. How the hell was he supposed to manage her?

"The dog isn't going to hurt you. He might jump up on you from time to time, but that's only because he's friendly," he said.

She jumped as if he'd hit her with a Taser. "Uh, sorry," she said, although he couldn't figure out what she was sorry about. Then she simpered a little, which annoyed the hell out of him. He wasn't going to fall for that poor-little-rich-girl routine.

"So Willow says you need this job, huh?"

She pressed her lips together and nodded, even though her chocolate-drop eyes watered up a bit. Crying was not allowed on his crew, so he steeled his heart against the adorable, sad puppy-dog look on her face. It was a toss-up as to which of them, Amy or Sven, had the poor-pitiful-me look mastered.

"So what do you want me to do, Dusty?" she asked.

Her high-handed and familiar tone seemed at odds with that sad look on her face. It chapped his butt. "First of all, you will call me Mr. McNeil."

Did she roll her eyes? Yup, she did. He folded his arms and glared at her while the silence unreeled.

She finally cleared her throat. "May I ask a question, *Mister McNeil*?"

"Sure."

"When do I get paid?"

"Paid? You gotta work first. Payday is every other Friday." He glanced at the whiteboard calendar on the wall. "So I guess you'll get paid in a week."

She paled but said nothing.

"As for stuff you need to do, first thing is you need to go home and change clothes."

"What?"

He waved at her outfit. "I've got a golf shirt for you, and you'll need to get a pair of khaki pants and some work boots. Everyone on the grounds crew wears a uniform. We supply the shirts. You supply the rest." He walked into the back storage room and rummaged through the boxes of golf shirts until he found a men's small. It would be too large for her, but he didn't have any women's shirts. Amy was the first female on his crew.

He tossed the blue shirt at her, and she managed to catch it. "It's a busy day. We've got a one o'clock wedding at the chapel with a small reception afterward and a two-hundred-guest reception here starting at 6:00 p.m. The setups are mostly done for the early wedding, but we've got boatloads of work for the evening reception." He checked his watch. "Be back in an hour, dressed for work."

About the Author

Hope Ramsay is a *USA Today* bestselling author of heart-warming contemporary romances. Her books have won critical acclaim and publishing awards. She is married to a good ol' Georgia boy who resembles every single one of her Southern heroes. She has two grown children, a couple of demanding lap cats, and a puppy named Daisy. She lives in Virginia, where, when she's not writing, she's knitting or playing her forty-year-old Martin guitar.

You can learn more at:
HopeRamsay.com
Twitter, @HopeRamsay
Facebook.com/Hope.Ramsay

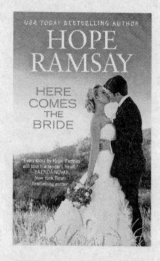

HERE COMES THE BRIDE
By Hope Ramsay

The newest novel in the Chapel of Love series from *USA Today* bestselling author Hope Ramsay will appeal to readers who love Jill Shalvis, Robyn Carr, and Brenda Novak.

Laurie Wilson is devastated when she is left at the altar. How long will it take her to realize that Best Man Andrew Lyndon is actually the better man for her?

Fall in Love with Forever Romance

THE PLAYBOY BACHELOR
By Rachel Van Dyken

New from #1 *New York Times* bestselling author
Rachel Van Dyken!

Bentley Wellington's just been coerced by his grandfather to spend the next thirty days charming and romancing a reclusive red-haired beauty who hates him. The woman he abandoned when she needed him the most. Bentley knows just as much about romance as he knows about love—*nothing*—but the more time he spends with Margot, the more he realizes that "just friends" will never be enough. Now all he has to do is convince her to trust him with her heart…Fans of Jill Shalvis, Rachel Gibson, and Jennifer Probst will love this charmingly witty and heartfelt story.

Fall in Love with Forever Romance

HARD JUSTICE
By April Hunt

Ex-SEAL commander Vince Franklin has been on some of the most dangerous missions in the world. But pretending to be the fiancé of fellow Alpha operative Charlotte Sparks on their latest assignment is his toughest challenge yet. When their fake romance generates some all-too-real heat, Vince learns that Charlie is more than just arm candy. She's the real deal—and she's ready for some serious action. Don't miss the next book in April Hunt's Alpha Security series, perfect for fans of Julie Ann Walker and Rebecca Zanetti!

Fall in Love with Forever Romance

WHEN THE SCOUNDREL SINS
By Anna Harrington

When Quinton Carlisle, eager for adventure, receives a mysterious letter from Scotland, he eagerly rides north—only to find the beautiful—and ruined—Annabelle Greene waiting for his marriage proposal. Fans of Elizabeth Hoyt, Grace Burrowes, and Madeline Hunter will love the next in the Capturing the Carlisles series from Anna Harrington.